A
SECOND
HAND
LIFE

A SECOND HAND LIFE

PAMELA CRANE

Rockin' C Reads
Raleigh, North Carolina

Thank you for supporting authors and literacy by purchasing this book. Want to add more gripping reads to your library? As the author of more than a dozen award-winning and best-selling books, you can find all of Pamela Crane's works on her website at www.pamelacrane.com.

This book is dedicated to the man who breathes life into my dreams with his unwavering support. My darling Craig, we both know you're my everything.

Sometimes the heart sees what is invisible to the eye.
— H. Jackson Brown, Jr.

Prologue

721 Willoughby Way
Durham, North Carolina
Wednesday, March 4, 1992
8:13 p.m.

I didn't wake up one morning and randomly decide to be a killer; rather, somewhere in the recesses of my soulless being, there it was—a primal urge for blood, for manipulating life and death. Yet all the while I was unable to control my own mind. I had become an animal.

I wasn't always a murderer, as far as I know. Born with it, or raised into it? Nature versus nurture. The question of the day. One that has baffled therapists for decades. As one of the monsters they studied, even I had no answers. Picking apart my gray matter proved fruitless.

I never tortured cats, pulled the wings off of butterflies, or watched too much graphic news. In fact, I hated what television represented, what it took from us. It stole our youth, our time, our minds. Yet our lives revolved around it. So much power granted to one inanimate object. Perhaps I was jealous.

But jealousy didn't mutilate my soul. Something else awakened within me over time, eroding my humanity to the point where I despised what society had become. Perverted. Impure. Corrupt. It was a shame what people had turned into with the help of a malevolent social order.

And I thought *I* was evil.

Look around you. Look at what people do behind closed doors. Neglecting their kids. Abusing their spouses. Drinking themselves into oblivion ...

They're the ugly ones, not me.

I was their savior.

So what exactly turned me into ... this? I will probably never know.

But today I challenged all theories of humanity's innate goodness as the girl's limp neck hung in my hands, my dirt-stained fingers wrapped around her flawless pink flesh like a snake coiled around its prey. I hadn't planned on squeezing until she vented a terror-stricken scream, potentially spooking the neighbors and sealing my red-and-blue-flashing fate. Reflexively my hands tightened their grip, summoning Death to take its victim.

If my chokehold didn't kill her, certainly the stab wound would. She had made it easy enough for me. Sitting in the recliner watching *Beverly Hills, 90210*—a filthy show no twelve-year-old should be watching—snacking on Doritos, unaware of the threatening shadow lurking behind her. Without hesitation I had placed my hand over her mouth, letting her struggle a bit as she kicked over several empty beer bottles from the coffee table in her frantic state, then I plunged the kitchen knife into her side, feeling the squishy flesh part beneath the blade. I had been pleased with how smoothly the metal edge entered her. A moment later, a pool of crimson drizzled down, soaking the chair in blood.

"Shhh ..." I had soothed. "You must remain quiet, Alexis. If you don't stay quiet, I'm going to have to hurt you more."

When I had sensed her terror prompting her to scream louder, I had shifted my hands to her neck to snuff out the noise and set her at ease.

First, a gentle rub. Under my kneading palm her shoulders tensed.

"It's okay," I had lied, blowing my hot breath against her cool ear. Pierced, of course, with a garish bauble dangling from the tender lobe.

That's when my grip tightened, and her fight-or-flight instincts kicked in.

She had chosen fight, and let out a scream meant to alert anyone within a quarter mile.

Silly girl.

In her last battle against surrender, I felt the girl squirm and reach up behind her—for I could not bear to stand before her and meet her eyes, a numbness that would take time to mature, I assumed—to claw at my wrists. Her neon-pink painted nails scraped against my sleeves, searching for traction in my flesh. Her hands gripped my wrists, pulling, tugging. Of course, her meager efforts were futile against my hundred-pound advantage.

Beneath my fingers her surging lifeblood slowed and weakened. I wrung harder, feeling the neck muscles relax. I choked out any last remnants of a scream, then the sweet release of the end arrived as I felt her pulse wane. A mixture of delight and fear overwhelmed me at that moment—a desire to watch the light of her youth fade from her green eyes, yet a debilitating dread held me back from looking ... from seeing my masterpiece as I purged the sin from her. I feared regret for something I couldn't change. I couldn't bring back the dead.

Tomorrow I would wake up different. Life would never be the same after my first victim. So young, she was. Only twelve. And prematurely snuffed out. Because of me.

Me. Once a nobody, now a somebody. The author of death.

I released my hold and looked down at her once-pure face tainted with whorish makeup. I pulled a wrapped alcohol pad from my pocket, tore it open, and dabbed gently at her skin. Each wipe restored more of her purity as the lipstick, the blush, and the eye shadow disappeared. Sure enough, she became a young girl again—who she truly was beneath the makeup mask. When I finished, I headed for the phone hanging on the kitchen wall and punched in 9-1-1.

"9-1-1. Please state your emergency," the operator said.

In my softest whisper, hoping it was sufficient to mask my voice, I said, "Please help."

Then I dropped the receiver. By the time they could trace the call and paramedics arrived, I would have sufficiently finished my staging.

I turned back to my victim, stumbled toward her, and stopped cold. I simply stared. Her black hair, braided in two pigtails, framed a sweet, cherubic face—eyelids closed like she was slumbering, an eternal sleep. Red handprints circled her pale neck, below which her Bart Simpson "Don't have a cow, man!" T-shirt hung loosely on her lithe frame. I hadn't noticed how tiny she was before now— seventy pounds soaking wet. Shame burrowed its way into me. I reminded myself why I had done it: so she might never lose that purity. She would become incorruptible in death.

What happened next, however, surprised me ... and little surprised me. In sympathy with her discovery of the afterlife, I felt my own life waver. Blood rushed to my head and a blackness crept to the corners of my vision, closing in on me. I was going to pass out.

The taste of bile lurched from my stomach into my mouth, its grassy tang lingering foully on my tongue for a split second. The floodgates opened. I spewed epically on the floor, deluging the rivulets of blood. The acrid scent of vomit wafted upward, prodding more. Hunched over, my gut pumped its contents out—a mixture of undigested lunch and afternoon snack.

It was at this point I knew my weakness would be my demise. I couldn't stomach the job.

And I left evidence everywhere.

Frenziedly, I grabbed a roll of paper towels and a bottle of bleach, and started slopping up my vomit, slipping on a bloody trail as I fell to my knees. A stinging pain coursed through my right kneecap. I paused to examine it and found a sliver of colored glass jutting out from one of the broken beer bottles. I pulled the shard out, but I'd have to nurse it later. Time was running out, and my hands were covered in blood. My jeans and shirt were stained.

I heard sirens in the distance and worked at a fevered pitch. When I figured I had gotten most of the evidence cleared, I threw it into the garbage and grabbed the bag. I tossed a glance at my first victim. Her glassy eyes had opened partway during her cleansing, but she appeared lifeless. In the background I heard Luke Perry talking his way into the pants of a dreamy-eyed girl. An adolescent just like Alexis.

Ah, yes. I was forgetting something.

I limped back to the living room and kicked over the television with my good leg, sending the Beverly Hills sluts into black-screen oblivion.

Take that, you life-sucking machine. You ruin young girls' purity, but I'm here to take it back.

With one last look at Alexis, I felt a twinge of sadness. She didn't appear as peaceful as I had expected. Instead, her head hung at a crooked angle, her shoulders slumped, her arms sprawled. What should have appeared serene instead looked dead and mutilated.

Nausea rose once again. The sight of blood and murder was too much. The smell of a bleach-infused metallic cocktail too much. The taste of bile too much.

I needed out. Air.

As I ran out the back door to the cadence of approaching sirens, I vowed to never be weak again.

Chapter 1

Duke Hospital
Durham, North Carolina
Wednesday, March 4, 1992
8:22 p.m.

The last thing I remembered was my life splintering—the crack of bones, the crunch of glass, the shriek of scraping metal ... normalcy as I knew it gone forever and in its place a ghastly existence. After the accident, my life would never be the same.

Gone were the days of carefree antics and childish joys. All that remained of my life was a higher calling, a calling I never asked for but had no choice but to accept.

Duke Hospital
Durham, North Carolina
Thursday, March 5, 1992
10:15 a.m.

I woke up to a bright light, which at first I thought was my entrance into heaven, but when a foreign face peered down at me, I realized I hadn't died. I only *felt* like death.

His honest eyes gazed into mine a little too intimately. "Mia, do you know where you are?"

My pupils hurt too much to get a sense of my surroundings. Only white. White everywhere. And beeping. I noticed his blue scrubs, but nothing registered.

"Um..." but I couldn't push the word "no" from my cracked lips. My throat felt like the Sahara. I shook my head faintly.

"Nurse, some water, please. She's parched," Scrubs ordered someone I couldn't see. I heard a door click shut. "You're in the hospital, Mia."

I wiped a layer of crust off my eyes and opened them a little more, then peered around. Tubes taped to my wrists, machines standing sentry on both sides of me, a stiff blue chair in the corner, a window shrouded by cheap aluminum blinds. Yes, it was definitely the hospital. And the pain ... the pain was intense. And everywhere in my body. But especially my chest. It ached like it had been ripped open.

After another door click, a nurse sidled up beside me and propped me upright with a pillow, holding a pink straw to my lips. With my tongue I guided the straw into my mouth and slowly sipped. Water—an oasis to my throat. When my throat was soothed enough for me to speak, I looked at Scrubs.

"What happened to me? Where's my mom and dad?"

"You've been in a car accident, Mia. Your mom is down the hall. Once she gets here we can talk about what happened, okay?" His voice was too nurturing. It gave me the sense that something was wrong. Very wrong.

But I didn't get a chance to plead for more answers, because that's when my mom came rushing to my bedside, her hands smoothing my matted hair aside.

"Baby girl, are you alright?"

"I think so," I said. "But everything hurts."

She planted kisses all over my face, and that's when I noticed her bloodshot eyes. She had been crying.

8

"Don't worry, Mom. I'm okay."

With my words the floodgates opened. Tears coursed down her cheeks. Apparently she knew something I didn't.

"Mom, am I okay?"

"Yes, sweetie." Her fingertip touched my lips. "Honey, a lot has happened."

"What do you mean?" That's when my brain suddenly caught up—a flash of me standing in front of my bedroom mirror wearing my gymnastics leotard, then Dad and I in the car, then my screams, and then ... nothing. Despite my neck's achy protest, I scanned the room of unknown faces. My dad wasn't here. "Where's Dad?"

Mom swiped at a tear and shook her head, clearly unable to speak.

All kinds of horrific scenarios swam through my head. "Is Dad ...?" I couldn't finish the sentence.

"Honey, you and your dad were in the car when someone hit you. Your dad is alive, but he's in a coma. We're hoping he'll wake up soon."

I was too shocked to cry, to react, to do anything. A somber silence enveloped the room, and I couldn't speak. Mom had run out of words too. There was no comfort available when the outcome felt so bleak.

"But I don't want you to worry about your dad," she finally continued. "Your dad is tough. And you are too. Just focus on getting better and getting home. You've been through a lot."

What was I supposed to feel right now? I couldn't feel what I needed to feel. I couldn't feel the sadness or anger that yearned to surface. I was emotionally void. All I felt was the throbbing in my chest. My hand touched where it hurt—my heart.

"It hurts so bad, Mom."

"You've had emergency surgery, honey. You needed a heart transplant. We were lucky, though. You were able to get one right away. It saved your life."

Odd as it seems, the thought of losing an organ jarred me more than news of the car accident or my dad's coma. It wasn't my heart anymore.

I pulled open my hospital gown and peered down at my chest. Large black staples ran up it, with dried blood clinging to where the halves of my chest cavity met. The skin was shiny and tight around the incision, and blotchy red with yellow crust all over the wound. Little bunches of flesh overflowed where each staple clipped it together. Could this really be my body? I was hideous!

Tears formed, then a sob escaped. After that I couldn't stop bawling.

"Oh, honey ..." Even my mom couldn't say anything reassuring. She knew it as well as I did—I was disfigured. Doomed to spinsterhood.

"Mia, it's okay," Scrubs chimed in. "Those stitches will heal, and you will hardly see any scarring. By swimsuit season you'd never know anything happened."

"Promise?" I needed his word.

"I promise. You'll have to put ointment on it several times a day, which will help nourish the skin. But I'll make sure you get the best cosmetic care available."

I felt a little relief, but something else was bugging me.

"So I have someone else's heart?"

Mom nodded.

Simple as that—one day I'm me, the next day it's like I'm someone else, with someone else's organ. And not a minor organ like an appendix. My *heart*. It might as well have been my soul.

"Someone died? The person who gave me the heart?"

"Yes, honey. Unfortunately that's what happened. But don't think of it as a girl dying; think of it as a girl living the rest of her life through you."

"A girl? A young girl, like me?"

10

Mom wouldn't answer. Just a barely perceptible nod.

"Do you know the girl who died, the girl whose heart I have?"

Mom tossed the question to Scrubs with a glance.

"We do, but when it comes to organ donation, we prefer to keep names confidential ... out of respect for the family."

I considered his words for a moment before more questions flooded me.

"Will I ever be able to do gymnastics again?" I had missed tryouts for the competition team when the accident happened. I wondered if they'd let me try out once I healed.

Scrubs shot me an avuncular wink. "Absolutely, you should be able to enjoy your usual activities just as if nothing happened. But you need to heal fully first. For the next couple of months you need to do as little as possible."

A couple of months? To a twelve-year-old that was forever! Although I was nodding, I felt like my world was falling apart. Though, with the size of my scar, I doubted I'd ever feel comfortable in a leotard again. My life was officially ruined.

"Did they find whoever hit us?" I asked.

"A teenage boy, I think," Mom answered. "Lost control of the car when he was coming around the bend. The police are handling it."

"Do you think he'll go to jail?"

"I'm not sure, honey. Probably some kind of punishment, though. But it seems it was simply an accident. Nothing he did wrong, from what they can tell." A pause. "Why are you asking these questions? You shouldn't think about this stuff. Just rest, okay?"

I nimbly agreed, though my musings had their own intentions. I thought it ironic how "justice" might require the life of another youth in order to avenge mine. Even if the kid who hit us didn't go to jail, he'd have to live with the burden of what happened on his conscience. Memory could be a bitch sometimes. And who would avenge the girl whose heart I now bore? Misery was making its rounds today. Three losses in one day.

I wanted to ask more questions, but I didn't like the answers. Yet my mind was relentless.

As my thoughts rambled on, my mother turned a grateful face to Scrubs.

"Thank you, doctor, for taking such good care of Mia. I can't imagine what could have happened if that heart wasn't available." She shuddered and added, "I can't bear to think of losing my baby girl."

"You've been through a lot, Mrs. Germaine. Let's just hope that your husband and daughter make a full recovery so that your family can get back to normal as soon as possible." He tenderly squeezed my shoulder as he spoke.

I hoped my prayers could reach high enough to appeal to God for such an outcome—being back to normal. But something inside me told me life would never be normal again.

My eyes slid closed and I conjured an image of "normal"—Dad, Mom, and me sitting around our dining room table chatting over the day's events, laughing and smiling as Dad teased me about the pink streak of dye in my hair or my Paula Abdul dance moves for the school talent show, picking at me good-naturedly as he was wont to do.

Then I wondered if I'd ever smile again.

Chapter 2

My glance wandered upward, noting how the cedar branches grabbed fistfuls of sunlight before tossing shards around me. Spring always came too late, in my opinion. If I could avoid winter altogether, I would, but Florida had never been a viable option. The mere suggestion of me moving that far away would have killed my mom—emotionally, that is. After my father's death, I was all she had. Though, the constant interrogations about when I would give her grandbabies was enough to drive me to the Eastern hemisphere.

A row of yellow daffodils and red tulips nestled against the walkway beneath my feet. Stray weeds peeked up through cracks in the concrete, a reminder that nature had the final say. No matter how much mankind bulldozed or built, all was vulnerable to Mother Nature's whims.

Each step was brisk as I approached my boyfriend's apartment door. I had endured an endless, grueling week of work, anxiously waiting to see Brad Thomas—the love of my life—until at last the weekend had arrived. I reached his door, knocked once, then pushed the door open.

"Brad?" I called out. "It's Mia."

I heard the news broadcasting from the living room, so I headed in. When I turned the corner from the entryway, I whiffed the heavenly aroma of bacon—and the salivating began.

"Hey, gorgeous," Brad called from his position at the stove. "Hungry?"

Even wearing an apron, he was all man. And gorgeous. He made brown eyes and brown hair striking. The dusting of scruff on his jaw gave this sweetheart a bad boy appeal that I could never resist. That, and his devilish grin. I was charmed, to say the least.

And as I told my mom in not-so-graphic detail, I could totally see myself making babies with Brad.

I threw my purse on the sofa and traipsed to the kitchen, sliding myself behind him. I slipped my arms around him and kissed his neck, where part of his back tattoo peeked out from under his T-shirt. "What's cookin', good lookin'?" I teased. It was a phrase my dad had used daily with my mom when he came home from work and dinner was cooking, one of the many things I fondly remembered about him.

"Eggs Benedict over homemade English muffins ... and of course bacon."

My favorite.

"Showoff," I said. "I would have been happy with Cheerios—Honey Nut, of course."

"You *are* a nut," he teased. "Besides, a professional chef serving Cheerios? I don't think so."

Brad's culinary genius was one of my favorite things about him. Although being a chef demanded sacrificing most evenings and weekends together, it sure paid off at home when he experimented with new dishes. I loved being his guinea pig.

"Though I'm thinking about skipping breakfast," he said with a suggestive grin as he swiveled around to pull me up against his chest, "and going straight to dessert. Whaddya say, Miss Germaine?"

"I do have a sweet tooth," I quipped.

His trail of kisses started at my lips and tiptoed down the ridge of my chin, further down my neck, then trailing the length of my collarbone until I squirmed away. Only a couple of inches further along was the beginnings of the scar that my cosmetic surgeons assured me would one day barely be noticeable.

Lies. That "one day" never came.

The angry pink line stretched vertically down the length of my breastbone, a constant and ugly reminder of my past. I spent years of my adolescence practicing the art of camouflaging it, but no amount of concealer could fully hide my disfigurement.

When I turned twenty-one I decided to get a tattoo over my heart—a rose. A symbol of my life, though I never told anyone the depths of what it represented. If I wore a shirt low-cut enough for the blossom's edge to peek out, or on the rare occasion I wore a swimming suit, viewers merely noted how "pretty" it was. To them it was a flower. To me it was much more. Yet no one, not even the current love of my life, seemed trustworthy enough to share that part of my soul and my past with.

So, eventually my chest became a no-see and no-touch zone with the men I dated ... which luckily were few.

Until Brad Thomas.

Brad had been the first "keeper" of the bunch. A tough gentleman who loved me, scars and all. Yet the insecurity of my scar forced a barrier between us, an obstacle that I wasn't going to be able to hurdle anytime soon. While he'd certainly caught glimpses of it when I undressed, I always shut off the lights and wore a shirt when we made love. We'd had a handful of conversations about it—mainly Brad telling me not to hide it, that he loved every part of me—but to me it was a disfigurement. It made me ugly. I would never accept it, even if Brad assured me he did. Luckily Brad wasn't in a race to overcome this emotional wall I erected, and neither was I. Things were good, and we were content—as far as I knew.

"Let's not burn breakfast," I said coyly as I pulled away, pretending my forestalling tactic was about eating, not my imperfections.

"It's just about ready. You wanna grab a couple plates and forks?"

I grabbed two beige ceramic plates and set the makeshift dining-slash-coffee table. I threw a pile of clothes and his Durham Bulls baseball hat on the floor beside me. Brad could be such a bachelor at times. His sparsely furnished apartment resembled a guy's college dorm room, boasting only the "necessities," he'd argue—a sofa, television, video game console, and two TV trays—until I gifted him a coffee table for Christmas last year. How could men live like this? It was so Third World.

With the last flip of the bacon, Brad carried his culinary masterpiece into the living room and served us both, then sat next to me. While we ate, an anchor from WRAL was covering the local news. Gunshots at Northgate Mall, a fire in Woodcroft. Local spring festivals, Durham Bulls baseball stats.

A panning shot of downtown Durham played across the screen, focusing on the packed Durham Bulls Athletic Park where fans decked in royal blue cheered on the local baseball team for their season opener two nights ago against the Gwinnett Braves. Our team opened with a win but lost last night. "The sorry bums," Brad grumbled.

Zooming across the street to the American Tobacco Historic District, the screen showed the newly renovated tobacco warehouse that now housed an eclectic and thriving mix of shops, restaurants, and office spaces.

Handsome red brick walkways and an industrial-style concrete waterway graced the popular venue. The Lucky Strike tower sparkled with lights in the epicenter of the campus, creating a romantic atmosphere that Brad and I had enjoyed several times when dining downtown.

On and on the perfectly coiffed female news anchor droned. Some bad news, some good news. The norm. Then something drew my attention with such force that I couldn't chew, couldn't swallow, only watch.

"In breaking news," the anchor said soberly, "a teen death has rocked the Raleigh area. Thirteen-year-old Gina Martinez was found last night in her Apex home with fatal stab wounds to her abdomen." A picture of a smiling, golden-skinned teen flashed on the screen. Her black hair cascaded down her shoulders in heavy waves.

"After an evening out, parents Roy and Amelia Martinez came home to find their daughter, Gina, passed out from blood loss. She was rushed to WakeMed where she was pronounced dead. There was no sign of forced entry, which leads investigators to believe the family knew the assailant. Police report stab wound patterns that are consistent with a murder committed last March, when police found twelve-year-old Violet Hansen brutally murdered in a local park. Investigators found Miss Martinez with her makeup removed, leading police to recognize this as the work of a serial killer now dubbed the Triangle Terror, though no suspects have been named. A memorial will be held for Miss Martinez at St. Thomas' Church on Monday."

As the anchor moved on, I couldn't. I numbly found the remote and turned the TV off just as the anchor cheerily segued into coverage of upcoming "Got to Be NC Festival."

"You okay, Mia?" Brad's voice was barely a whisper above my crowding thoughts.

I shook my head.

I was going to hurl.

Rising to my feet, I darted to the bathroom and frantically flipped up the toilet seat. I dunked my head inside and emptied my eggs into its awaiting porcelain maw.

A moment later I felt Brad's hands pull my shoulder-length hair back. When I felt sure there was nothing left in my stomach, I stood and leaned over the sink to wash the sweat from my face. I swished a mouthful of cold water to get rid of the taste of bile.

Brad sweetly stood by, rubbing my back.

What a gem.

I rested my weight against the sink, staring at my own vacant hazel eyes in the vanity mirror. Brown strands of sweat-soaked hair stuck to the side of my face, and I pushed them away. I knew food poisoning when it hit me. This wasn't a reaction to rotten eggs. It was a reaction to bad news. It seemed preposterous. Why would a random sad news story make me sick? It didn't make sense. But I sure as heck didn't want to find out. I preferred blissful ignorance.

"My cooking that bad, huh?" Brad said with a chuckle.

"I don't know what came over me," I said after one final mouth rinse. "I'm so sorry." I wiped my mouth on the hand towel. "And I promise not to gripe about you leaving the toilet seat up again. I didn't think I was going to make it ..." I said, attempting humor.

"It's okay, Mia. Don't apologize. Just sit down and rest."

He guided me back to the couch, allowing me to sink into his able arms. Arms that seemed to ward off all fear. They felt safe.

I closed my eyes, but all I could see was blood splatter. A sharp pain surged through my chest, and I grabbed

18

where my heart was. Was I having a heart attack? The pain intensified, and I couldn't catch my breath.

"I think I'm having a heart attack!" I said between hard breaths.

"What? Should I call 9-1-1?" Brad asked frantically. "Try breathing slowly, Mia. You're hyperventilating."

I dropped my head between my knees and concentrated on breathing. Inhale. Exhale. Inhale. Exhale. Within a couple of minutes my breaths slowed and my chest pain began to subside.

"Do I need to take you to the hospital, honey?" Brad asked again.

"No," I answered, sitting upright. "I think I'm okay now."

"What happened?"

"I don't know what's wrong with me. My heart just started hurting really bad." But then I remembered something.

"Do you think it was a heart attack?" Brad probed.

"I'm not sure."

I hadn't thought about it in years, but now the memory was as fresh as if it had happened yesterday. Brad's hand cupped mine, giving me the courage to speak.

"You know how I told you that when I was a kid I was in a horrible car accident?"

He nodded.

"Well, this young guy lost control going around a sharp turn and somehow ran into the side of us as we were turning. I got crushed underneath the side door and almost died. When I got to the hospital, they had to give me a heart transplant—you know, the reason for my scar. I never had complications or anything, but this heart pain just made me think about it."

"Is this the same accident that killed your father?" Brad asked tentatively. It was a touchy subject, one we had only discussed once before.

"Yeah."

"I'm so sorry."

"Well, stuff happens. Gotta move on, right?"

Brad squeezed me tenderly.

"Did the guy go to jail?"

"No, my mom never pressed charges. It really was a no-fault. Since he wasn't drunk or anything, he didn't deserve to do jail time. And I was okay with that, since there's no point in one mistake taking two lives. He was just another typical teenage driver who probably considered himself invincible and lost control of the wheel. It happens. I'm sure the pain of knowing he killed a man was more anguish than a jail sentence could've inflicted. I never did find out who he was, though. My mom felt it was better I didn't know."

I shrugged. Water under the bridge.

"What about your heart donor—did you find out who that was?"

"Nope. I only know that she was a girl my age—twelve. And local. I don't even know how she died. Part of me wishes I could find out, you know? But the hospital wouldn't disclose organ donor names when I looked into it in the past. It's a sealed record, they told me. Other than through hospital records, how am I supposed to figure out who she was?"

"I dunno, Mia, maybe you're not supposed to know what happened. That sounds kind of morbid to know whose heart you have and what killed her. Besides, how will knowing be of any benefit?"

"It's not about benefiting anyone. It's about closure."

"Closure from what? You had nothing to do with her death."

"But someone did, Brad. Someone, or something, killed her. And she's a part of me now. She's what keeps me alive." My voice rose an octave as my words grew terse. A passion that was never there before surfaced. I didn't know why I cared so much now, but it didn't change the fact that she died and I lived. "I want to know who, and why. She was only a child. She didn't deserve to die."

"Are you saying you think she was murdered? She could have died of natural causes, you know."

"A twelve-year-old suddenly dead, and not from a disease? Because they wouldn't have harvested her organs if she had a terminal illness. Sounds like something shady to me."

"I don't know ..." Brad said, shaking his head.

"I suppose I'll never know the truth, will I?"

Brad eyed me skeptically. He obviously had no idea what it felt like to be in my position.

"Look," I said with a razor's edge to my tone, "you can't possibly understand because you're not borrowing someone else's time. Her heart was alive inside her before I took it. It bothers me, okay?"

"Okay, okay. Don't get upset with me. Do what you want to do." I heard the bite to his voice.

Was this our first fight? It was beginning to sound like it, and I had never intended the subject to escalate. Though I didn't feel I owed him an apology. I was right, after all, even though I wasn't sure what I was right about.

Surrender was never pretty when pride was at stake, especially among couples. I'd yet to meet a humble married couple.

"Let's just try to salvage the rest of this day before it's ruined," I said, trying to smooth over the tension. The last thing I wanted was our first fight to be about my scar. It should be about picking up dirty clothes off the floor, or whose turn it was to do the dishes. Not about my past. "I just hope nothing's wrong with my heart," I added warily.

"Don't worry, baby. It's probably nothing, but get checked out just to be sure. Okay?"

"Yeah, I will," I mumbled.

But Brad's offering was no reassurance, for somehow, deep in the recesses of my now-empty gut, I knew something was wrong. Something big. And it had to do with murder, a serial killer, and a dead girl.

Chapter 3

I was twelve years old. I sat in the backseat of our red 1989 Subaru station wagon, antsy to get to gymnastics class. I urged Dad to hurry, but he shushed me, assuring me we'd be plenty early.

As he turned his head back to calm me, in that split second the side of the wagon imploded. I blinked and found my body contorted into a mangled cluster of limbs. My eyelids slid closed. A cool breeze chilled me as I was ripped out from beneath the crushing weight of metal. But as soon as I was released from the vehicular coffin, I found myself sitting in front of a television. Only it wasn't my television. Not the one I remembered from my childhood, at least.

Rabbit ears poked up from the TV, which sat on the floor. Next to my pile of Pogs, a line of bottles—various beers, but mostly Budweiser—lined the coffee table in front of me, blocking my view. I kicked several over onto the hardwood floor, stained and scratched with years of abuse, though I was sure there was nothing left to spill. Wherever I was, I felt at home, and after a commercial break for Super Soaker, I was ogling Luke Perry and despising Jennie Garth, both at the same time. It wasn't fair how perfect her life was—gorgeous and rich. A combo that none should be worthy of, for it was too much power for one person to properly handle.

I possessed neither beauty nor riches. Instead, I was homely and poor—a typical girl from the ghetto.

The recliner was a scratchy wool monstrosity upholstered in green plaid, so I wrapped my legs in a soft knitted blanket, creating a leg cocoon. Cuddling into the nook of the cushions, I let my imagination wander into the pleasures of angst-soaked high school TV melodrama at its most outlandish and idealized best/worst—depending on your point of view.

Donna's blond hair was styled in cute braided pigtails, so I decided to braid my own. I fingered my hair, twisting it into two braids. Satisfied with my new look, I envied the latest fashion trends that Mom's minimum-wage-plus-tips job would never be able to afford.

My bag of Doritos crinkled as I placed a cheesy chip in my mouth. I shivered from a brief wave of cold, the last vestiges of winter's chill. The back door creaked shut, but I ignored it, too engrossed to care if it was Mom arriving home from the bar with a new boyfriend on her arm. Sober or drunk? It was better I didn't find out.

When I heard a shuffle behind me, I twisted my neck to glance behind me but saw nothing. As I turned back to the television, a grip tightened around my mouth and I couldn't breathe. The fingers locked down too hard for me to open up my jaw and bite my way to freedom. I tried to inhale through my nose, but his hands covered my nostrils. Shaking my head frantically, I leaned forward, but he was too strong. He jerked me back and held me still. Then gripped harder.

Seconds were passing. Precious seconds of air bidding me farewell.

I whimpered, hoping my unspoken message would reach my attacker:

Please let me go. Please let me breathe.

Still, no air.

I began blacking out, my eyes watering, wondering if Luke Perry's face was the last I would ever see.

As an ebony cloud shrouded me, my mind screamed for help. Then a picture flashed before all went black. A familiar face.

It was Gina Martinez.

I needed air ... needed air ... needed air ...

◈◈◈

"Help!" I cried, gasping as I bolted upright in bed. My lungs couldn't get enough oxygen as I sucked in lungful after lungful. In an effort to calm down, I examined my bedroom. The teal walls, the tastefully simple décor, and my digital clock revealed the ungodly hour of three thirty in the morning. Sure enough, it was my apartment, and I was alone ... or so I hoped.

The dream had felt so real, like a memory, yet so foreign, like it belonged to someone else. I had never been allowed to watch *Beverly Hills, 90210* at that age, and I hadn't bothered to catch up on the show as an adult, so how did I know those characters? And where had I been? It felt surreally like home ... but certainly not my home. Mom never drank, and she kept a pristine house, even during her mourning. And despite her full-time work, a chef-approved dinner was served every night, dishes and kitchen clean before bed. The Rolodex of my mind ticked through my childhood friends, houses I'd visited. Nothing clicked.

Was it some long-buried memory, or a figment of my imagination? Then I recalled the last image I had seen. Gina Martinez, the girl who had been murdered two days ago. Was it her house? How would I know that? I'd never met the girl.

I wanted to forget it all and go back to sleep, but I couldn't let it go.

After nearly an hour of lying in the dark, afraid to close my eyes for fear of returning to the nightmare, I decided it was morning enough to start my day. I threw on a pair of sweats and a UNC sweatshirt. I brewed a cup of chocolate mint tea and sipped the sweet warmth, staring into the emptiness. My eyes darted at every shadow. Every sound sent me jumping.

I could tell already that it was going to be a long day. And worst of all, I couldn't shake the feeling that I was going to die. More than a feeling, in fact. I *knew* it. The nightmare fueled this premonition.

When the tea couldn't sooth my frazzled nerves, I picked up my cell phone and texted Brad.

Babe, u up? Need to talk.

A minute passed before my phone beeped in reply.

Up now. Wzup?

Can i come over?

U serious?

As a heart attack. Pls?

Is this abt yesterday?

I'll explain when i get there. So can i come over?

Of course, babe. Door's unlocked.

I grabbed my coat and keys and double-locked my door on the way out. I rarely locked the bolt and knob, but I wasn't taking any chances. As the cool early morning temperature helped clear my head, I realized something.

I needed air.

When I arrived at Brad's, the lights were off and he was still in bed. I snuck in, bolted the door, and slipped under the covers, spooning next to him and hoping to subtly wake him. I needed to talk through my thoughts.

My restless shifting around must have worked, because soon his brown eyes groggily opened.

"Sorry to wake you," I said.

"Liar," Brad teased. "So what's the problem? You need some of my lovin'?" he said with a coy grin as he nuzzled my neck.

Refusing to feed his advances, I went on talking. "Something is wrong with me."

"Mmm, nothing's wrong with you, baby. You're perfect." He kissed my jaw, tempering my urgency, but I leaned away.

"Brad, this is serious. I need you to listen to me right now."

He shifted upright and circled his arm around my shoulders.

"All ears. Is this about what happened yesterday?"

"Sorta ..."

He sighed heavily. "What's going on?"

Where should I begin? I could find no logical beginning.

"Remember how when we were watching the news yesterday I got sick?" Brad nodded, silent. "Well, I went to bed thinking about that girl, Gina, and her death. I ended up having a horrible nightmare and she was in it. I think my dream is trying to tell me something about her murder. Like I might somehow know who's murdering these girls."

Even as I said it I winced at how ridiculous I sounded. As if I had some prophetic ability to see things, to reveal things that the cops couldn't. But the look of incredulity on Brad's face pissed me off. I was the only one allowed to think myself crazy.

"What's that look for?" I growled.

"You realize what you're saying, right? That you are connected to these murders."

"No," I corrected, "not connected to them. Let's call it a"—I fumbled for the right phrase—"supernatural hunch."

"Supernatural, as in ... what exactly?" he queried.

"I dunno. Something beyond the natural, I guess."

"That's pretty crazy stuff, Mia."

"I know it sounds nuts, but ... well, I can't explain it. Something in me knows who's behind this, and I need to follow my gut on this. This could save lives, Brad."

"And how do you propose to do that—to catch this killer?" His sarcasm was biting.

"I don't know yet. I guess I'll figure it out as I go."

"As you go? Are you kidding me? Mia, this isn't Nancy Drew. You're talking about a serial killer and actual murders here. You could be killed! Stay out of it. You have no business playing detective."

"And you have no business telling me what to do," I retorted. Sure, I sounded childish, but I couldn't think of anything more adult to say. My ire was rising to the point where I couldn't keep my thoughts—or my words—straight. Or it could have been the meager three hours of sleep making me nonsensical. Either way, Brad was pushing my buttons and I didn't appreciate it.

"Mia, I just want you to be safe. I care for you. Please promise me you won't pursue this."

"I can't do that," I said matter-of-factly.

"If you can't assure me that this is over, then I can't guarantee that I'll be around to watch you get hurt."

Whoa. Brad took the argument to a whole new level, and he definitely wasn't playing fair anymore.

"Are you breaking up with me?" I asked point-blank.

"That's up to you, Mia. If you don't let this go, then I guess you're forcing my hand. I don't want to break up with you, but I can't sit idly by watching you chase danger like it's a toy."

"Whatever." With that, I scooted to the other side of the king-sized bed, as far away from Brad as I could get without falling off, and pouted until the sun peeked through the cream, metal blinds, casting the bedroom in hues of orange.

Maybe my mom was right about me all these years—I had indeed inherited my father's stubborn streak.

PAMELA CRANE

Chapter 4

I watched from the Starbucks window, observing how the people flowed with antlike organization. A line through the door, a line at the register, a line through the drive-thru ... all following one another, all mindlessly moving from point A to point B. Who among them valued life, cherished each moment? My speculation: none.

That's what was wrong with people these days. They didn't cling to the joys of life until they were gazing down at their own funerals from heaven, or perhaps upward from hell, wondering where all the time went. They lay waste to their lives until the end comes—that's when they mourn over their regrets.

The children are our only chance. Start by changing their attitudes early on and you kill the root problem. Remind them to embrace each moment ... yet I knew how stubborn adolescents could be.

Gina Martinez had been stubborn. She spent her last moments fighting, screaming, crying ... what a waste. Apparently my message wasn't clear enough. I'd keep working on it, though. It had taken me years to perfect my message, and still I had so far to go. I wondered how many lives it would require.

Twenty years, and still they were ignorant. They thought Violet Hansen was my first victim ... the blind fools.

There had been many others before the blue-eyed brunette was stumbled upon by a group of kids at the American Village Park where I buried her beneath a shallow bed of leaves. It would only be a matter of time before they connected the dots to reveal two decades' worth of victims. Though I couldn't boast and take the credit. For it wasn't my work, but the work I was sent to do.

One by one, I would help the young girls of America see the truth.

A black Lexus pulled up to a parking spot in front of my window view. A gorgeous yet overstated car. Was someone compensating for something? Probably a workaholic, neglectful husband trying to keep his wife faithful by buying her expensive toys. We'd see just how devoted she was ...

A girl stepped out of the front passenger seat, then entered the coffee shop with her mother trailing her. The girl was probably twelve years old, though she wore the trampy clothing of a woman, revealing far too much leg. A hooker in training, apparently. Her mother was no better, showing boob job cleavage and pants suctioned to her jacked-up rear. They were both in need of some truth.

The girl's natural red hair was pulled into a ponytail, and her cheeks and nose were dusted with freckles. She was every bit the image of fleeting innocence.

A perfect illustration.

Chatter about the Triangle Terror infiltrated the conversational din, and a grin crept along my lips.

"Oh, it's just awful what he's doing to those poor girls," a white-haired lady whined to a mother of two across the aisle. "What has this world come to?"

"I'm afraid to let my kids out of my sight," the mother replied, clutching her toddler to her side.

A SECONDHAND LIFE

I had become a celebrity overnight. But hearing about my achievements wasn't what brought me here. More important matters beckoned me.

I stood up from my table by the window, discarded the rest of my black coffee, and headed for the register, pretending to examine the pastry selections.

"Amy," I overheard the mother say as they approached the cashier, "order what you want." The two ordered their beverages, then Amy's mother pulled out her wallet.

I made my move and rested my hand on the counter. "Actually, allow me." I delivered my most charming smile, a surefire winner. None had been able to resist it yet. I visibly eyed her up and down, resting my eyes on her chest for appearance's sake. No one suspects a typical pervert of murder, after all. It's always the nice, normal, charismatic guys—the Ted Bundys—who are the crazy ones.

I tossed a twenty-dollar bill on the counter. "Hi, I'm Jude. And you are?"

The mother looked at me warily. "Married," she said, flashing her wedding ring. At least two karats adorned her finger.

But I was easily five years her junior, so that gave me an advantage against money.

"Mmm, that's too bad. Well, still, let me treat you both. I insist. Two pretty ladies like yourselves shouldn't have to pay their own way."

Amy's mother laughed. "Quite the gentleman, huh?"

"I like to think so," I said.

"Well, thank you for the coffee, *Jude.*"

Judging by her emphasis, I knew she suspected that wasn't my real name. Clever woman. Apparently she knew this game all too well.

"You're quite welcome. Oh, and I didn't catch your name," I prodded.

"That's because I didn't give it to you."

Oh, this woman was good. I was immediately hooked.

No matter. I'd find out what I needed to know in due time.

"Well, then, if you're ever not married, I hope to run into you again." With that I winked, collected my change, and left. Yes, I would definitely be seeing her again ... at her daughter's funeral.

On my way to the parking lot I slowed my gait as I passed their car. The interior was immaculate, not a car one would throw dirty cleats in. I found nothing noteworthy inside, but the back window gave me just what I needed. An Orange High track team bumper sticker. I might have to make it to a few track meets this season.

I typed the license plate number into my notepad on my cell, along with the name "Amy," and headed for my car, intentionally parking across from the main entrance to Starbucks. My silver Honda Accord was perfectly forgettable and blended nicely with the thousands on the road. I sat behind the wheel, turned on some Journey, and tapped my hands against the wheel to the beat of "Don't Stop Believin'." I waited, keeping an eye on my rearview mirror for their exit.

Thirty minutes into my vigil the two ladies walked out the door, a bounce in their step, to-go cups in their hands. They got into their car and drove through one light, heading for the main intersection. I wondered how long I'd be following them, especially on a Sunday—shopping day. As most men can attest, it was grueling lingering about while women shopped.

As luck would have it, twenty minutes and six turns later they pulled into the driveway of a reasonably unpretentious two-story home in a generic subdivision. I pulled my car over to the side of the road as they headed into the garage.

The home was normal enough. No apparent bells and whistles. Hell, it didn't even look like they had a security system. I typed the address into my cell's notepad and made a mental note of the surroundings. Trees lined both sides of the yard, obscuring nosey neighbors' views of the house. I looked for motion lights and saw none. The backyard was small but separated from rear neighbors with another line of trees. How much more perfect could it be? I admit, I had a knack for picking the right girls at the start.

It was turning out to be a perfect Sunday, brimming with opportunity.

Chapter 5

I spent the rest of Sunday alone. I wasn't sure where things stood with Brad. After our argument the night before, we both needed a break to cool off, to think things over. Although, my mind was unwavering in its determination to figure out what was happening to me. I only hoped he'd get on board.

I hiked the day away on Little River Park's trails, using the solitude that nature offered to indulge in some much-needed contemplation. The chaos of home was too distracting. There, laundry, dishes, and work beckoned my attention. Here, I was free to think and let go of the burdens of everyday chores.

Nestled on the outskirts of the town of Hillsborough, North Carolina, the park attracted hikers and cyclists to its miles of wooded trails traversing its 300-plus acres. My favorite amenity was the butterfly garden whose colorful flowers were normally matched by the fluttering beauty of butterflies of every description, relishing the banquet of nectar, though today's April chill sadly deterred them from making an appearance.

I wiped trickling sweat from my forehead as I trudged up the hill heading back toward the parking lot. Streaks of sunlight speared through the burgeoning leaves, as branches laden with blossoms hung low. I stopped and closed my eyes, savoring their sweet fragrance. A bench, cleverly crafted from two tree stumps, emerged up ahead. After hiking the dirt trail up to the bench, I sat down. As I looked around, sunlight caught something on the ground. Glass. A nudge from my sneakered foot turned it over. A Budweiser bottle.

In an instant I felt my heart spasm, and I clutched my chest, praying for the pain to subside. Tears surfaced, and I squeezed my eyes shut to block out the world, helping me to concentrate against the wrenching within me. An image flashed in my head. A girl. Black pigtails. Green eyes—a brighter version of my own hazel color.

Although the chest pain seemed to diminish, the mental picture grew more vivid ... transitioning from a series of images—a beer bottle, a television, a green blanket—into a moving scene. The television flickered to life, and the beer bottle hit the floor with a clunk. During the first few seconds I felt distanced, foreign, but then it started to feel more intimate, as if I was *in* it. I was watching myself, only it wasn't me ...

❧

His hand held my mouth closed, blocking any chance of air through my mouth or nose. I clawed above me, aiming to scratch his eyes, but I only found empty air. My fingers attempted to pry his fingers loose, but he was too strong. I felt my head growing heavy with blackness seeping in. I was on the verge of passing out.

Then something flashed in the corner of my vision. My shriek was smothered by the palm as my flesh tore open. The side of my torso was being ripped apart by a blade as he plunged a knife in, then ripped it out. I hunched over, holding my side. If the lack of oxygen didn't cause my blackout, the excruciating pain in my abdomen would. I felt the side of my shirt dampen, and an apprehensive glance downward confirmed my fears. Blood was oozing out by the gallon, it seemed, soaking my favorite shirt. An odd, fleeting thought went through my head: Mom would never buy me another Bart Simpson shirt, and I doubted I could wash the bloodstain out.

"Shhh ..." I heard him say in my ear. A familiar voice. "You must remain quiet, Alexis. If you don't stay quiet, I'm going to have to hurt you more."

I nodded as best as I could beneath his firm grip. I couldn't imagine any worse pain, but I couldn't risk finding out what that would be. If being quiet meant not suffocating, I would do anything. His palm went lax, and he tentatively removed his hand, though always maintaining contact with my skin, and slid it downward. He rested it on my neck, rubbing gently.

"It's okay," he soothed. Again, a voice I recognized. I knew this person.

Despite his spine-chilling nurturing gesture, I knew worse was to come. He was either going to rape me or mutilate me ... maybe both. I had watched enough movies to know what psychos did to their victims. My mom exhibited little supervision when it came to what I watched, leaving it to my discretion.

So the moment his fingers tightened around my throat, I screamed as loud as I could, hoping the sound would reach the *neighbors. My first mistake. This caused him to grip my neck like he was going to snap it in half. Any chance at survival was now gone.*

I began kicking wildly, knocking several beer bottles to the floor. I heard glass split and shatter across the hardwood. My fingers pried at his to loosen them just enough to breathe ... but I wasn't strong enough. Searching the space around me for any kind of weapon, I noticed a few bottles remained on the coffee table. I reached forward to grab one. My fingertip brushed against the closest one, but I needed another inch. One measly inch.

Before I could gain that inch, I was thrust against the back of the chair. He must have seen where my reach was heading.

My adrenaline was running out. Time and air were running out.

Numbness in my side eventually allowed me to focus my efforts away from the pain and, instead, on breaking free. But no matter how much I scratched and scraped at his wrists, his grip was steadfast, and my strength was waning at the rate my blood was letting. The room was fading ... then no more.

❧❧

A phone chirped.

I bolted upright to a throbbing, cramping pain in my side. Scanning my surroundings, I saw that I was still in the park, sitting on the same bench, but in a lot of pain—

throbbing that I knew wasn't from my workout but from the daydream.

My cell rang again, tugging me out of my confusion. The caller ID showed it was Brad.

"What do you want?" I answered, more gruffly than I had intended.

"Wow, nice to hear your voice too. I just wanted to check in on you. I guess you just answered my question if we're done fighting," he said.

"Are you done being a jerk?" I retorted.

"Mia, I know you're angry with me, but please understand that I'm only concerned about you. Look, I don't want to break up with you. I love you. But I don't want to stand by while you chase a murderer. If something were to happen to you—"

"Nothing is going to happen to me, Brad. But if you can't stand by me through this, then get out of the way."

Silence. I knew I had hurt his feelings, but my adrenaline was rushing too fast for me to care right now.

The rustle of leaves pulled my attention upward toward a man approaching along the path holding a walking stick. I smiled tightly as he passed, his eyes and grin warm with friendliness. Yet in the back of my mind I didn't trust what lurked behind that façade. No one could be trusted these days.

I waited until his back was lost amid the sprouting foliage before I spoke again.

"How about we talk this over later?" I suggested. "I'm kind of in the middle of something right now."

Brad muttered an "okay" and hung up. I'd deal with him later. Right now I had something more pressing on my mind. The vision.

The daydream was too similar to my previous nightmare to be coincidence. The events had felt so real, so much so that I had to double-check for blood on my torso. Satisfied that there was none, I began to pick apart the events, searching for clues. There had to be a message in there somewhere. But what was it?

My mental inventory began with a name: Alexis. It wasn't much to go on without a last name, but it held meaning of some kind. It had to.

I wanted to talk to someone, but Brad didn't want anything to do with it, and I had no one else I could entrust this kind of secret to. Mom would freak out if I told her. And in the girl friends department I was lacking. But it was a secret that had to be told. Now more than ever I was convinced that lives depended on it.

An hour later I sat in front of my computer with my Google search box waiting for me to type. My fingers keyed the first thing that came to mind:

meaning of dreams

A long list of websites about dream interpretation popped up. I scanned the list of sites, pausing on the website of a local dream analyst: Dr. Avella Weaver. I clicked on the link, which took me to a professional-looking site.

Skimming through each page, her credentials seemed sound. Certified psychologist, impressive academia, and she utilized alternative medicine methods like acupuncture, hypnotism, and dream analysis. It was worth a shot, though I doubted my insurance would cover it.

On the contact page it listed her work hours. Surprisingly enough in the Bible Belt, where even some gas stations were closed for the Sabbath, she was open on

Sundays from one to six. I checked the clock. It was only 4:30, so I dialed the office number.

After two rings I heard an elderly woman's voice on the other end. "Hello, this is Dr. Avella Weaver's office. How can I help you?"

"Uh, hi. My name is Mia Germaine and I wanted to make an appointment ... today, if possible."

"Hmm, yes, I think we can fit you in before we close, Mia. Are you seeking dream analysis or psychological care or something else?"

To be honest, I had no idea what I was seeking.

Answers. So I said, "Dream analysis, I think."

"Okay. You sound unsure, so when you get here we can figure out what you need. Each session is usually an hour long, and I take my last appointment at five, so if you can make it here by then, we can squeeze a full session in today. Would that work for you?"

"Yes, thank you! I'll be leaving now. Thank you again for taking me on such short notice."

"That's what I'm here for, my dear. I look forward to meeting you."

As I hung up, I wondered if I was on the verge of going bat-crap crazy. Meeting with a dream interpreter? Should I follow it up with a palm reading? It sounded like something super-spiritual, like from the book of Daniel in the Bible when Daniel had the crazy prophetic dreams about Babylon. Prophecy was certainly not something that I was into.

I had a nagging feeling that I was beginning to lose myself to whatever had taken hold of me.

Chapter 6

Dr. Avella Weaver's office was as strange as her first name.

Nestled between an adorable antique store and an upscale restaurant in downtown Hillsborough, I nearly passed by the nondescript front door, adorned only with a simple brass plaque bearing the doctor's name. Almost all of the shops were closed as I walked from the parking lot behind a row of random businesses—an old-fashioned ice cream parlor, a handful of upper-scale restaurants, an insurance company. Catching my reflection in the large, streak-free storefront windows, I couldn't help but admire the jewelry and art on display, while potted pink azaleas and purple pansies framed their entrances.

A wrought-iron bench marked Dr. Weaver's.

Past the plain door whose old-fashioned bell jingled as I entered was an office full of unusual knickknacks, and heady with the mingled perfume of fragrant oils, incense, and greenery. Sculptures of various exotic animals—a Bengal cat, a squirrel monkey, a giraffe—littered every table, and the walls were adorned with images of bonsai trees. The décor created a mystic-meets-rainforest atmosphere.

Several chairs in vibrant fuchsia and teal fabrics lined three walls, and since I didn't see a reception desk, I picked a chair and sat. I had barely planted my rear down when a woman in a tie-dyed tunic and matching loose linen pants appeared around the corner. Her gray hair was close-cropped with a hint of curl to it.

"You must be Mia?" She extended her hand, and I accepted it and shook. I felt her bones jutting out from beneath the wrinkles and loosened my grip.

"Yes, and you're Dr. Weaver?"

"Call me Avella. Please follow me." She gestured for me to follow her down a hallway with carved tribal masks hanging on the walls. I felt a particularly penetrating Hopi Indian mask bore into my soul with its dead eyes as I passed.

At the end of the hallway was a large, open room, much simpler and less cluttered than the waiting room. A red sofa sat to one side, with two beige chairs in front of it. Two end tables held exquisitely carved wild animal figures—wildebeest, zebras, gazelles, a Serengeti tableau— and colorful coasters with the same exotic motif. Incredibly prolific potted plants decorated a rough-hewn table beneath a windowsill upon which marched a family of miniature elephants. Several degrees hung on the wall—bachelors, masters, doctorate, all in psychology. And from prestigious universities. Perhaps she wasn't a quack after all.

She gestured to the sofa. "Have a seat, dear."

The cordiality of her words made me feel like this was a visit with my grandma.

"Coffee, tea, water, juice?" she offered.

"Tea, please," I answered. She held a tray out for me, which displayed a wide variety of bagged teas. I picked a chai and she took it.

"Sugar and cream?" she asked.

"Yes, both, thank you."

Avella busied herself at a quaint refreshment nook. A moment later she handed me a steaming cup and, holding her own mug, sat across from me.

"So," she began after a sip, "tell me a little about yourself. Why you're here today."

I was stumped at where to begin and fell mute. It was hard to explain without sounding insane. When the hush lasted for more than a moment, she prodded, "Why don't you start by telling me what happened before you called me. Something prompted you today. What was it?"

"I guess you could say I've been having trouble sleeping."

Avella set her teacup down and folded her hands on her lap. "That's a good start. But don't be afraid to speak your mind, Mia. This is a safe place. Anything we discuss is confidential. Can you share why you've had trouble sleeping? Is something on your mind?"

"Okay, well, I had a dream. One that I've had before. And it kind of scares me."

"Why does it scare you?"

"It involves … a girl being murdered."

Avella nodded in understanding.

"Do you wish to know the significance of the dreams?"

"I guess, although I think they are more than dreams. I think they've actually happened and are perhaps unsolved murders. Cold cases. Does it make me crazy to think that?"

I wondered how much lower I could go—I was a patient asking my psychiatrist if I was crazy. Of course she wouldn't tell me if she thought I was.

"No, not at all. Dreams aren't always figments of our imagination. They can be glimpses into reality. We've had quite a few unsolved murders at the hands of the Triangle Terror lately, Mia. Perhaps your dreams are related to what's happening in the news?"

The thought hadn't escaped my attention, though I sensed it was more than just that.

"That's what I was wondering. You see, the dreams didn't start until just recently, right after I saw the news coverage of that girl Gina Martinez's death. But my dreams aren't about Gina. They're about some other girl, someone named Alexis. And the dream events seemed to have happened a long time ago."

"Why do you say that?"

"Because the details of the dream are from the '90s, I think. That's when I was a teenager, and everything in the dream—the furnishings in Alexis's house, the Pog collection—points to that era. And she's watching *Beverly Hills, 90210* on TV—the biggest giveaway."

Avella leaned forward, placing her chin on her hands, intent on my words. "Very interesting, Mia. Do you feel a connection to the girl—Alexis—in your dreams?"

"Definitely. More than a connection, though. It's like I *am* her."

I paused, not sure where to go from there. In the ensuing lull, Avella examined me with sincere eyes. "Tell me about your childhood, Mia. I'd like to know more about your life so that we can dissect this dream's bond to you."

I heaved a sigh. "For the most part it was pretty normal. Middle-class family. Raised well by loving parents. A happy home until I lost my father in a car accident, which happened when I was twelve. Even after that, though, my mom held it together for the both of us and helped me move past it. Sure, I was broken by the loss, but we healed together. I don't think I'm messed up by my dad's death."

"So you don't feel any lingering emotional scars from that loss?" Avella asked. Her eyes penetrated me, and I realized how very blue they were. Not dark aqua, but almost translucent. They were quite striking.

"Not so much emotional as physical scars." I tugged the neckline of my shirt down past my tattoo, just enough to show a faint white line running down my chest.

"I had a heart transplant as a result of the accident."

Avella's jaw dropped slightly. "You say you were twelve when that happened?"

I nodded.

"And I assume your donor was roughly your age?"

"I believe so, though I never found out who she was. It bugged me for a long time, and part of me thinks that has something to do with what's happening to me right now."

"Happening to you?" Avella's eyes explored mine.

"I'm not sure how to explain it, but I've been having chest pain right before or after those flashback episodes. It's weird."

"Hmm, yes, odd. But not unheard of."

"What do you mean? This kind of thing has happened before?"

Avella rose from her chair and went to a large bookshelf along the far wall. Her finger traced the spine of several books until she found what she was looking for and pulled the book down. She returned and showed me the cover:

A Change of Heart

"This book," she explained while flipping through several pages, "discusses organ memory. Organ memory is a theory positing that cells retain traits exclusive to the individual. Thus, each person's organs preserve a part of them, not merely blood type but actual personality characteristics. This particular book shares Claire Sylvia's experience with an organ transplant back in 1988. She recounts distinctive personality changes after her transplant."

"Wow," I said. So I wasn't the only one? Hope surged through me that I wasn't crazy after all.

"Yes, wow is appropriate," Avella said with a chuckle. "Additional research since then has shown that it's common among organ transplant patients to experience the onset of particular changes presumably brought about by the donated organs. For example, in one case study, patients noticed a change in preferred tastes. Before the transplant they might have liked the taste of white chocolate, then afterward they hated it. Or even changes in entertainment—movies, music, for instance—or recreational preferences. Before they liked swimming, afterward they couldn't remember how to swim. It's quite fascinating. Further studies revealed that in most of these cases the new preferences aligned with that of the donor."

She handed me the book to peruse.

"They originally ran these tests on volunteers who donated a kidney or lung, and they maintained contact with the donors and recipients so that they could facilitate further studies to confirm the nature of any changes in preference among the transplant patients. They did this since there was no conclusive way to validate changes from donors whose organs were harvested upon death, except for anecdotal testimony from family and friends."

"But I haven't noticed a change in my tastes or anything. Just weird memories."

"Well, there's more. In many of those documented cases, studies showed memory recall among several organ recipients who claimed to have memories of events not from their own lives."

"So other people had memories from their donors, and these memories were confirmed as real?"

"Yes. In one instance an infant who received a heart transplant recognized the mother of the boy whose heart he received years after his transplant. It made news, in fact, since he was a mere baby at the time of the organ donation. How could a child have known who the donor's mother was if not for organ memory? There are countless other examples, although the topic doesn't get much positive coverage in the mainstream media. Quack science, they call it. Needless to say, I would agree that it may teeter on a fine line of speculative science, but we can't discount empirical data, now can we?"

I couldn't believe what I was hearing. This wasn't science fiction? I had walked in here ready to be psychoanalyzed, but instead I was getting answers. Okay, maybe hippie-dippie, pseudo-scientific answers, but at least it was a start. Perhaps therapy wasn't so bad after all.

"So you think my heart is revealing the donor's actual life, maybe a memory of her murder?"

"It's a distinct possibility."

"You've given me so much clarity, Dr. Weaver—"

"Avella," she corrected with a smile. "And I'm happy to have helped you. But be careful in your pursuit of answers, dear. This sounds rather dangerous."

We both stood, and I reached out my hand, but she stepped forward and pulled me into a hug. "I'm a hugger, dear."

I thanked her again and pulled out my checkbook.

"How much do I owe you for the session? It was invaluable to me."

"This one's on me," she said. "As long as you promise to stay safe and keep me informed. It's not every day I encounter a session as enlightening and unusual as this one has been."

I assured her I'd keep in touch and try my best to stay out of trouble. Though lately trouble seemed to have a way of finding me.

PAMELA CRANE

Chapter 7

Movies make detective work seem so easy. But they never tell you how time-consuming it really is. After my appointment with Avella on Sunday, I wrote out a list of what I knew and what I didn't know— my own real-life version of Clue. It looked something like this:

Know:

The girl's name was Alexis.

She was roughly twelve years old in 1992.

She was stabbed in the abdomen.

Her mom was possibly an alcoholic.

She died at Duke Hospital on March 7, 1992.

Alexis recognized the murderer's voice.

Don't know:

The murderer's identity.

Alexis's last name.

How she died.

Where she lived.

Why she was targeted.

Despite its vagueness, the list gave me hope. So far I knew more than what I didn't know. If I could figure out who Alexis was, how she died, and why she was chosen as the victim, I hoped that would lead me to the killer.

So Monday afternoon, after slogging through editorial meetings that lasted through lunch, I stopped by Jackie O'Toole's office, my managing editor and only real friend, to ask about an early leave.

Since day one at the publishing house I worked for as an editor, Jackie positioned herself as friend and boss—in that order. Though our social lives intertwined less and less after I met Brad, Jackie never failed to be there when I needed her. And the woman could never tell me no.

"Hey, Jackie, do you mind if I skip out of work early today? I've got some errands to run."

With overdone black liner rimming her gold eyes, and a short bob of black hair wisped with gray, she reminded me of a ring-tailed lemur I had seen at the Museum of Life and Science.

"Sure, sweetie. Is everythin' okay?" she cooed in her Southern accent.

"Yeah, all's well. I just have some things to do to get a head start on the week."

"Mmmkay, but be careful out there, with that murderer on the loose. You know I worry 'bout you livin' all alone."

Was the Triangle Terror the only thing on peoples' minds these days?

"You know I'm tough as nails, Jackie."

After stopping by my desk to grab a stack of manuscript proposals that I was overdue to review, I decided to take a detour from my usual route home to do some investigation of my own. I'd start with the easiest stuff and build my foundation on that. Hopefully all the pieces would connect to give me the identity of her killer.

A tall order, I knew.

My first step was to figure out Alexis's full name. Newspaper archives dating back that far weren't online, so my best option was to hit the Durham Public Library. Their newspaper archives dated back to 1897, the year before the first public library opened in Durham, and they collected every paper since, though I was only interested in the year 1992. Alexis's obituary would naturally include her last name.

Twenty minutes after two, I walked through the library's front door and stopped at the help desk. I knew the date I was looking for, so I hoped my research would go quickly.

"Can I help you?" a bookish, balding man with glasses perched precariously on the tip of his ski-jump nose asked.

I resisted the strong impulse to reach out and push his glasses up on his nose. Most people didn't appreciate a stranger poking them, I figured.

"I'm looking for the newspaper archives."

He pointed to a room at the far end of the building. "The archive room is behind that glass door. Do you need help finding something?"

Was it safe to tell him? I couldn't imagine why not.

"I'm looking for *The News and Observer* records from 1992."

"Sure thing. The newspapers are collected in bound volumes according to year. The '90s will be on your immediate right as you enter the archives. Good luck!" He smiled and greeted the person behind me.

I walked past stacked rows of books and movies organized by genre, and computers huddled in tiny cubicles. The click of fingers typing away mingled with the whispered conversations around me. At the end of the building was a glass door with the word "Archives" on it. I went in and closed the door behind me. I followed my gaze along the spines of vertically arranged bound volumes until I came to one reading THE NEWS AND OBSERVER—

JANUARY-JUNE 1992. With a grunt I pulled the heavy volume off of the shelf, plunked it down on one of the tables, and flipped to the March 5, 1992, edition.

I pulled it out. The once crisp white newsprint was yellowed now and appeared so ancient and worn, though it was printed during my lifetime. It was a strange feeling realizing how much time had passed ... and suddenly I felt old at thirty-four.

It didn't take me long to find what I was looking for. The front-page headline read:

TWELVE-YEAR-OLD DURHAM GIRL FOUND DEAD, VICTIM OF BRUTAL MURDER

Durham, NC

Alexis Worthington, age 12, died Wednesday from a brutal stabbing. Her mother, Jennifer Worthington, came home to find her daughter lying in a pool of blood with a puncture wound in her side at their Willoughby Way residence Wednesday evening. Paramedics responding to a 9-1-1 call transported the youth to Duke Hospital where she was pronounced dead later that evening due to extreme blood loss.

There were no signs of forced entry, and police investigators are currently searching for evidence that might lead to the apprehension of her killer.

Worthington was a student at Lowe's Grove Middle School and enjoyed playing soccer. A memorial will be held March 9th at 10:00 a.m. at Christian Assembly of God on Pebble Road.

My eyes stung with fresh tears as I read the summary of a girl's life—all her hopes and vitality summed up in three short paragraphs. My heartbreak over the loss fueled my anger and desire for justice for this little girl.

Her killer had to pay, and I was collecting.

I pulled a notebook out of my purse and jotted down:

Alexis Worthington, Willoughby Way

Below that I scribbled:

Jennifer Worthington, mother

I wondered if Alexis's mother still lived at the Willoughby Way house. I doubted it, considering the nightmares that probably had haunted her there, the ghost of her daughter lingering in every room. Returning the volume to the shelf, I headed to the central part of the library.

A moment later I found a vacant seat and sat down. Retrieving my iPhone from my purse, I pulled up the White Pages and typed "Jennifer Worthington, NC." Half a dozen records popped up, so I screened the ages of each listing to gauge a likely fit. I guessed her to be around my mother's age, mid to late fifties. Two women met the profile, and sure enough, one still lived on Willoughby Way. I couldn't imagine why. Maybe the memories held her hostage.

No phone number was listed, so I'd have to make a personal appearance. I checked the time. Three fifty. By the time I got there it'd be after four, so I probably wouldn't have to wait long for her to get home from work, assuming she had a day job.

I MapQuested the directions to her house, set my navigation to guide me, then left to meet a mother who had lost her daughter to a killer.

I had no idea what I was going to say.

It was 4:38 when I finally pulled into the driveway of 721 Willoughby Way and parked next to the walkway. I had already wasted fifteen minutes circling the block, rehearsing what I would say, and still, as I stepped out of my car, I drew a mental blank. How should I introduce myself? I couldn't come right out and tell her I'd been having dreams of her daughter's murder from twenty years ago—unless I wanted to get outfitted in a straightjacket.

My nerves were fatigued from the anxiety of meeting Alexis's mother. What should I say? What shouldn't I say? I had no idea how to approach a mother who had lost her child two decades ago with the brazen announcement that I planned to find her killer.

Forcing unsteady steps, I made it to the front porch. I stood there staring at a lion's head knocker, his bronze mouth open and fangs jutting out like he'd snap his jaw shut at any moment. Before I lifted my hand to knock, the outer screen door trembled as the wooden front door swept open. I jumped, startled by the movement.

"Stalk much?" a man asked me behind the screen.

For a moment I was shocked silent, but when he smiled, the fear switched to immediate attraction. Although I didn't usually like clean-shaven men, it worked for him. And even through the haze of screen, his eyes were a striking green that seemed to penetrate me. I suddenly felt exposed.

"Um, what?" I blustered.

"I saw your car pass by the house, like, eight times. Care to explain?" the man said without emotion.

"I'm looking for a Jennifer Worthington," I replied meekly.

"And who might you be?"

"Mia Germaine. Do you know Mrs. Worthington? Does she still live here?" I caught him looking me over, examining me. Heat flushed my cheeks as my nerve wavered. For a fleeting second I prayed he'd say I had the wrong house so that I could retreat to my car.

"Yeah," he said, propping the screen door open with his arm, "she lives here. Do you want to come in and wait for her to get home? It won't be long. She's usually home by five."

"Uh, sure," I said, though I wasn't so sure. Being alone in a strange house with a strange man ... it wasn't my most street-smart moment.

I walked past him as he held the door open for me. Our chests bumped as I slid by, and I whiffed the subtle fragrance of cologne—a manly musk. He was hotter up close, even wearing pajama pants and a rumpled T-shirt.

Not sure how to proceed, I waited in a cozy foyer while he shut the door behind him. "And you are?" I asked as he turned and led me into the nucleus of the house—a modest-sized living room adorned in burgundy and beige hues.

"Landon. Landon Worthington. I'm Jennifer's son." Instead of shaking my hand, he stuffed his hands in his pockets and rocked back on his feet. The pose showed off his muscled arms and toned shoulders, two of my favorite body parts on Brad. Landon's dark brown hair reminded me of Brad, and I instantly felt a stab of guilt. I never got around to calling him back.

"Oh, I didn't know she had a son."

"Do you even know her? I don't recognize your name ... Mia, was it?"

"Well, it's kind of a long story. I'll have to explain when she gets here."

"Why don't you explain now?" Landon said matter-of-factly, waving me to sit down on a trendy microfiber sofa. "I was just sleeping, but I'm wide awake now. Thanks to you."

"Oh, sorry for waking you." I wondered who slept at 4:30 in the afternoon, other than jobless people. Then I realized this guy lived with his mom. There was definitely a story there.

"No worries. I had to get up anyways. So, what do you want with my mom?"

I sat and inspected the room. Despite significant remodeling, I could detect the similarities to the room in my dream. Where the recliner had sat was now a love seat. The floors were no longer dirt-stained but polished to a mirror shine. A potted snake plant had replaced the floor model TV, which had undergone a major upgrade to a wall-mounted 52-inch LCD TV. Artsy pictures of flowers adorned the walls. It was quite a modern and clean transformation.

Landon plopped down next to me. His expression said he was still waiting for an answer to his question.

"Was Alexis your sister?" I boldly asked.

Landon's emerald eyes narrowed into slits. "What do you know about Alexis?"

I took a deep breath and released it slowly. "When Alexis … passed away, I received her heart. I mean, her heart was donated to me. Anyways, her heart saved my life, and I never really had any side effects from the transplant … until now. It's those side effects that I wanted to talk about with your mother."

"How did you get our information? I thought that was confidential."

"It is … but I kind of pieced it together."

He pursed his lips in thought. "So, what kind of, uh, side effects do you need to talk to my mom about?"

"I'm sorry, but I'd prefer to keep that between me and your mom."

Landon leaned back into the sofa and folded his hands on his lap. "Let me level with you, Mia. I'm not trying to be a jerk. It's just that it was really hard on us to lose my sister, and you coming here dredging up the past … well, I'm not so sure that's a good idea. My mom's been through enough already. I don't think she'll be too happy to hear about your 'side effects,' whatever they are."

"I understand," I said. But I couldn't give up so easily. Not yet. "So Alexis was your sister," I repeated. "I'm sorry for your loss. Did the police ever find out who killed her?"

Landon shrugged weakly. Although it was well hidden, I noticed the sadness creeping into his eyes. "No, there weren't enough leads. That always bothered me—not knowing. But it was twenty-two years ago. Sure, I miss Alexis and wonder what she'd be like now, if she'd be married with kids, things like that ... but there comes a point when you have to move forward, y'know?"

"Yeah," I whispered. "I lost my dad shortly after you lost Alexis, so I know what you mean." I stood up and started walking toward the entryway. "I'm sorry to bother you. Maybe this wasn't a good idea. I'll get going now—"

"Wait," Landon said. "Would you mind sharing with me what you came to tell my mom? I mean, maybe it will help."

"You sure?" I asked hesitantly.

"Humor me," he said with a weak grin.

"Okay," I agreed with a warning tone. "But promise not to whip out the straightjacket once I tell you."

"Now I'm really curious."

"This might be painful to hear, Landon."

"I can handle it."

I headed back to the sofa and sat at the far end, pressed against the arm. Overlooking my desire for distance, Landon shifted himself close enough so that our knees touched. I felt pink embarrassment color my cheeks. I couldn't help myself. The guy was gorgeous. But I didn't want Landon. He only reminded me of how much I missed Brad.

Dismissing those thoughts, I took a cleansing breath and began my story. I opened with an explanation of organ memory, giving the disclaimer that this information came from a doctor, not a sci-fi movie. After a few jokes at my own expense, I went on to describe how I started having nightmares about Alexis's murder shortly after Gina Martinez's death, and they were growing more detailed and clearer with each dream.

"I'm hoping that somehow these dreams will lead me to her killer. And before you tell me to drop it, sorry, no can do. Whoever did this to her needs to be brought down, even twenty-two years later."

Landon looked offended. "Why would you think I'd tell you to back off? I want to find out who did this to my sister more than anyone. If you think you can find him, let me help you."

"Really?"

"Yeah, really. But for now let's leave my mom out of it. I don't want to get her emotionally involved yet, not until we have something more concrete."

"Totally," I agreed.

"So what do you know so far ... about the killer?" Landon asked.

"Not much, unfortunately. Until today I didn't even know Alexis was the girl in my dreams. But I get the sense that he was familiar to her, so it'd be someone she knew. And although his voice was kinda distorted, it sounded like a man."

"A man ... she knew. That's it?"

I laughed at his clear sarcasm. "For now. Give me time. I'll have more."

I heard a car pull up the driveway and a door shut.

"That's my mom. Just pretend to be a friend, okay? I don't want to raise suspicion."

"Sure," I said. "You *are* a friend now, so it's not lying."

"Maybe we should kiss or something?" he jested.

"Ha! Nice try!"

A SECONDHAND LIFE

When Jennifer Worthington walked through the front door, I immediately recognized her to be Landon's mother, a near-exact female replica—though strands of gray mingled with her dark brown hair, and fine wrinkles creased the corners of her mouth. Her green eyes crinkled up in a smile, accentuating the friendly laugh lines around them.

"Hi, I'm Mia Germaine," I introduced myself, though my voice sounded strained. I could barely push the words past the lump in my throat.

Something within me ached so hard that I nearly wept. The compulsion to touch her overwhelmed me.

I couldn't stop myself as I strode up to her and wrapped my arms around her frail shoulders, pulling her into a hug that I never wanted to release. Her torso stiffened under my embrace, but she didn't push me away from her.

"It's okay, honey," she soothed, awkwardly patting my back.

"I'm so sorry. I'm sorry I couldn't keep my promise," I whispered, not sure where the words were coming from. I had no clue what I was doing, what I was saying. It was like my body had taken control and I could do nothing about it. For a brief second I wondered if this was what having a mental illness felt like.

"What did you say?" she asked, holding me at arm's length, searching my eyes. After intense scrutiny, her arms slowly circled me and squeezed tenderly.

A moment later I found myself sobbing. I couldn't stop heaving as I held her, tears streaming down my cheeks, until after a minute or two she joined me in tearful release. We both stood there crying for several long moments before she pulled away and held me at arm's length.

"Alexis?" she asked hopefully.

I patted my heart. "Yes. How did you know?"

"Alexis's promise—you just spoke her final words to me the night she died. She wasn't fully awake when she said it, though. She was in some kind of a coma, but she spoke to me the moment before her heart stopped—said she was sorry. To this day I wish I could have said good-bye."

"That's so sad," I whispered.

"Yes, but that's not the only reason I know you, Mia."

"You know me?" I asked, perplexed.

"I visited you in the hospital when we heard that Alexis's heart would be donated to another young girl at Duke. You haven't changed much since then. Still a beautiful young lady." She rested her palm on my cheek.

I chuckled. "I was twelve years old. I sure hope I've grown up since then. Wait—I thought that donor records were confidential ..."

"They are, but the hospital couldn't turn down a grieving mother. I begged the doctor to tell me your name so that I could have some kind of closure, and reassurance that Alexis would live on, in a sense. He couldn't say no. Of course, I swore to never contact you, but I had a feeling that someday I would meet the one who keeps my baby girl alive. It's nice to finally meet you ... and to be reunited with Alexis."

Jennifer—she insisted I call her—offered to have me stay for dinner, which I politely declined for now. It had been a long, emotional day and all I wanted was to drop into bed and sleep the exhaustion away. But I vowed to visit again as we exchanged contact information.

As Landon walked me to the front door, I turned and spoke cautiously, "Jennifer?"

"Yes?" she said.

"May I ask what Alexis's promise was—what she was referring to before she died?"

"Of course," Jennifer replied with heartache etched in her words. "That morning she had promised to be a better daughter and give me a reason to quit drinking."

"Oh, I'm sorry."

"No, don't be. In a way she kept her promise. She did give me a reason to get sober and become a better person. After her passing I made a lot of changes for the better, and it's all because of her. Her legacy lives on."

At least Alexis's death held some meaning after everything the family had been through.

As I headed into the brisk dim evening, Landon trailed behind me to my car. I inhaled a sweet scent of lilac drifting from the next-door neighbor's yard. Stopping at my car door, I turned and met Landon's gaze, barely visible against the dusk's deep blue backdrop. Twilight's chill kissed my cheeks and I blushed.

"I'm really glad you showed up on our doorstep, Mia," he said, opening his arms in a hug.

"Me too." With a tentative step forward, I hugged him back, unsure what it meant—to him, to me, to us. Was this the creation of "us" unfolding before me? It couldn't be. I longed for Brad. So before either of us had a chance to interpret—or misinterpret—the moment, I glided backward and slid behind the wheel.

As Landon stood with his hand on the edge of my driver's side door, propping it open, I saw a seriousness pass over his face as his jaw clenched and his eyes darkened. "Now let's catch us a killer."

PAMELA CRANE

Chapter 8

Wednesday, April 9
5:23 p.m.

I was surprised to get a call from Landon so soon after our first meeting on Monday. While my thoughts raced back and forth between Landon and Brad for two days straight, my main focus lingered on Alexis. I couldn't let boy-craziness distract me from my purpose.

It was Wednesday afternoon when Landon left a message on my cell phone, so I called him back on my way home from work.

"Remember me—your cohort in crime?" Landon teased when he answered my return call.

"More like my sidekick, Watson," I retorted.

He laughed, a good-natured, deep laugh. I smiled at its sound.

"Busy?" he asked.

"Not really. Why?"

"Wanna meet up for coffee and chat?"

"Sure. I'm on Erwin Road right now—heading home from work. You know the Port City Java near the Duke University East Campus? I can be there in fifteen."

He paused.

"Got it. I'm on my way. I'll meet you there."

After we hung up, I noticed the oddly titillating sensation of butterflies flapping wildly in my stomach.

❧❧❧

Landon beat me to Port City Java and met me at the cash register. Carrying both of our coffee cups—his treat, he insisted—he picked a corner table away from a crowd of undergrads clad in Duke Blue Devil sweatshirts noisily laughing and hogging three tables in the middle of the trendy shop. Was I already old enough to find college students irritating?

Warding off the elder side of me, I instead grinned at their overpowering banter as I sat in a red faux leather chair across from a shiny, knee-high chrome table. Landon took a cushion on a thick leather sofa across from me, hugging his cup to his chest.

"Kids," Landon grumbled with slight agitation, nodding toward the group.

"Kids? Those are adults, old man."

"Whatever. They're loud and obnoxious."

"It doesn't bother me. We were kids once too."

"But doesn't it seem like they get more inconsiderate with each passing decade? Kids these days are so much worse than in our time. I don't remember being like that."

"Selective memory," I teased. "I guarantee *all* kids are frustrating to deal with at that age. So anyways, what were you calling about?"

"You sleep well this past week?" he asked with a wink.

"What's that supposed to mean?" Was he implying that I was up at night dreaming about him?

"You know, the dreams about Alexis ..."

Flustered at my own misinterpretation, I faltered over a hasty *oh, right, that.* "Nothing new to report," I added.

"What did you think I meant?"

"Nothing," I assured him.

"I was just wondering if you're hot on any new trails,

Sherlock."

"Two nights of blissful slumber, unfortunately. And no new clues." I shrugged. "But that doesn't mean we can't keep digging. Although, I do have something to show you. I made up a list that might be helpful. I'm not sure if this is how the cops do things, but I figured it would help me get the facts organized."

I pulled out my updated notepad of *knows* and *don't knows*. The killer's unknown identity was still at the top of the list. I placed the notepad between us and pointed to the handwritten script:

> *Know:*
>
> *The girl's name was Alexis Willoughby.*
>
> *She was roughly twelve years old in 1992.*
>
> *She was stabbed in the abdomen.*
>
> *Her mom was possibly an alcoholic.*
>
> *She died at Duke Hospital on March 7, 1992.*
>
> *Alexis recognized the murderer's voice.*
>
> *Died from blood loss.*
>
> *No forced entry.*
>
> *Lived at 721 Willoughby Way.*
>
> *Murderer is a man.*
>
>
> *Don't know:*
>
> *The murderer's identity.*
>
> *~~Alexis' last name.~~*
>
> *~~How she died.~~*
>
> *~~Where she lived.~~*
>
> *Why she was targeted.*

Landon sarcastically oohed and aahed over the paper.

"Seriously, though," he said sincerely, "it's a great start."

"This is everything I know and everything I still need to find out. In my dream the killer was familiar to Alexis, so if I could find out a little more about her life, who her friends were, it might lead us to him. Based on his ability to overpower her, plus his voice, he's a guy. Even the method of attack—a stab wound, which isn't something female killers generally do, though I've known a few women who like to stick the knife in figuratively—points to a man."

"How do you know that?"

"Saw it on *Criminal Minds*. I'm guessing it's true, or else they wouldn't put it on television. Right?"

"I hope you don't base all of your knowledge on television shows," he said with a laugh. "Unless you're telling me that dogs can talk and Godzilla is traipsing around Manhattan."

"Ugh, you watched that version?" I chided with a scowl.

"Apparently you did too," he replied.

I looked away in unspoken shame.

Landon picked up the notepad, his eyes following the lines down the page. "How do you know it's a man ... and not a teenage boy? Wouldn't a teenager fit the profile too, since you said it was someone she knew? Maybe it could be a guy from school."

"I hadn't thought of that, but if he was strong enough ... absolutely." I scribbled an amendment:

Murderer is a man/teenage boy.

"So, that's it. That's all we got." I frowned. It wasn't anything. The cops probably had much more and still hadn't solved the case. "Do you know if there were any fingerprints recovered from the scene of the crime?" I asked.

"I was pretty young back then, so I wasn't privy to a lot of the details. But I do know they never found the murder weapon and I don't think any prints were found. He probably wiped them. We could always go down to the police station to see if they can give us any information. Since it was my sister, I'm sure they'll be willing to pull the file and tell us what they know."

"Yeah ..." the word trailed off as another thought plowed through. "What about a relative—could it be an uncle, cousin, someone like that?"

Landon took a careful gulp of his house blend and stared through me to the space beyond where the door jingled open and patrons swept in and out. His eyes darkened. Something lingered on the tip of his tongue, but I had no idea what it could be. Something painful.

"You okay?" I whispered, placing my hand on his.

As if stunned to find my hand touching him, he jerked back and muttered, "No, yeah ... I mean, yeah, I'm okay. Just thinking. Remembering."

"You don't have to talk about it if you don't want to."

"It's nothing. Just my dad. The day Alexis died was shortly before my dad was sentenced for first-degree burglary, felony theft, and attempted manslaughter. At least Alexis wasn't alive to watch her father stand in that courtroom and be declared guilty, then hauled away in handcuffs. I'll never forget it. Although, I suppose Alexis had seen her fair share of his screw-ups."

My heart broke for this damaged family, for Landon especially. Losing a sister and father so close together. I wondered how lives ended up so crushed and out of control.

"Things were a mess at home," he resumed after a solemn moment. "Neither of my parents were ever sober. My mom was cheating on my dad, my dad was living with my Uncle Derek at the time, and then Dad gets accused of robbing a house and shooting the lady who lived there. Luckily the lady survived or he'd be facing murder one. To this day he claims he didn't do it, but who knows? I wouldn't trust my dad as far as I could throw him ... and he's a big man. Life was crazy." Each sentence ran on the heels of the next as he rushed through the gory details.

And I thought my past was messy.

"I'm so sorry for what you went through."

"It's not all bad. Because of all the rough stuff, my mom actually got better. She found God, got sober, went back to school, and landed a good job. Despite losing everything, she got a second chance, and she's happy now. Doesn't need the revolving door of men or booze to get through each day anymore."

I wanted to ask him if he found healing too, but it felt too personal a question.

He paused.

Then cleared his throat.

"Do you think my dad could have done it ... killed his own daughter?"

I couldn't imagine that being the case. But I didn't know the man. He almost killed someone else, so why not?

"I don't know. Maybe we should talk to him."

"Ha! He's in jail, Mia. And knowing him, I doubt he'll ever make parole."

"He's allowed visitors, isn't he? Can't we go see him?"

Landon emphatically shook his head. "I don't think so. I haven't talked to my dad since he was sentenced. I don't even know what I'd say when I saw him. It's been twenty years."

"I'll be there with you. I can do all the talking. He might be able to help shed light on some things."

"I dunno ..." he said with reluctance.

"You don't have to decide now. Just think about it."

With a little strong-arming on my part Landon agreed

to think about it—no promises, though.

I tipped my head back and gulped the remainder of my caramello leche. But as my gaze leveled, I suddenly wanted to climb under the table and hide. Standing at the counter was Brad, and I knew that if he saw Landon and me together, no amount of explaining could fix things. I grabbed a newspaper that sat a table away, opened it, and hid my face behind it.

"You okay?" Landon asked.

"No—my boyfriend is standing in line. I can't let him see me," I whispered, shading myself from view.

"Why not?" a voice replied, but it wasn't Landon. It was Brad.

The newspaper fell limply to my lap as I searched for words—any words would suffice. My face flushed at being caught, though I didn't quite know what I was guilty of. I hadn't been doing anything wrong. I was totally innocent … yet somehow I didn't feel so blameless.

"Hey, Brad," I mustered. "This is Landon Worthington, Alexis's brother. Landon, this is Brad." The introduction was awkward and tense. Clearly Brad noticed the lack of a qualifier "boyfriend" attached to his name.

"Alexis—as in the girl you dreamed about?" Brad clarified.

"Yep," I said.

Landon held out his hand, which Brad ignored. When no one spoke, I continued uneasily, "Sorry I never called you back. Things have been a little—"

"Busy?" he finished for me. "I can see that." He gestured at Landon while glaring at me. "You move on quickly. And here I didn't even realize we were officially broken up. Next time send a memo, okay?

"Brad, it's not what it looks like …" I pleaded.

It sounded cliché even as I begged.

"Stop, Mia. I don't want to hear any more. I just

wanted to say hi … and bye. For good, I guess."

As he briskly turned to go, I jumped from my seat and grabbed his arm. "Wait, please. I can explain."

"Famous last words," he said under his breath. "Save it, Mia. I thought we had something special. I even began to come around to the idea of supporting you on this whole investigation thing, but now I'm wondering how I could have been so stupid and naïve to buy into your drama. Just leave me alone. Don't call me." He yanked his arm out of my grasp and stormed away from me, a tinkling jingle echoing as the door slammed shut behind him.

As I shot down my mind's debate of whether to run after him or not, begging and pleading for another chance—knowing Brad was the type who needed to cool off before another confrontation if I wanted to avoid World War III—I sadly wondered if I had lost him forever. While my brain conceded that letting him go was perhaps best for us both, my heart didn't agree.

I was in love. I'd always love Brad.

Yet in our short relationship, I'd already lost so much of my identity over this man, and I knew it was only going to get worse if I stayed with him while fighting my demons. Over the past few weeks I felt myself slipping into co-dependency. I slept, breathed, longed for him. I … *needed* him. I'd never needed anyone before. It was unhealthy. I had to shut it off before *it*—love—consumed me.

Here I was, torn between avenging the lost life of a young girl, or embracing love with a flesh and blood man who made me giddy. It felt selfish to pick Brad over Alexis … so it was the honorable thing to let him go, right?

It didn't feel so honorable at the moment as I watched his retreating form—head hung low, shoulders stooped, as he strode against the harsh wind to his car.

A SECONDHAND LIFE

My mother always called me an empath—someone who feels what others are feeling, and often magnified—to my own detriment. Seeing a person get injured, for example, shot pain through my legs that nearly crippled me. Or the tears of a friend could send me bawling. But that's not the worst of it.

Love was the worst of it.

Feeling things so deeply could be a blessing or a curse. A blessing when the love is as deep as the ocean and as pure as mountain air, but a curse when heartbreak sent me over the edge and into a pit of oblivion.

I had stumbled into my pit.

PAMELA CRANE

Chapter 9

As the workweek took its sweet time lumbering toward the weekend, Landon's calls filled Brad's void and kept me company ... until they started coming later and later into the night. I began to wonder if he ever slept. But when his phone calls started interfering with my own sleep, I made a mental note to talk to him about boundaries the next time I saw him.

That day came the next Tuesday.

Tuesday afternoon my cell phone rang as I was walking to my car from work. With things so dire between Brad and me, I had lost any incentive to put in extra hours editing the growing pile of books demanding my time. Clocking in late and leaving early—deadly ammunition any normal boss could use against me, but Jackie wouldn't. Besides, at this point, I didn't care. They were lucky I showed up at all as my pit of depression sucked me in deeper.

I answered my cell and recognized Landon on the other end.

The wind whistled over the sound of his voice, so I ran across the parking lot and jumped into my car to better hear him.

"Hey, what's up?" I said with a glance in my mirror. I was a hideous flashback from the big hair days of the '80s—a frizzy, brown mess that the wind had whipped into a mile-high wad of cotton candy. I tamed the unruly 'do with my fingers, then dotted my lips with a shimmery Burt's Bees lip balm—the most makeup I ever dared to wear.

"I thought about your offer ... to go to jail with me to visit my dad. I want to take you up on it."

"Really?" I exclaimed with a little too much fervor. It was the best news I had all week, which wasn't saying much. Brad had refused all twenty-six of my calls, and my dreams were MIA. "When do you want to go?"

"You free tonight? I scheduled a visitation for six o'clock."

It wasn't exactly how I planned to spend my evening, but since Brad and I hadn't reconciled yet, I was plan-less and had nothing better to do than veg on the couch with a book.

"Sure. Where's it at?"

"The Durham County Detention Facility on South Mangum Street. You know what—how about I pick you up at your house and we can drive together? It'd do me good to have you in the car with me so I don't chicken out and drive home instead."

I gave him my address and told him I'd need about an hour and a half to get home, grab a bite, and change out of my work clothes into something more casual. "Wouldn't want your pop to think I'm a mouthpiece you hired to spring him from the big house," I joked.

Landon didn't laugh.

Two hours later Landon and I were sitting at a metal table in front of a bulky, nearly bald man who introduced himself to me as Dan. The visitor's room was a sparsely occupied pod with a Plexiglas wall separating inmates clad in rumpled jumpsuits—some orange, some green, depending on how long you'd been there—from their loved ones and not-so-loved ones. Guards loitered around the room, pacing with a watchful eye.

Amid hostile arguments over child-rearing and sentimental tears of hope at being reunited with their families soon, a sense of longing permeated the room. For we all knew that at the end of the hour, those of us on the outside would return to freedom's embrace while the prisoners trudged through their harsh reality of bland prison food, cramped and squalid living quarters, endless boredom, and an oppressive atmosphere of violence and hopelessness.

The conversation was stiff at first as Dan and Landon sat in solemn silence. With meager participation from the men, I chattered about nothing in particular just to fill the void between them, as promised. The belated spring weather. The skyrocketing price of gasoline. The latest Steelers draft picks. Since my father loved the Steel Curtain, he raised me with the same passion, thus saving me before I could jump on the Carolina Panthers bandwagon, despite being a born-and-bred Tar Heel, and danged proud of it. However, after 2013's middling 8-8 season, I wondered if I had made the right choice.

When it became clear that Dan wasn't interested in idle chitchat, current events, or sports, he blurted out, "Landon, why are you here? You haven't visited me once since I've been in here. Why now?"

I heaved a sigh of thanksgiving that the conversational burden was finally off my back.

"Long overdue, I guess," Landon said half-heartedly.

Dan snorted. "Twenty-two years overdue. So suddenly you care about me enough to stop by? Are you here to announce an engagement, kid on the way—what?"

"Nope, still single and kid-less."

"What, then? I have no idea what's going on with you, and you're my son, my flesh and blood. You getting my letters? You're still living on Willoughby with your mom, right?"

"Yes, and yes." Landon's stilted answers dropped like lead amidst the din of the animated conversations elsewhere in the visiting room.

"How's your mom? It's been a couple weeks since I've seen her."

Landon finally perked up. "Wait—Mom's been visiting you?"

"Has been for years. Almost every month. Got a heart of gold, your mom. Even when things've been busy, she never fails to stop in, God love 'er."

"Then you *do* know what's going on with me."

Dan heaved an exaggerated sigh. "Landon, I'm just trying to connect with you. Your mama's forgiven me; why can't you? One more time: Why are you even here? Finally feeling guilty for shutting me out of your life, or what?"

Landon growled and rose to his feet. "I'm here to ask if you killed Alexis."

"What?" Dan shouted, clearly taken aback.

From the corner of the room an armed guard pointed to our table and yelled firmly, "Is there a problem over there?"

"No, sir," I answered sweetly. Then I turned to Landon. "Both of you need to take a breath before we get kicked out." I switched to Dan. "And Dan, that's not what Landon means. We're trying to figure out what happened to Alexis and we thought maybe you might know something."

Dan lifted his chin and scrutinized me. "Something like who killed my baby girl? If I did know, I'd be in here for murder—for taking the life of the man who stole my Lexi from me. I may have been a drunk, but I was no killer. And I loved my kids—even you, Landon, when you were a teenaged prick."

Landon returned to his metal folding chair and propped an elbow on the table. "I was never a prick."

Dan chuckled heartily. "Aren't all teenage boys? I'm kidding, son. No, you were a good boy. Always helping out, trying to mend our messes. And you took care of your sister when your mama and I were too caught up in our own selfish games."

He exhaled as if his secrets weighed a thousand pounds.

"You and Lexi were gifts that I squandered. I wish I had been a better father to you back then ... and to you now. But here I am ..." He gestured pathetically around his dismal surroundings.

He paused, and Landon said nothing.

"You deserved better, son. I wish I could go back and redo my life. Take you to your baseball practices. Help you with girl troubles. Make you clean up your room. Watch you grow up ... you know, just be there for you as a dad rather than a failure."

"Dad ..." Landon interjected, the single word touched with more sympathy than any longwinded oratory.

"No, don't make excuses for me. Since I've been sober I got some perspective. It's hard to explain from behind bars, but I have changed. I'm a better man. I hope to prove it to you one day. I just wish I had learned sooner, before it was too late. Before my mistakes cost your sister her life and caused you God knows how much emotional trauma."

"I'm fine, Dad. And I know you meant well," Landon replied sincerely. "The drink changed you. But when you were sober we had some good times, didn't we?"

"Remember that time I took you driving when you first got your learner's permit? I thought we were gonna die!" Dan threw his head back, laughing.

"Hey, you wouldn't stop screaming. How was I supposed to concentrate with you crying like a little girl? And you were a terrible driving teacher, by the way, telling me to gun it through the yellow lights."

"Squeeze the lemon, I would tell you. Yeah, I remember those days. They get me through the tough times in here."

They both shared a long, healing chuckle.

"I love you so much, Landon," Dan said softly when the laughter died.

"I love you too, Dad. I'm sorry I never visited before now. I just wasn't ready, I guess."

I felt slightly awkward sharing in this sentimental moment, but neither seemed to care that I was present.

"I didn't deserve a visit, son. But I'm glad you came. Hopefully I'll be out of here by the time you decide to settle down and marry a nice girl. Which reminds me, so what exactly can I do for you and—Mia, is it?"

"Mia is trying to help us find Alexis's killer. Remember when Alexis's heart was donated? Well, this is the girl who received her heart. Alexis saved her life, so she wants to return the favor by finally putting Alexis to rest."

"That's noble of you," Dan said to me. "I hope you find who did it. The police were useless."

"Do you remember the details of their investigation?" I asked.

"I couldn't forget if I tried. No forced entry, no murder weapon recovered, tons of prints, but the fingerprints were all accounted for."

"What do you mean?" I prodded.

"Back in the day Landon's mother was a bit of a—"

"Tramp?" Landon finished for him.

"I was going to say 'lady of the night,' but tramp works too. Back then she had more men coming and going than a Thai whorehouse—pardon my French, little lady. I always suspected it was one of her boyfriends. God knows where she found them or what they were capable of. Which would also explain the lack of forced entry. But the cops couldn't pin it down on any one guy. There wasn't enough evidence to convict anyone, and half the guys Jennifer was with at that time she didn't have names or contact information for."

"Maybe if I talked to her ..." I offered.

"And say what?" Landon interjected. "*I know you don't know me very well, but can you tell me your sexual history? I think one of your one-night stands might have killed your daughter.* And I sure as heck am not asking my mom about her former sex life."

He was right. It wasn't exactly a tactful conversation to broach.

"It wouldn't matter," Dan chimed in. "Jennifer doesn't remember much about that part of her life. She was always drunk, rarely lucid. Like I said, she didn't know full names anyways. Plus, it would hurt her to have to travel back to that period of her life again. She's finally doing good, living right, living in the present. Leave her here. Besides, hurting your mother to avenge your sister wouldn't help anything."

Dan was right.

So there it was.

Another dead end.

Chapter 10

Friday, April 18
10:08 p.m.

The bedside clock said it was only a little after ten o'clock, but to my heavy eyelids and spasming back it felt well past midnight. It was Friday night and I was already in bed. Pathetic.

Was my age catching up with me?

Although my head insisted no, my body told me yes.

I had bid farewell to my twenties four years ago. While all of my friends were married with kids, worrying about play dates and mortgage payments, here I was—single, asset-less, and on a road to nowhere fulfilling. Brad had been my last hope for a family of my own. Once a girl hits her mid-thirties, men are like parking spots: taken or handicapped. Although I had never envisioned myself as an apron-wearing, baby-toting wifey playing house in the suburbs, it was what people did if they wanted a nice life.

I pulled my comforter down below my waist and flipped over on my side. I considered fixing myself a bowl full of ice cream and popping in a movie—nothing too romantic, since it would only depress me more—but I wasn't in the mood. Since that fateful Saturday night when I experienced my first nightmare, all I could think about was Alexis, and finding her killer. It consumed me.

Two weeks ago I never would have considered visiting a felon in jail. I would have never showed up on a stranger's doorstep unannounced. I never would have given up Brad in pursuit of some harebrained idea of solving a murder. Who was I? I didn't recognize myself anymore. But I had to admit, I liked certain aspects of the new me. Adventurous. Daring. Brave. Up for a challenge. And I was feeling things I hadn't felt in a long time.

Sure, I loved Brad. It was the purest love I could imagine. But our relationship lacked passion ... an intense can't-ignore-it, risk-everything-for-it urge. I couldn't imagine how strong a grip obsession could have on a person until this case. I was passionate to figure it out. To find her killer. It gave me purpose. Never had I felt this way about anything. In a way, Alexis was saving me from myself. Instead of leading a bland, typical life I would later regret, I was living on the edge. But it was costing me everything.

Next to my notepad on the nightstand was a pencil topped with a Troll doll. I don't know why I had hung on to that pink-haired monster since childhood, but his goofy expression and wild Don King hair—not to mention his adorable, pot-bellied nakedness—added character to my otherwise boring pencil, I suppose. My new task was drafting a list of possible suspects. Any guy in Alexis's life was a suspect, though I didn't have a single name for my list. So I started with the basics:

Possible suspects:
Dan, father
Uncle Derek
Neighbors
Classmates
Cousins
Friends from church, extracurricular activities
Jennifer's boyfriends

While I trusted Dan's sincerity, I couldn't rule him out just yet. Had it been a drunken rage that sent him after her? Perhaps she said the wrong thing at the wrong time and spurred on his mean, inebriated side? I didn't know much about him when he drank, but people did all kinds of horrendous things while under the influence. But something told me it wasn't him. He loved his little girl, and if the same killer was tied to the current murders, it couldn't be him.

Moving down my list, I doubted any of Alexis's male classmates at that age would have the strength to overpower her or the stomach to kill. Logically it had to be someone bigger, stronger, who knew the family and their schedules and could freely come and go.

So for now I drew a tentative line through Dan and the classmates. I needed to find out more about the uncle and extended family to see who was in her life back then.

And then there were the neighbors. I wondered how to find out who lived on Willoughby Way in 1992 and who was still local. It'd been twenty years—surely people had moved. Especially if they were trying to avoid murder charges. Either way, I'd dig through property records to turn up what I could and see where it led me.

Since Jennifer's list of boyfriends could be a mile long, I would save that for last. For the time being I'd focus on eliminating whom I could.

It felt like an impossible task to weed through, and I was too drained to start tonight.

❧❧❧

The muscles in my gaping abdomen painfully constricted as I heaved. With each precious second I grew weaker, losing any fight left in me. Although I temporarily obliged his request to remain silent, he wrung my neck harder. A liar—that's what he was. And a killer—that's what he was becoming.

As his grip tensed, I was certain he'd break it. But luckily I'd be passed out and on my way to heaven before I felt it. At least I hoped I was heading to heaven. It wasn't a concern I gave much thought to until now, but I hoped I was right with my Maker enough to scrape by.

My eyelids drooped, then dropped shut as all went black and my body went limp. A bittersweet end from the misery.

I thought I was dead, until I felt him release his hold, but I was too afraid, too weak, to show any sign of life. I heard the tear of paper, then felt a coolness on my face. The pungent smell of Old Spice mingled with rubbing alcohol wafted into my nostrils as he leaned over me to wipe my lips, then my cheeks, and lastly my eyes. He was removing my makeup. I remained rigid throughout his strange ritual, praying I didn't accidentally flinch as he finished his final swipe of my skin before moving to my fingertips.

Upon completion, he released me, and I felt a rush of cool air as he left my side.

Then I heard footsteps. A crunch of glass underfoot. Was he leaving? Opening my eyes a mere sliver, I watched the back of my attacker as he headed for the kitchen. The living room shadows obscured him from outside view, due to my earlier mistake of drawing the heavy, forest green curtains to keep the glare off the TV. The white light of the television illuminated the room.

As he reached the kitchen, the contrast in brightness silhouetted him. He picked up the phone hanging on the kitchen wall and dialed, his back still toward me.

I considered for a moment grabbing the beer bottle closest to me, but a quick self-assessment warned me that he'd easily subdue any attempt I made to attack him.

He spoke into the phone, but I couldn't make out what he said. Then he dropped the receiver to the floor.

A moment too brief for me to flee, he turned back to me, stumbling toward me as if drunk. As he neared, I knew I only had mere seconds to react. Should I jump up and run? No, I didn't have the strength. He'd easily overpower me and finish me off. Playing dead was my only choice. But I needed to keep an eye open just long enough to see his face.

When he stopped to watch me, I feared I'd been caught. But when he didn't advance—his face still too deep in the shadows for me to see his features clearly—I felt optimistic. I might survive this after all ... though did I even want to survive with this memory?

PAMELA CRANE

Chapter 11

Friday night's dream wasn't much help in filling in the gaps or solving the case. Even though Alexis's memories were becoming my own thoughts, my own translation of events, I lumbered through a clueless haze, unable to piece the puzzle together.

Without a clear picture of the elusive killer's face, I had nothing. So I decided to apply more conventional investigative methods. I called Landon, telling him to meet me at the police precinct that originally handled the murder investigation.

He talked me into grabbing a bite to eat first, which sounded perfect since I hadn't eaten breakfast and it was approaching eleven o'clock. Despite my fears of a repeat coffee shop episode with Brad, I met Landon at a diner down the road from the station, the Silver Spoon, and ordered typical lunch fare—sandwiches and fries. Seated at a picture window that overlooked the busy four-lane stretch of concrete with unruly, untapped forest beyond that, I got comfortable in the booth. The cushion squeaked under my fidgeting.

After triple checking the parking lot for Brad's car—just in case—I told Landon about my suspect list, which he wanted to see.

When I showed it to him, he pointed to

Friends

"You can scratch that off the list."

"Seriously?" I asked. "She didn't have any friends?"

"There was no one she hung out with regularly outside of school. One visit to our house would send kids running right back out the door. They were kind of afraid of Alexis because of my parents and where we lived."

"What about church? You did grow up in the Bible Belt, after all."

"We didn't go to church back then. I think my mom thought she'd catch on fire if she entered a holy place." Landon's finger rested on

extracurricular activities

"And we weren't involved in any sports or extramural activities."

"I thought Alexis played soccer?" I recalled the newspaper article.

"Yeah, when she was, like, five," he said between bites of his club sandwich. "Neither of us could get into sports seriously because our parents were too self-absorbed or trashed to take us anywhere on time. I had to drop out of Little League for that reason."

I remembered Landon and his dad mentioning that at our meet-and-greet. I couldn't imagine a childhood so ... lonely.

"How did you end up so normal?" I wondered aloud as I ran my pencil through another item on the list. I was down to

Uncle Derek

Neighbors

Cousins

Jennifer's boyfriends

"You think I'm normal? Thanks!" he said with mock gusto.

"Maybe I don't know you well enough." I grinned.

My finger traced Dan's penciled-out name on the list. "Are we fairly sure your dad is innocent? I don't know what he was like drunk, but before I write him off, I wanted to ask you … unless that's too personal, Landon."

He shook his head. "No, that's not a bad question. But he wasn't usually a mean drunk, didn't beat on us constantly or anything like that … More excitable than anything, wanting to party harder. But not violent. Usually he'd just get loopy, then fall asleep."

I felt satisfied with that answer.

Next he pointed to

Cousins

"No cousins. My mom was an only child, and my Uncle Derek never married or had kids—well, that he knows of, that is."

"A bit of a player?" I asked as I scribbled a line through cousins.

"You could say that."

"What's his story?"

"My guess is he hit midlife hard and has Peter Pan syndrome—no matter how old he gets, he can't handle growing up. Into drugs and perpetually jobless. And a total user, in my opinion. He was always using my dad for money and stuff."

"How about murder—is he the type to kill someone, you think?"

Landon scratched his chin. "Maybe … Uncle Derek—he could be worth talking to … just to see if he has an alibi or some information about that night. While I have a

93

hard time thinking he'd be capable of something like that, Uncle Derek was kinda shady. Always a little ... off. And a tad perverted."

When Landon didn't elaborate, I prodded him on. "What do you mean?"

"Well, he'd been in jail a bunch of times for petty theft, and he had a couple of inappropriate relationships with, uh ... girls."

My eyebrows shot up. "*Girls*—as in prepubescent, Watson?"

"Not as young as Alexis, but not much older. Way too young for him. Like seventeen years old when he was in his thirties. Even as a kid I remember him preying on girls in my grade—asking me about them, you know? Creeped me out seeing him with girls from my class."

This was getting juicy. "Girls—plural?"

"Yeah, he dated a couple of them. Back then he could charm the pants off of anyone, and he constantly worked out. He was kind of a bad boy, which was appealing ... total opposite of me, the book nerd. You know how girls love a bad boy."

"Aw, I'm sure you weren't that geeky."

"My pocket protector testifies otherwise."

We shared a laugh.

"You probably dated the quarterback for the football team," he added.

"Not my type."

"So, what *is* your type?"

I giggled. He was fishing and I found that incredibly funny. For despite his charm and my new singlehood, I wasn't interested ... was I?

"I don't know if I really have a *type*. Confident, interesting, adventurous ... I haven't really dated enough people to know what I like or don't like in a person. I guess I just know it when I feel it."

"Are you still seeing that guy we ran into—Brad?" The way he asked was tinged with a subtle shyness. It was cute.

I wasn't sure how to answer, though. Were Brad and I officially over? Or were we just taking a break? We hadn't spoken since our exchange at the coffee shop, which was a telling sign of doom. We used to talk daily. The thought made me miss him. I was nowhere close to over him. It took a lot longer to fall out of love than it did to fall in love.

"I'm not sure. We were pretty serious not that long ago, but he wasn't too thrilled about my latest activities—this whole investigation." I rolled my eyes. "So we're on a break. In guy-speak, does that mean we're over?"

"Nah," Landon assured me, "he just needs time. He's probably worried something bad is going to happen to you. It's not like you're investigating the latest Bigfoot sighting. You're dealing with a bona fide murderer, not a cryptid. That puts you at risk. I wouldn't want my girlfriend—if I had one—to be doing this either."

"I suppose that's reassuring—the part about my relationship not being over with, not the life-threatening killer-catching part." I smiled weakly.

The realization of just how dangerous my research was hadn't sunk in until that moment.

I had never been in a police station before. It wasn't quite what I expected. I imagined cement block walls, bare light bulbs hanging from exposed wires in shadowy interrogation rooms, and donuts. Lots and lots of donuts.

Instead, I was pleasantly surprised. While there weren't more than a handful of windows, I found standard overhead waffle lighting and desks organized into neat cubicles. A couple of ferns added ambience, and the gurgle of a modern water dispenser rose above the chatter. A plump woman at a semi-circular front desk greeted us, offering to help "y'all" in her thick-as-sorghum-syrup Southern accent.

"Is Detective Williams in today?" Landon asked.

"Sure, hon, he's at his desk in the far right corner over yonder." She pointed and answered a ringing phone with a chirpy, "Dur'm Police Department. How can I help you?"

We wove through a sea of puke-gray metal desks, Landon leading the way. When we reached Detective Williams' desk, the two men hugged.

So they were friends—friendly enough to hug. It wasn't shocking, since they appeared close enough in age to have gone to high school together, and they even looked similar. Clean, chiseled jaw, same lean build, same average height … only Detective Williams' blond hair gave him a slightly boyish look. But I wondered why Landon hadn't told me just how effortlessly he could access inside information. My excitement skyrocketed. This could give us a break in the case!

"Landon, how ya doin'?" the detective asked, patting Landon's shoulder.

"Doing okay, Evan. You?"

"Just staying out of the line of fire until retirement," he joked. "And who is this?" Detective Williams glanced at me.

"Mia Germaine," I said, shaking his offered hand. "Nice to meet you, Detective Williams."

"Please, call me Evan. You make me sound … professional or something." He winked. "Girlfriend finally?" he directed at Landon with a raised brow.

Landon and I responded with a simultaneous "No."

"Just friends," Landon clarified.

"So you two know each other?" I asked.

"Evan lives on Willoughby Way. I've known him my

whole life."

"Did you go to school together?" I wondered aloud.

Landon chuckled. "No, Evan's got half a dozen years on me. I'm still a young'un compared to this old geezer."

"Yep, forty's come and gone for me, broheme, but it's coming for you soon," Evan chided.

"At least I'll be looking good as I hit forty. Back in the day Evan was nice enough to let me play ball in the street with the big kids."

"You never thanked me for taking it easy on you back then," Evan joked.

"And you never thanked me for taking it easy on you now," Landon retorted. "Anyways, we wanted to talk to you about Alexis."

Evan shook his head solemnly. "Man, don't go down this road. It's been twenty years, dude. You still trying to find out who did it?"

"She never got justice, man. But Mia may be able to help."

"I want this killer brought to justice just as much as you do. I've made it my life's work trying to catch this guy. But I don't know anything new."

"I don't need new," I cut in. "If I could have whatever's old, that would work."

"First of all, Mia, I can't just hand over evidence to a civilian. There are proper channels for handling and distributing case files—despite what the media may think."

I sensed a defensive tone.

"Who was the detective handling her case?"

"He's retired and living in Florida. You need his address?"

Now I knew he was being sarcastic, but I was about to call his bluff. Landon rested a hand on Evan's shoulder.

"Take it easy, man. She's just trying to help."

Evan was taking this Q&A way too personally. I wondered if something happened that I wasn't supposed to know.

"Fine," Evan grumbled. "What do you need?"

"If the detective in charge of the case isn't here anymore, is there anyone else who would know the details? I only have a couple of questions."

"I was the first responder to the 9-1-1 call, so I know a bit about it, but since I was still green, I wasn't the lead on the case. What exactly do you want to know?"

Ah, at last his skeptical attitude toward me was starting to make sense. My guess was that as a newbie he had screwed up the investigation. But I didn't dare say what I was thinking.

"So you have firsthand knowledge of everything."

"Yep."

"Did you ever have any suspects? I mean, who would want to hurt a little girl, and why Alexis specifically?"

"Why any of these recent victims?" Evan threw back at me. "We've had two young girls—Gina Martinez and Violet Hansen—murdered in the past two years. If you look back over the past twenty-two years, there've been eight girls in that age group whose deaths are mighty damned suspicious—all killed by a fatal stabbing."

"Eight?" I stammered. "That's a lot of lives. Why hasn't the FBI gotten involved? You would think they'd have taken over by now."

"My thoughts exactly. We've tried involving the FBI, but they don't see any hard connection between the murder victims other than approximate victim age, and considering the long time span, I guess it's not convincing enough for them."

Evan shook his head wearily as he went on. "We're presenting them with archaic cases over a span of twenty years that appear unrelated. Because of the locations, demographics, and race, the FBI argues that it's most likely gang related, since the girls were underprivileged and had known ties to gang members. The girls were black or Hispanic, and from the ghetto, other than the case of Violet Hanson—the only Caucasian other than Alexis."

"Seriously—they don't think serial killers target poor people too?"

"Look, I don't know what else to tell you. Hopefully the public outcry about the Triangle Terror will finally prompt FBI involvement, but when the murders are so spread out and don't involve the socially elite, they won't step in. Even I have to wonder about the timeline logic—I mean, why wait years between each victim?"

He sighed heavily, clearly distraught.

"While I can't prove all the victims have been killed by the same person, it seems awfully coincidental to me when young, healthy girls pop up dead for no reason other than some psychopath is getting his jollies. All starting with Alexis."

"You seem pretty convinced it's the same killer, though," I said. "Why?"

"Well, the common threads we *can* find are the method of attack, age, and around the Triangle area. While it's not a slam dunk, it's enough to convince me that we're dealing with the same guy over a period of twenty-two years."

"Wouldn't that make him pretty old, though?"

"Maybe, maybe not. Depends on how young he was when he started killing."

"So we're dealing with a genius serial killer, then, if he's been getting away with murder for two decades."

"My guess, yes. But because the deaths are stretched out over such a long period of time and all of our victims have questionable associations, I can't convince anyone else of this. My entire career has revolved around catching this scumbag, yet I'm nowhere close to solving it. We're not equipped to handle this kind of criminal activity. We don't have the forensic capabilities to find everything there is to find. We're overworked, understaffed ... and with budget cuts, there's just not enough money to go around. I wish I could help you, because I believe we're looking for the same person, but I don't even know where to start."

Evan's big ham of a fist struck his desk in frustration. Precinct chatter ground to an expectant halt for a good five seconds, then resumed. There was no doubting his devotion to his duty. He seemed so distraught that I felt extremely bad for him—the empath in me coming to the fore.

I wanted to tell him about my visions, but I knew better than to confess to having dreams about murders. Cops believed in hard evidence, not pseudo-science. I'd only make a fool out of myself.

"So you think the murders are connected—Gina, Violet, and Alexis?"

"I think it's very possible. They were all around twelve years old, same stab wound pattern in the abdomen, and all within a short drive of Raleigh. And when I pull up all of the similar murders in the past twenty-two years, I noticed a subtle trend. It takes some imagination, sure, but I think the killer perfected his craft over the years. Each one is a little less sloppy."

"How so?" I wondered aloud.

"At Alexis's crime scene, presumably his first, he left her for dead. She survived until they reached the hospital, and had she lived, she could have identified him—big mistake on his part. But a year later in 1993—same date, the fourth of March—another girl, also age twelve, is stabbed in her home. Same scenario. Stab wound, 9-1-1 call from the house, but this time he succeeded in killing her. Though his mistake that time was leaving prints on the phone."

"So you have the killer's prints?" I asked eagerly.

"Unfortunately we couldn't pull an ID from them. The mother got home as the ambulance arrived and she unwittingly grabbed the phone to call her husband before we pulled the prints. As a result she smudged them. But the killer was sloppy back then, and increasingly more meticulous with each kill. That tells me it's the same guy."

"Why didn't they make a connection to the two murders if they were only a year apart?"

"You want the truth?"

I nodded.

"Because the victims weren't noteworthy. Lower class families never are. People don't care when so-called expendables are murdered. It's sad but true."

How awful. How could anyone determine one person's value over another based on where they lived and how much money they had? Society—and I use the term loosely—was royally screwed up.

"Is there anything else that ties the murders together?"

He shrugged. "There's one thing that popped up with Gina that caught my attention. Back when Alexis was killed, the killer left an alcohol pad with her makeup on it at the scene of the crime. It was the first thing I noticed about Gina's crime scene—another alcohol pad. It could be his calling card."

I wondered what message the killer was trying to send. Girls are growing up too fast? Losing their innocence too young? I jotted down a note to reflect on it later.

"But no leads otherwise?" I asked.

"No, nothing concrete. But I'm going to find this guy if it kills me."

"Let's hope it doesn't," Landon muttered.

Evan smirked at him, then shifted his glare to me. "Well, I worry more about you, Mia. You're getting a little too close to the heat. You could get burned."

"What's that supposed to mean?"

Evan's eyes were unblinking, his words deliberate. "It means: Stay out of police business."

"Are you telling me to back off? Because I'm not backing off," I said through clenched teeth. This guy was really starting to get on my nerves.

"Let me be clear, then. You're out of your league and you're going to end up hurt if you don't back off. Leave the police work to the police."

I raised my hands submissively. "Message received."

It sounded like a threat to me, so I'd have to do my research discreetly, which made things a little more difficult. But I had an advantage. I had Alexis helping me.

"I'm not trying to be a jerk, Mia, but you don't know who you're dealing with here, and I'd hate to see another innocent person die." If it was an apology, I had to really read between the lines of his stern tone to find it.

After an uncomfortable good-bye, Landon and I headed to the parking lot. A surge of hope rushed over me. The killer was still local, which meant he could be found. Sure, I was playing a dangerous game of hide-and-seek, but I was determined to win.

Chapter 12

Through slitted eyes I could feel his gaze burrow into me, awakening me from momentary blackness as I slipped in and out of consciousness. Watching me, yet somehow gazing through me. To him I wasn't a girl, rather an object to torture. A wild animal ... just like him.

The sting of his handprints lingered on my neck. I wanted to reach up and soothe the ache, but I knew the slightest movement would be my last. Play possum, I repeated to myself. It wasn't hard to do, since the blood loss made me feel too weak to move.

The silhouette across the room moved, then swayed.

I heard a groan, then a moment later he was hunched over, throwing up all over the floor. The smell made my nose wrinkle in disgust, but he was too occupied with his own sickness to notice my movement.

When he was done retching, he ran to the kitchen, grabbed the entire roll of paper towels off the counter, and furiously started wiping up his mess, spreading bleach across the floor. I heard him yelp in pain when he slipped on the blood-vomit concoction and fell on his knees. He grabbed his right knee, giving it his brief attention as he pulled a shard of broken beer bottle out, then continued to mop.

Even in my semiconscious state I heard sirens in the distance, and my hope for survival soared. With each second he wiped faster, then jumped up and shuffled to the kitchen. He pulled the bag out of the can and tied it shut. I was certain it was over, that he was gone as the sirens neared, until he looked back at me, watching me for a long moment. Willing myself to remain motionless, I held my breath.

He hurriedly limped toward me, I assumed to finish me off, until ... he didn't.

Instead he hobbled to the TV and viciously kicked it like it was the devil. He either broke it or the fall pulled the plug, because the screen went black before he gave me one last glance. I caught a momentary glimpse of short blond hair as he passed through the kitchen and ran out the back door, clicking it locked after he slammed it shut.

When I knew he was long gone, I shifted my chin downward to examine my abdomen. So much blood! Oozing all over my blanket, soaking Bart Simpson, trickling to the floor. I briefly wondered how much blood I had left in me before my eyelids grew too heavy to force open anymore. Then I closed them in shuddering relief.

⁊⸙

I woke up to sweat-soaked sheets the morning after that dream ... rather, nightmare. My heart thumped painfully against my ribs, and my temples throbbed from the aftershock of what I had seen.

Yet I wasn't afraid ... not like I was the first time it happened.

Sadly, I was becoming numb to the anguish of Alexis's torture. When the dreams had first started I couldn't stomach them, couldn't handle witnessing her murder, smelling the blood, sensing the fear. But with each sequence, that sickness fueled my lust for vengeance. Instead of being appalled by the scenes unfolding before me, I was subconsciously looking for clues.

Somehow these dreams would lead me to the killer.

I vowed to avenge this poor, lost life.

I scoured my memory, bringing to recall every detail from the dream. My mind was slightly hazy at waking up so abruptly, but most of the particulars still stood out. I grabbed the pen and pad that never left my side. The pen tip hovered above the paper as I closed my eyes and imagined the location, the atmosphere, then Alexis.

I first conjured the scenery.

The smell of stale beer. The flicker of the television. The clink of bottles falling.

Then an image popped into my head: the back of a blond head.

Whoever it was had blond hair. I didn't know many blond men, which could help narrow down my list.

I continued to squeeze my eyes closed as I let the scene unravel moment by agonizing moment.

I focused on the back of his head, willing him to turn around. In fragmented slow motion he turned toward me, yet the distance masked his features. The cut of his jaw blended into the cheekbones, creating a hazy blob of a face. As if zooming in with a camera lens, I examined harder, but the face was still a blur.

Sighing, I gave up on the face and continued searching for clues elsewhere. His clothing—blue jeans and a blood-soaked shirt—were nondescript and forgettable. Just average men's clothes. Typical black boots, wiped clean so no footprints would give him away.

The bag of garbage hung over his left shoulder, but I caught something I hadn't noticed before. His right hand reached into his pocket and pulled something out. Something small and shiny, but I couldn't tell what.

He exited my field of vision and slammed the kitchen door shut before I could get a better look.

Then I heard a click.

The sound nudged me from my trance. It sounded too real to be in my head. My eyes popped open, searching the room to see if something—a strong gust from the vent, God willing—had closed my bedroom or bathroom door, but both doors hung open. Had I actually heard something?

Get a grip, Mia.

My nerves were too shot to sit around anymore, so I got out of bed and paced the room, pooling my thoughts.

I was looking for a blond, male killer. It wasn't much to go on, but I hoped the rest of the pieces would come together soon.

I figured a morning run might do me some good and help clear my head, so I changed into a T-shirt and shorts, stepped into my running shoes, and grabbed my keys. As I closed my apartment door behind me, I locked the deadbolt—a habit I had only recently developed.

Click.

That sound—that was what I heard in the dream.

The killer had locked the door behind him ... using a key.

A SECONDHAND LIFE

Oh my God, he had a key!

What did that mean? He was someone they knew well enough to hand a key to. Landon had said that Jennifer had a series of revolving boy toys coming and going, but did they have keys? Doubtful she would give a one-night stand a key. So that eliminated them.

The only remaining suspects were the uncle or a neighbor, assuming a neighbor had a copy of the key. Although, if they left a key hidden somewhere outside, anyone who knew of its hiding place would have access ... which for a stranger would require some thorough surveillance. Either this person knew the family well enough to know where they kept the spare key, or the killer was that good at watching them.

A shiver caused goose bumps to pop up on my arms and legs as I imagined a ghostly figure parked across the street studying their routines, their guests ... their children.

As my feet hit the sidewalk, my pace increased from a walk to a jog as my black, pink-soled New Balance running shoes—in bad need of a good deodorizing—slapped the pavement in an easy rhythm. Passing the last row of gray apartments, I turned the corner and headed into a subdivision of cute houses with their friendly sidewalks and homey landscaping. I shook away a fleeting image of Brad and me as lord and lady of our own picket-fenced manor, lazily rocking on our wraparound porch, surrounded by tortoise-shaped planters spilling forth vibrant blooms.

Brad had often spoke about getting married and buying a place together in the 'burbs—our own piece of paradise, he'd say—while I had continuously avoided the talk by throwing in a joke to change the subject. *Why ruin a good thing, babe?* I'd say. *'Cause your toilet-seat-up privileges will be revoked if we live together. And the moment a woman says "I do," she becomes a nag. You sure you want that?*

He'd assured me that wouldn't happen to us, but I was always afraid of taking that chance. Brad was perfect enough to ruin me, for sure.

I had ventured half a mile into the subdivision when I finally caught myself daydreaming about Brad and mentally slapped myself.

"Focus!" I scolded. "We're probably done with, anyways. No point dwelling on it." I hoped no one heard me talking to myself as I picked up speed.

With my head back in the zone, I began formulating possible scenarios about how the Triangle Terror and Alexis knew each other while my blood flow revitalized my brain.

If indeed Alexis's killer and the Triangle Terror were one and the same, I had to compare facts. Just like Alexis's murderer, the Triangle Terror also got in and out of homes undetected. How? It couldn't be possible that all of his victims left a key under their doormat. Somehow he appeared trustworthy enough to gain entrance without breaking in. I needed to find out how.

As I trudged up a windy hill that circled back toward my complex, I decided that I needed to pay Alexis's uncle a visit. It had all started with Alexis; she was the first victim for a reason. Someone close to the Worthington family had to be her killer. Someone they trusted ... which meant I could trust no one.

Chapter 13

23 Miller Bend Road
Hillsborough, North Carolina
Tuesday, April 29

When Amy Watson opened the red front door to her cookie-cutter house, looking five years older than her actual age with her skimpy clothes and heavy makeup, I knew I had picked the right girl. Luckily she hadn't recognized me from Starbucks when I "randomly" approached her at the mall two days ago posed as a talent scout. While it had required some of my best stalking skills to find alone time with her over the past couple of weeks, eventually the perfect moment arrived.

Sunday afternoon her mother dropped her off at The Streets at Southpoint, a popular mall that satisfied the needs of the shopaholic upper class with its luxury stores nestled side by side along a fake indoor "street" to give the appearance of trendy outdoor shops.

Because of its upscale market, it had a feeling of "safe" to it, giving parents security in letting their children wander off in unchaperoned herds. As if the rich weren't capable of heinous acts! All the same, the parents' naiveté spelled their children's doom.

Today, standing confidently on Amy's front porch stoop, I came prepared. I adjusted my ball cap emblazoned with the Ace Talent and Modeling insignia—the acronym ATM in fancy lettering. Understated yet witty. It was the same hat I'd worn at the mall, and as long as I kept my chin down, no mall camera should have gotten a good angle on my face.

Despite my lack of practice, it was so easy to play the talent agent role—one I had pulled off only once before—as I preyed on her vanity. What young girl didn't want to be a famous model or actress these days?

"Hello," I introduced myself as Amy stood in the doorway, "I'm Gary Billing from Ace Talent and Modeling. We met a couple days ago at the mall."

She looked at me stupidly, her head cocked. I smiled ingratiatingly and repeated, "Gary Billing. The mall. Ring a bell?"

I watched her memory jog to catch up, then recognition dawned on her face. "Oh yeah ... the agent, right? Uh, hi."

"You filled out a form with your contact information. I hope you don't mind my dropping by. Are your parents home?" I asked, already knowing the answer was no. I had watched them both leave for work that morning and knew their schedules didn't bring Mom or Dad home for another hour and a half. Two working parents made my choice of victims so much easier.

"Sorry, but they're both at work."

"Hmm," I contemplated aloud, "well, I wanted to talk to them about your modeling potential and doing a photo shoot. We're looking for fresh faces to represent, and you have the look we're searching for. Height, build, facial qualities, and sense of fashion ... you could be a star if you got serious about it. Is that something you would be interested in doing—modeling?"

Another question I knew the answer to. We had briefly touched on it at the mall when I had first approached her with the proposition. Even then I watched her self-esteem blossom as she was singled out among her friends for this once-in-a-lifetime opportunity.

She nodded eagerly. "Yeah, of course I'm interested! What kind of modeling? Like, could I get on TV?"

"Mainly print ads, but we also represent actresses as well, so that's a definite possibility." Oh, how fun it was to feed the ego, knowing that moments later it would be crushed. "I'll need to speak with your parents to go over the terms of our contract and to arrange a portfolio for you, but I can leave them my contact information to get in touch. Do you mind if I come in and jot down some information so they can contact me?"

"Sure."

Silly, silly girl. It was pathetic how simple it was to manipulate people these days. Feed the ego, harvest wealth.

At this point the door swung open, granting me entrance. I sauntered past Amy into the living room like I owned the place. She trailed me, awed by my poise and supreme confidence, sitting catty-corner to me on the sofa when I dropped onto the love seat. I opened my briefcase and pulled out a handful of brochures. I handed her one.

"What's this?" she asked.

The glossy, professionally designed brochure depicted several famous faces that Ace Talent supposedly represented, along with a list of what Ace clients could expect. I owed Kinko's a hearty thanks for making my ruse even easier to pull off.

"This is some general information about the company, how you can prepare for your career as a model—or actress—and some things you'll need, like a portfolio. Feel free to look through it and let me know if you have any questions."

As Amy flipped through the colorful brochure, her concentration presumably on the glowing reviews for Ace Talent and Modeling Agency, I planned my attack. I waited until she got comfortable, and I knew I had about two minutes' worth of Amy reading to get into position. I had timed it several times, adjusting the length of the brochure to buy me exactly the minutes I needed. Murder was a meticulous craft.

Once I knew she was fully absorbed, I made my move.

"Do you mind if I get a glass of water?" I asked.

"Sure, I'll get it." Amy shifted to stand, but I urged her to stay seated.

"No, you get acquainted with that brochure. I can find my way around the kitchen. I'll be right back." I rose and headed to the kitchen, quickly circling back around through the dining room and across the entryway, but this time with gloves on. I peered in, and sure enough, she was engulfed.

She never saw me coming.

Never noticed my approach behind her.

With a swift movement I grabbed her neck, squeezing hard as she reached behind her to claw at me. I basked in the beauty of the moment. Her gurgled screams. Her hysterical kicking. Her terror as she attempted to twist her neck free while I wrung the life out of her. I held my grip for one eternal minute, then another, until her arms and legs slackened, then her head drooped to the side. With one hand holding firm to her neck, my other yanked out the concealed knife hanging inside my belt and jammed it into her side. She flinched and groaned—still alive, but barely. And not for long.

The knife sliced through her abdominal tissue up to the hilt, tearing the muscle beneath it. She reflexively tried to push my hand and the knife away, but it was too late. The damage had been done. She'd bleed out all over her forty-dollar Hollister T-shirt before help arrived.

Every moment I savored ... her whispers of breath, the death that glazed over her eyes, her innocence at last returning. I was saving her from the impurities of the world, from the malicious bite that the media—that false prophet—had taken from her flesh. Death nipped at her, and it enthralled me, because it was only through me that she could be saved.

Moments passed, then minutes ... I'd spent too much time, I knew, but I couldn't pull myself away from the sweet indulgence of watching her die. I waited for that climax, that pinnacle of satisfaction. Then it came, and I knew I had stayed too long.

I had one thing left to do, then my work would be done.

I walked to my briefcase, opened it, and retrieved a sealed packet, inside it a pad saturated in rubbing alcohol. With careful, delicate strokes I wiped all remnants of makeup from her porcelain skin, revealing the youth concealed beneath caked-on foundation and blush. In several dabs she returned to her childhood. The sight made my heart flutter. I tossed the pad on her lap as a *screw you* to the police, tucked the knife in a plastic bag to clean later, and shouldered my bag. As I headed to the door, I heard a *thump*. I turned around to find her fingers twitching.

She was still alive.

I wasn't finished after all.

Her chest rose with ragged, wheezing breaths.

Just as I stepped toward her, I heard the expensive-sounding *thunk* of a luxury door closing outside—too close for comfort. I ran to the window and peered out.

A large man in a tailored suit walked around the front of his black Mercedes. Her father was home ... an hour too early. I wouldn't have time to snap her neck, but I hoped the blood loss would finish her before an ambulance arrived. I ran to the kitchen, looking for the back entrance. Spotting the door, I hastily opened it and bolted out, being sure to silently close it behind me. I squatted along the back porch in wait, then slowly crouched my way along the back of the house, before turning the corner and running the rest of the way to my car, with my briefcase bouncing wildly against my thigh.

When I reached my car, which I wisely parked in the street and not the driveway, I tossed my gloves on the passenger seat and sunk into the cushion, allowing a moment to catch my breath. My eyelids felt heavy as I bowed my head, resting it against the steering wheel. Exhaustion was catching up to me, either from the adrenaline rush dying down or the sleepless nights spent planning my next kill. Tonight, however, I'd sleep satiated … until the hunger for blood roused me once again.

I hit the gas, knowing that as I peeled away a father was pressing his daughter to his chest, weeping into the phone for help, losing his baby girl in his arms.

It brought a smirk to my face.

Chapter 14

I'm here at the home of Rick and Jolene Watson," the reporter said, "where their daughter Amy was the victim of a near-fatal stabbing yesterday afternoon." The camera zoomed in on the two-story colonial house that was no longer a home. It had become a mausoleum of memories.

"Shortly after the murder of teen Gina Martinez, another attack leaves the Triangle citizens in a panic," the reporter continued. "Twelve-year-old Amy Watson was found bleeding and unconscious in her Orange County home this afternoon when her father, Rick Watson, arrived home early from work. He immediately called 9-1-1, and EMTs were able to resuscitate Amy. The trademark abdominal stabbing and removal of Amy's makeup lead investigators to believe this to be the work of the Triangle Terror."

A candid photo of the redheaded youth, smiling and holding a lacrosse stick, popped up in the top corner of the television screen. "Amy is in critical condition at Duke Hospital where she is receiving around-the-clock police protection while the suspect is at large. Like the other similar cases, there was no sign of forced entry and no weapon found. Police are offering a reward for anyone who can provide information about the attacker."

A phone number flashed across the bottom border and I jotted it down.

I hit the power button on the remote and the screen

went black. My egg and cheese breakfast sandwich churned in my stomach as I felt a pang of sadness for the victim—Amy Watson. Another day, another target. How was the killer picking them? What made him tick? It was yet another question piled on top of more unanswered questions, and the heap got bigger by the day.

After washing the sink full of dishes from several days' worth of meals—the simple act more therapeutic than loading the dishwasher—I called my editorial manager.

"Hey, Jackie," I said when she picked up.

"Mia, what's up?"

"Do you mind if I work from home today? I'm on a roll with this book I'm working on and could probably finish the proofing today if I keep going." A half-truth, politician style. I had indeed logged a couple of hours so far this morning, and *if* I did keep going I'd finish ... but the truth was that I had no intentions on working today.

"You've been working from home a lot, Mia. I hardly see you anymore. Is everything okay?"

"Yeah, you know how it is. I'm more productive at home ... less distractions."

"True, but I miss my lunch date. It's quiet around here without you. But sure, stay home. It's fine by me."

Thank God for lenient bosses. I knew she never minded me telecommuting occasionally as long as I met my deadlines, though I felt guilt jab at me for lying. "Thanks, Jackie. I promise to make it up to you. Maybe we can plan to have lunch tomorrow?"

"Sure. How about at Bella's Cuisine?"

Ugh. Brad's restaurant. I hadn't told her things were ... what were things between us, anyway? I didn't even know. It was probably time to reach out to Brad and reconcile, though lunchtime was not the time.

"About Brad and me ... we're sort of ... not talking right now."

"You broke up and didn't tell me?" Jackie screeched.

"I'm not sure what we are yet. Don't go saying anything. I still need to talk to him. But for now let's avoid Bella's Cuisine. We can do Pomodoro's instead."

"Alright." Jackie sighed. "But don't stand me up. I wanna know what happened."

"I'll be there with bells on."

Now I just needed to figure out what to tell her, since I was clueless about the state of my relationship.

After hanging up I logged back on to my computer and searched for the White Pages. I typed

Derek Worthington, North Carolina

Only two Derek Worthingtons popped up on the screen, but one was way too young. I picked the fifty-five-year-old, and his address came up.

It wasn't exactly the best part of town, but safe enough to drive through during the day. It was still early enough to possibly catch him before he left for work ... if he even had a job. Living in that part of town, he was probably on welfare. It was time to find out more about creepster Uncle Derek.

I pulled up to a ramshackle duplex in desperate need of some TLC. Alligatored paint chips flung from the rotted wooden exterior, and ivy scrambled up the siding, reclaiming the structure for Mother Nature. I parked in front of a broken, uneven sidewalk that appeared as if it had barely survived several earthquakes. Knee-high grass brushed against my bare legs as I carefully climbed the rickety steps—some partially splintered, all slick and black with mildew—to the front porch. It was unseasonably warm for April, so I pulled my long hair up into a ponytail and cursed my fashion choice: jean shorts and a tank top, an outfit far too provocative in what appeared to be Rape Central.

I tiptoed up the stairs, praying I wouldn't drop through them. Luckily I weighed barely a buck and change, or else the creaky landing might have caved in beneath my weight.

The screen door squealed in protest as I opened it and knocked on the front door.

My heart raced as I waited, anticipating a drug-dealing gangbanger on the other side.

To my amazement, a clean-shaven man in a crisp uniform greeted me. Almost an exact replica of his brother Dan—except a full a head of hair and oddly attractive. And thin as the proverbial rail. I wondered if he ever ate.

"Can I help ya?" he offered as I stood there silently, working my brain overtime to think of what to say, how to explain who I was and why I was there. I now realized I should have planned ahead.

"Uh, hi. My name is Mia Germaine and I'm looking for Derek Worthington."

"That'd be me." His gaze ran up and down my body, inducing pangs of nausea.

A brief image flashed in my head—a younger version of Derek sprawled out on a sofa with a beer in hand, laughing cruelly and wearing a stained and tattered wife-beater. Before I could analyze the flashback, it was gone, and the real thing stood before me, his hip cocked and arm resting on the doorjamb.

I took several deep breaths to hold my gag reflex at bay. When I felt I had the queasiness under control, I met him stare for stare.

"I'm a friend of your nephew's—Landon."

"How is that there douche bag?" he asked in a mush-mouthed, hillbilly-esque dialect I could barely comprehend. "I ain't never hear from him no more."

"He's doing good. But I'm not here about Landon. I actually wanted to talk to you about something else ... if you have a moment."

He fussed proudly with his beige and green polo shirt, blazoned with a Ralph's Delivery Services patch. Two knock-kneed legs protruded from his shorts like a pair of hairy stilts. "I only got a few minutes 'fore I leave for work, but for a purty lady like you, I got time to hear you out."

He waved me into a dimly lit living room with a threadbare sofa, tattered rug, and massive state-of-the-art television and latest gaming technology. Huh. Priorities.

I nudged aside a stack of video games on the floor with my toe, making room for my legs as I sat down. I thought I heard a rat squeak when my rear hit the raggedy cushion with half the stuffing hanging out ... or maybe it was the springs I heard? Whatever it was, I didn't want to stay long enough to find out. The place gave me the creeps.

Derek sat beside me, picking up a dirty mug that had been sitting on the floor and crusted over with some long-ago beverage.

"Coffee?" he offered, holding out his cup.

"No thanks," I said. "I'll be quick."

"So, what can I *do you for*, sexy?" he said with a suggestive smirk as he got a little too comfortable.

I rolled my eyes, noting his tactless play on words that I'd heard a million times before.

Noting my displeasure, he added, "Relax, little lady. I was just kiddin'. You be too old for my tastes." He waved me off. "What can I do *for you*," he said with emphasis.

Deciding to ignore his comment about my age—like he should talk, clearly being twice my age!—I knew I needed to be discreet and careful with my words. I couldn't outright accuse him of anything, and I needed to earn his trust if I was to get anywhere with him.

"I'm not sure how to explain this. I was a friend of your niece, Alexis. Recently Landon and I were discussing how her murderer was never found. So, I kind of wanted to just, I don't know, follow up on that with friends and family to see if anyone remembers anything that could help find her killer."

"Shee-it," he snorted. "That be a long time ago, darlin'. Why y'all digging around in this now?"

"Like I said, Landon and I were just talking about it, and wishing we could have closure."

Derek eyed me skeptically. "How do you *really* know Alexis and Landon? I don't reckon you were school friends with Alexis, cuz I never met no one named Mia. I'm purty sure I'd remember if I did—especially a fine-lookin' fox like you." He winked. "And Landon—well, he never mentioned you before neither. So who are you *really* and whatcha want?"

Darn. My cover was blown. I wasn't sure how to recover.

With a stutter I replied, "Um, well, I was more Landon's friend than Alexis's ... and Landon and I weren't really that close until more recently." I hoped he'd bought it.

"Lookee here, lil' lady, I wish I could help ya. But I don't know much of anything about it."

"Do you remember where you were the day she was murdered?"

Derek cocked his head and his eyes narrowed. His jaw tightened, and suddenly I felt very afraid. No one knew I was here.

"Are y'all 'cusing me of sumpthin'?" he spat. "You git Landon over here right now and I'll straighten that boy out."

While I wanted to cower in fear and beg for my life, I

120

needed to stay firm and calm. "No, sir, no one's accusing you of anything. I'm just asking."

"You sound like them damn cops."

I laughed nervously, trying to appear amused. "No, I'm no cop, sir. Do I look like a cop?"

"None that've arrested me," he conceded. "You be way too purty."

"Thanks, I guess." I forced a grin. "I just want to give Alexis peace. I'm sure you didn't hurt your own niece, but I thought you might know something that can lead me to who did. I'm sorry for bothering you." I rose from my seat, ready to make a speedy exit.

I gripped my car keys tightly, ready to use them as a weapon in case he tried to grab me. *Aim for the eyes then run like hell.*

But Derek never flinched.

"Alrighty, I respect that. Take a seat."

I warily sat.

"Ask away," he ordered.

"I appreciate this. So, can you tell me anything you recall about that day?"

"Same as every other day, I guess. I been drunk off my ass. The whole day was a blur, but I remember gittin' the phone call about it and being too smashed to git up. I think Jinnifer called me from the horspital. I didn't pick up the first couple times, but then 'ventually I musta woken up. She was on the other end crying, screaming that her baby girl was gone. I remember hanging up on her and falling back asleep. Jinnifer—Lexi's mama—never did forgive me for that. I still feel horrible 'bout it, but I was too wasted to know what I was doing."

"I'm so sorry," I whispered. I really was. "Were you alone that night?"

"To be honest widja, I don't know. I had started the day partying with some friends, but by mid-afternoon I was out of it. Bad mix of weed, cocaine, and vodka. You know what I'm talkin' 'bout!" he said with a wheezy chuckle.

I had no idea. But the vices certainly helped explain his skeletal appearance.

"Anyways, all I know is that the next mornin' I woke up alone ... and hung over as hell."

"Do you remember any of your friends' names?"

He laughed. "Let's just say my friends didn't have last names. None of us used real names. We went by nicknames, just in case one of them bastards was an undercover cop. Lookee here, lil' lady, they was just drug buddies, with no reason to kill Alexis. I mean, what would be the point? Besides, I don't keep tabs on them guys no more. I be tryin' to get clean now. Can't hang with the trash if you wanna git outta the Dumpster. You know what I'm sayin'?"

Yeah, I knew what he was saying. He had no one to account for his alibi.

I noticed a couple of beer cans crunched up at the foot of the sofa. Derek must have followed my gaze, because he said, "I'm a work in progress, 'kay?"

I nodded and grinned weakly. "No judgment here."

The key information I needed would be a little more difficult to obtain: Where was he during the times that Gina Martinez and Amy Watson were attacked? These questions lingered in my mind, but I didn't know how to ask without getting myself kicked out—or killed. I needed a tactful, roundabout way of finding out those details. So I subtly tugged my tank top down, fiddled with my bra strap, and leaned forward just enough to give him a peek of my cleavage.

The sacrifices we women made to get things done.

Derek took the bait, his gaze falling appreciatively on my chest.

"Sorry for detaining you, Derek. You said you had to head to work now?" I said, perhaps a little too huskily. After all, I wanted to get information, not be molested.

"Yeah, in a few. But it's no bother."

"A package delivery guy, huh? It seems like a fun job." I twirled stray strands of hair playfully, acting the part. I almost impressed myself, if it had been a role I actually enjoyed. "You must get to drive around and pretty much set your own schedule, right?"

"You think it be fun? Man, it ain't leisurely like that. Half the time I gotta piss in a cup 'cause I ain't got no time for a bathroom break. They be rigid sumbitches about time and deliveries. You take too long with one package or git stuck in traffic, you screw up the whole day. It's tough work. But it pays the bills."

"I like a man who can pay his bills." I smiled sweetly. "So, um, what do you do on your time off? Like, what'd you do yesterday?" *As Amy Watson was being murdered,* I added in my head.

A huge, proud grin spread across his face as he took my words as an invitation. What was I getting myself into? Regret hit me hard.

"Well, yesterday I worked part of the day, then last night I beat another level in *Call of Duty.* Wanna watch me play?"

Groan. No thank you. My approach was getting me nowhere but in trouble. I just needed to get my information and get out.

"Sure, maybe later. Um, I forgot, I did have one other question for you."

"Shoot," he said slyly, as if expecting a proposition.

"You might not remember this far back, but what were you doing the evening of April fourth? It was three Fridays ago."

His playful expression dropped and was replaced with

irritation.

"Why do you ask?"

"Oh, um, Landon tried calling you several times but couldn't get a hold of you. He was worried and mentioned it to me. He cares a lot about you." I'd have to remember to fill Landon in on my lie in case Derek questioned him about it.

"Hmm ... I cain't 'member what I was doin' last week, let alone three weeks ago. Reckon nothing, really. Workin', I guess."

It was no use. "You've been most helpful, Derek. I can't tell you how appreciative I am. And if you ever get another Friday night off, maybe we can hang out." I threw that in for good measure, just in case he got around to remembering anything.

"Wait a sec, hon. You ast 'bout a Friday—April fourth? Yeah, I 'member that night. If memory serves me, I was having a bad day that day. Backslid a little. Ended up in the drunk tank, I think. Though it's hazy, the date. But I'm purty sure it was the fourth ... or maybe the fifth? Shee-it, I can't even remember what I did two days ago. Weed kills brain cells, y'know?"

"No kidding," I said derisively. Apparently the man smoked more than his fair share.

"But I be doin' much better now."

"I can see that," I muttered under my breath.

I left Derek's house five minutes later feeling uncertain after an apologetic good-bye for bringing up painful memories. He assured me it was okay, then asked if I wanted to come watch him play video games and have pizza next week. I politely declined, saying that I was on medication for a really bad STD that made me tired a lot. The lie worked like a charm as his interest immediately vanished.

As I hustled to my car, I wondered, was he telling the

truth about Alexis? It sure seemed like genuine emotion to me, but then again, a murderer was capable of anything and could certainly fake remorse. I couldn't justify scratching Derek off the list of suspects yet. I still had some digging to do.

After all, if the Triangle Terror was Alexis's killer, Derek fit the profile in more ways than one. First, he worked as a delivery guy. It was the perfect occupation for manipulating his way into a home without breaking in:

Good afternoon, miss. I have a large package to deliver. Can I bring it inside?

The unsuspecting girl would unwittingly oblige.

Then he's in. Undetected and without arousing suspicion.

Secondly, he had no alibi for the night of Alexis's murder, or for Amy's attack, for that matter. His alibi for Gina's murder seemed shaky at best—he couldn't even remember when he was in jail! I made a mental note to check on that. I was sure Landon could pull some strings with Detective Williams to find out.

Thirdly, he was close to Alexis, which made her the perfect first victim.

And finally, he was a druggie alcoholic—which meant he had addictive tendencies and was likely emotionally troubled. While those attributes didn't automatically brand him a serial killer, they definitely made him a likely candidate. To top it off, he clearly had some bad connections. Even if he didn't do it, he might be linked to the one who did.

I didn't yet have enough evidence to put him at Alexis's crime scene twenty-two years ago, but I had a feeling that if I kept an eye on him, I'd have the information I needed to know if he killed Gina and attacked Amy.

As I opened my car door, I felt eyes watching me. I glanced around the empty street, then back at Derek's house. In my peripheral vision I saw the curtains sway and a shadowy figure back away from the window. Derek was watching me, so I'd need to watch him closer if I was going to outwit him. Though based on our first encounter, it wouldn't take much.

Chapter 15

Thursday, May 1
1:11 a.m.

The darkness of my bedroom yawned before me as I regained consciousness, opening a chasm of mysteries. Mysteries about who I was and what my purpose held. Since I was sixteen years old I knew what I was put on Earth for, but lately ... lately I wasn't so sure.

Questions etched themselves into my heart, causing me grave doubt.

Damn every one of them.

Wasn't I supposed to free the innocent from this purgatory that we call life? Vanity overran society, and it was killing us all. How dare others pass judgment on my work! Was I truly the torturer? How about the cosmetic surgeons performing facelifts, or the Botox injections of botulism toxins women willingly subjected themselves to? That, indeed, was more torturous than anything I did. And I was the crazy one?

I think not.

True beauty had been slandered for far too long by the aged seeking eternal youth in potions and masks, but ever so sneakily the young were also falling victim to the whims of narcissism. Once upon a time adults were adults and children were children. But now that wasn't the case. The lines were blurred. Girls dressed like whores—acted like them too. Younger and younger they were deflowered, and so many were to blame for the trend. Negligent parents, ego-based media, Facebook, selfies, retailer targeting, schools teaching it in the classroom. Children were trapped at birth to one day succumb to this inflated sense of ego.

I had hoped my message would change all that. Slowly but surely the masses would understand their plight. But at each purging, my intent was covered up—by the media, of course. The newspapers called it "murder," "horrendous," and "sick." They girls were "victims." All lies! The girls were set free, and I was their hero! How could my point be mistaken? Either the media was blind to the truth, or they were in on the scam to corrupt the lost. My bet was on the latter.

Tonight, in the twilight glow, I came alive while others slumbered, and for once I felt like myself. In the safety of night I took off the mask that hid who I truly was underneath. A man searching for peace and hope in a fallen world and doing his part to fix it. That was more than most could say.

As I tossed off my down-filled covers and stepped out of my bed, my mind was riddled with questions—a wonder to me, as I rarely questioned anything.

What had I done? What had I become?

I had killed again, and beneath the sense of obligation, I liked it. My actions weren't purely to free the world from the clutches of sin; they made me happy.

Perhaps my motives weren't so pure after all.

Was I a monster like they said?

No, that couldn't be the case.

Yet recently something had changed. After years of killing, my body was beginning to reject my vigilantism … an intolerance I hadn't anticipated. It reminded me of my very first murder when my stomach sickened at the sight of a dead-eyed girl I cared about.

My own flesh was revolted back then, and it was happening again.

I noticed my weakness for the first time after purging Amy Watson, while I was in the car.

It started with cold sweats. Heart racing. I shrugged it off as the rush of anxiety before the kill waning at last. But it didn't end there. I was being haunted. Ever since Amy, I began having dreams. At first they were just snippets, tidbits, but they were growing, expanding, evolving ... into macabre visions of mayhem, mutilation, murder. They say dreams are the mind's way of working through issues. What were mine that I found such comfort in chaos, jubilation in mutilation, revelry in rancor? In these dreams I no longer saw myself as the savior, but as a killer. And it scared me.

But what frightened me wasn't so much the debate over what I was—villain or not. What truly struck fear into my heart was how much I *needed* to kill. To watch life's final escape, to inhale the wafting scent of blood, to grasp control over life and death. It was exhilarating, yet it was also my Achilles heel.

I no longer had control over myself, and that was a line I could never cross.

For three days I had remained hidden, lurking underground to avoid exposing myself so soon after Amy's death. But today it was time to come out and play. I was on a warpath in a battle against society, and there was no time for reprieve.

I headed into my kitchen and decided to make a sandwich—first mayo on sourdough, then two slices of ham, one slice of Swiss cheese, a leaf of lettuce, and two slices of tomato. I ran a knife diagonally across the bread and took my two halves into the living room. I hadn't indulged myself in reading about Amy Watson's death yet—a delayed gratification of sorts. A copy of the NEWS &

OBSERVER sat on the end table, taunting me with its headline:

THE TRIANGLE TERROR STRIKES AGAIN

I smiled the paternal smile of a proud father, then I continued reading:

Hillsborough, NC
The elusive serial killer dubbed the Triangle Terror has apparently struck again, with his intended victim narrowly escaping death, thanks to her father's timely advent on the scene.

Amy Watson, a 12-year-old Orange County girl, was viciously stabbed Tuesday in her Miller Bend Road home by a man posing as a talent scout. According to the victim's testimony, the alleged killer, using the alias Gary Billing, first approached her at The Streets of Southpoint, claiming to represent the fictitious Ace Talent and Modeling Agency. He later sought her out at her residence and, after gaining her confidence and distracting her, stabbed her in the abdomen.

Her father, Rick Watson, arrived home from work in the nick of time, rushing to Amy's aid as the alleged killer made his escape. Paramedics arrived on the scene in time to resuscitate Amy, who is now in protective custody at Duke Hospital.

With Amy's cooperation police hope to identify and apprehend the alleged killer before he attacks again.

Barbed wire felt caught in my throat as I tried to swallow but couldn't. Amy was alive? She had survived? Impossible. I couldn't have failed. I never failed.

The failure wasn't the worst blow, however. Amy's survival meant she could identify me, or already had.

There was no way to know what she had told the cops, but I aimed to find out. If, God willing, she hadn't yet given a detailed description, I'd extinguish any inclination to do so. But I had to act fast.

Today was a new day, a day of reckoning. And I reckoned it was time for me to finish what I started with Amy Watson.

Chapter 16

Thursday, May 1
1:46 a.m.

One o'clock had come and gone and I still couldn't fall asleep. Creaking floorboards and the glaring headlights of passing cars made me restless, jumpstarting my imagination to conjure up images of Derek slaughtering me alive—choking me, gutting me, raping me. It was almost as frightening as my nightmares.

Outside my window, a car door shutting aroused my curiosity. Who would be coming home this late in an apartment full of elderly widows and families with young kids? Having met nearly everyone in my complex, I stood out as pretty much the only young-ish/single-ish person who lived there … only I wasn't that young anymore. Lately I was feeling every moment of my thirty-four years, and I looked it too. My vibrant hazel eyes had dimmed with unresolved anger, and my supple skin sagged beneath the weight of insomnia.

I glanced outside my bedroom window and noticed an unmarked white van parked across the street. My eyes strained to see a silhouette of someone inside, but it was too dark and the streetlamp cast too many shadows. I closed my blinds, haunted by the foreboding sense of someone watching me.

With sleep nowhere on the horizon, I impulsively picked up my phone and texted:

You awake?

After about two minutes my phone chimed with a response:

I am now. jk. Can't sleep.

So I typed:

Me neither. Talk?

I dialed, and it rang several times before he picked up.

"What took you so long to answer?" I asked, seeing as he had just replied to my text.

"I wasn't sure I wanted to know what you're up to at this hour. Then I caved. What's up?" he replied sleepily.

"You home right now?"

When I heard a timid, "Yeah, why?" on the other end, I ventured to see if I could come over. Another groggy affirmative.

I hung up, grabbed pepper spray and my keys, and headed out the door, sprinting the entire way to my car and hastily locking the driver's door once inside the safety of my vehicle. The white van along the road was gone, but my fears weren't.

It was time to put my anxiety to rest for the night.

I showed up at Landon's wearing cornflower blue sweatpants and a UNC sweatshirt. He hushed me as I stepped through the front door.

"Keep quiet, okay? My mom's sleeping." He waved me to follow him into the kitchen.

Like the living room as I remembered it, the kitchen seemed recently updated with a fresh coat of white paint on the cabinets and tasteful wallpaper decorated with tiny pastel pansies—though not my taste. More the taste of a modern grandma. Framed pansy paintings decorated the walls, and a similarly-themed spice rack was tucked next to the oven. It felt cheerful, even in the dim glow of the frosted-glass ceiling fixture, which apparently boasted a miserly 25-watt bulb. The counters looked original, however—an old-fashioned sunflower yellow with a silver rim lining the edge. The avocado green wall oven was a relic from the '70s; incredibly, the kitchen boasted no microwave.

"Want a midnight snack?"

"Sure," I said. That actually sounded really good right now, since I had picked over my dinner. Even with a murderer on the brain, a girl's gotta eat.

Landon grabbed a bag of Utz tortilla chips and a package of shredded Mexican cheese and tossed them on the counter. Then he handed me a tomato, fresh chives, and a knife. "You like loaded nachos?"

"Heck yeah."

"Good. Let's see how good you are with that knife."

I groaned and gave him the stink-eye.

"Poor choice of words. I mean, I'd appreciate it if you'd do the honors."

As a lull descended on the kitchen, I started dicing, embracing the calming silence. For the first time in nearly a month I actually felt secure.

When the oven had preheated, Landon tossed the cheese-covered nachos inside and set the timer. We each grabbed a seat at a breakfast table nestled in the corner of the room.

"What had you awake at this hour?" I asked as I propped my chin on my hand.

"Eh, I don't sleep much. Insomnia." His yawn affirmed his exhaustion, which prompted me into a sympathetic yawning fit.

"Me too, lately. You look tired. Now I feel bad for calling."

"Don't feel bad. I wasn't dozing off anytime soon

anyways. So, what's going on? I don't often have girls showing up at this hour. I'm usually kicking them out by now." We both laughed like old friends.

"I couldn't sleep. And I had something to tell you," I said cryptically.

"I don't like the sound of that. What do you need to get off your chest?"

I inhaled a deep breath before replying. "I, um, talked to your uncle earlier today—well, yesterday, actually."

"Wait—my Uncle Derek?"

I nodded meekly.

"Why didn't you tell me you were going to talk to him? You could have asked me first, Mia. I've been honest with you, and I would have appreciated the same from you."

Perhaps I hadn't taken the most open road of going about it, but I suspected Landon's reaction would be, well, exactly this—defensive and difficult.

"I wanted to tell you, Landon, but I knew you'd say no and try to convince me not to talk to him."

"There's a reason for that. Because he's not guilty."

"You don't know that for sure," I retaliated like a teenage girl in a fight with her mom.

"Whatever. Let's just move on. What'd you talk about?"

"He's on the suspect list, Landon. I wanted to find out if he had an alibi the night of Alexis's death."

"Does he?"

"Nope. He was supposedly drunk … and alone."

"You're speculating. I just don't know, Mia. I can't imagine that he would kill someone. He's done a lot of bad stuff, but murder? It doesn't sound like him."

"Landon, no one pegs murderers for being murderers. It's not like they go around handing out business cards. They can be the boy next door, your pastor, your own spouse, even your friendly neighborhood barista at Starbucks—heck, they can be anybody! I know you don't want to think of your own flesh and blood as being a killer, but let's face the facts. He fits the profile."

"How so?"

"Works for Ralph's Delivery Services, so he can easily gain access into people's houses."

"Coincidental," Landon muttered with a shrug.

"Plus," I added, plowing onward with brute force, "he doesn't log his time, so he can come and go as he pleases. He has no one he's accountable to, so he can stay under the radar. And let's face it—he's messed up."

"So is half the population of the United States."

"He's a grown man—old enough to be a young grandpa—who preys on young girls! C'mon, Landon."

Landon shook his head. "I'm sorry, but I think you're off base with this."

"If not him, then who? We could keep going in circles, or we can stop the killer. I'm telling you, my gut says it's him. Trust me, I'm an empath."

Landon snorted. "An empath? What kind of metaphysical crap is that? You're going on a hunch here, not facts. Besides, don't you think he's a little old to be able to overpower another person?"

"He's not even sixty, Landon, and while he's thin, he's muscular. And we're talking about girls. Easy to manipulate, easy to subdue. I'm telling you—he's our guy."

As the argument was getting heated, the oven timer beeped, momentarily cooling the tension. But I wasn't done discussing it. Talk would get us nowhere without action. If Derek was our guy, he needed to be stopped immediately—before he claimed another victim.

"Other than the fact that he was home alone, give me some other evidence that points to him attacking my sister—his own niece," Landon demanded as he tossed a handful of tomatoes and chives on the nachos, then scooped a spoonful of sour cream on top. He grabbed a cheesy chip and gestured for me to help myself.

He didn't need to ask twice.

I heaved an exasperated sigh. "I don't know what else to say. Her killer knew her and had a key, and I'm assuming there weren't many people who did. But a family member might. So just that alone is enough to raise suspicion. What more do you need to at least consider him a suspect?"

"Assuming Alexis's killer is the Triangle Terror, which is more than likely, are you saying my uncle is intelligent enough to have been killing girls for two decades without getting caught? You met him—does he strike you as an evil genius?"

Landon had me there. The man-child played video games and seemed to be a reckless drunkard. Unless ... could it be a well-executed façade to throw the authorities off his scent?

"I don't know him well enough to answer that."

"What about the other girls—did you ask him about them? Does he have an alibi for their attacks?"

"He said he had been working and playing video games when Amy got attacked, and as for Gina, he thinks he got picked up for public drunkenness that night. I'm not sure anyone can corroborate his whereabouts, since even he seemed unsure. Though the police would be able to determine if he got arrested during the past month, right?"

"Yeah, let's check it out," Landon agreed reluctantly. "But I still think it's a wild goose chase."

"Maybe, but it's a lead, and a plausible one. The guy sure does like to party, and when I asked him for names of his friends, he didn't exactly spit out the phonebook. Let's just see what we come up with. If it doesn't fit, I'll drop it. Okay?"

I popped another loaded chip in my mouth, deciding to change the conversation before Landon kicked me out. I was enjoying the snack too much to storm out of there.

As I savored the melty mixture, a thought occurred to me. It could be nothing at all… or something profoundly important. Assuming Derek was innocent, I expected a serial killer to have some kind of record—and in this case, one related to children in particular.

"Do you have a computer around here?"

"In the living room." Landon grabbed the tray of chips and headed to the living room sofa. His laptop sat on the coffee table, already open and humming.

In the Google toolbar, I searched for the National Sex Offender Registry, then clicked on North Carolina.

"Mind telling me what you're doing?" Landon asked.

"We know this guy targets girls—*young* girls. Something tells me he may have a sexual offender history. I just want to look up any offenders in this area, see if anyone pops up that has lived here back when Alexis was alive. I know it's a long shot, but I've got nothing else."

At five miles, a staggering number of names showed up in the area. A sad reality that I couldn't comprehend. After narrowing down my search to a one-mile radius, I hit the jackpot:

Jeremy Mason, residing at 801 Willoughby Way, registered sexual offender, convicted for indecent liberty with a minor on 02/21/1992—two weeks before Alexis's death. The only information about the victim was that she was twelve years old, which made me wonder if it was Alexis. He was slapped with three years of probation—a gutless slap on the wrist. Since he wasn't sentenced to do any time in jail, he was free and clear to murder as he saw fit.

His picture revealed a blond guy with glasses. Blond—just like in the dreams.

It was too coincidental to ignore, but also too circumstantial to be viable. If he had sexually assaulted Alexis—and was convicted—wouldn't he have been a prime suspect in the police investigation?

"Well, I'll be damned," Landon said, ripping me from my reverie. He had been reading the entry over my shoulder. "I know this dude. I had no idea Jeremy was a sex offender."

"You know him?" I echoed.

"Yeah, since I was a kid. He's lived on our street forever. Grew up with my mom. They weren't close friends or anything, but he was always … neighborly."

"Probably because he was trying to molest your sister," I mumbled under my breath. "Do you want to check him out with me tomorrow? Stop by and ask him some questions?"

"Yeah, might as well. It's the only lead we got."

I wanted to remind him that good old Uncle Derek wasn't off the hook yet, but I bit my tongue. No point in arguing. It was way too late and I was way too tired to make a good case.

Eventually talk about the case segued into ice cream for dessert and banter about shared passion for the television show *Breaking Bad,* our respective taste in music—me: all styles REM and Collective Soul; him: Nickelback meets Marilyn Manson—and what we would do with a million dollars. Landon confirmed that I probably couldn't buy my own private island for a million bucks. Too bad.

In the wee hours of the morning Landon offered to take the couch and give me his bed—he, a grown man, actually had *South Park* sheets—but I wasn't comfortable with the idea of running into his mother during my "walk of shame" out of the house that morning … even though I had nothing to be ashamed of, I assured myself. Yet I couldn't deny the attraction. In the dim living room lighting, I dared to sit a little too close to Landon, allowing my fingers to occasionally brush against his when we reached for a chip at the same time.

A stab of guilt struck me when I rested my head on Landon's shoulder and his arm encircled me, hugging me against his chest. Brad would have been devastated if he'd witnessed the intimacy—wouldn't he? I still didn't know where things stood with Brad, but I knew I still loved him. I wouldn't have felt guilty if I didn't. But I refused to chase him like a besotted schoolgirl. He left, not me. His choice, not mine. He knew where I was and how to contact me, and I'd leave it at that. Call it pride, call it stubbornness— but I called it dignity.

Amid this volley of thoughts, I never saw it coming. Landon's hand brushing against my chin. His fingertips tipping my face upward. His lips wavering above mine, then gently joining our mouths in feather-light consummation.

I caved in to the hunger, yearning for his affection. The gentle caress of lips grew ravenous as each kiss became harder, firmer, more intense—a battle of tongues and hands grabbing at flesh, wanting more and more. Needing to feel passion, reaching for rapture beyond my bodily constraints.

We consumed each other as teeth scraped, mouths sucked, and his lips journeyed slowly down my neck. I moaned in ecstasy as he found the tender muscles beneath my cotton neckline, and my nipples hardened as he expertly nibbled at my exposed skin. Pain became pleasure. Pleasure became ecstasy.

The voracious grip of his fingers clawed at the small of my back, his hand rising upward to unsnap my bra. His hips pivoted toward me as he pulled me onto his lap. I felt heat smoldering in my loins and an eager wetness inviting him in as his other hand joined in lifting up my top. The sudden coolness of the air on my skin alerted my mind to what was happening.

My first thought was of my scar. I couldn't let him see it.

Second came a thought about Brad.

I can't do this to Brad. I still love him.

"Wait," I muttered beneath Landon's mouth, pulling back just enough to catch my breath. "We need to stop." I turned away and slid off of him, tugging my shirt back down and wiping my lips clean of the lingering moisture. I felt naked and vulnerable; I wondered if Landon had seen my scar. Shame swept over me for succumbing to this overpowering moment of weakness.

"I'm so sorry ... I don't know what I was thinking," Landon apologized.

"It's okay," I assured him, trying more to convince myself of its truth. "Can we pretend that never happened?"

"What never happened?" Landon winked playfully at me, then swatted my shoulder as if we had just played a friendly game of truth or dare—and took the dare a little too far.

"Thanks."

With Brad on the brain but Landon in my arms, that was my cue to leave.

I got up and headed for the door. As Landon walked beside me, he graciously brought up our next move—learning more about Jeremy Mason, the neighborhood molester. It wasn't exactly the follow-up that a girl looks forward to after a heavy make-out session, but it was the perfect cure for banishing my persistent thoughts about it.

We made plans to question Jeremy later in the morning, and I settled into a comforting belief that he could have done it—which freed me from further nightmares of death at the hands of Derek.

Feeling a bit more secure with the idea that perhaps I wasn't yet a blip on the killer's radar and could safely sleep alone in my apartment, I left Landon at his driveway and headed home. The streets were mostly deserted. As I made my turn into the parking lot, I noticed in my rearview mirror a car swerve off to the side of the road without entering the apartment complex and turn off its headlights. It seemed peculiar to me, since the car was parked conspicuously on a main road without much of a berm. *Curiouser and curiouser, cried Alice.*

I didn't want to waste time outside—alone—speculating, so I jumped out of my car and bolted toward my apartment's front door, then climbed the stairs two at a time.

Engaging the doorknob lock and securing the deadbolt behind me, I scurried to my bedroom window, which gave me a view of the main road. I peered out from the darkness of my room. The car was still there, and I could barely make out a profile. He was wearing a hat, but other than that, his face hid in the shadows. Then a moment later the headlights flicked on and the car drove away. At my angle I couldn't see a license plate or guess the make and model of the vehicle.

One thing was for sure, though. I wouldn't be getting any sleep that night after all.

PAMELA CRANE

Chapter 17

After a combined two hours of sleep, comprised of fifteen-minute bouts of dozing off here and there, I poured a hot cup of coffee—more cream and sugar than coffee, I suppose—and prepared for my interrogation of Jeremy Mason, prime suspect of the day. I couldn't approach him with guns a-blazin', or wild accusations, in this case. I needed to finesse the truth out of him without putting myself on his hit list. It would take careful planning and even more precise execution ... no pun intended.

I had arranged to meet Landon at his house at eight o'clock—fifteen minutes from now—at which point we would walk over to Jeremy's house together, posing as friendly neighbors on a casual stroll, stopping by to chat. According to Landon's wakeup phone call thirty minutes earlier, Jeremy's car was still parked in the driveway.

With the coffee carafe still halfway full, I poured the rest into a travel mug, stirred it into a milky confection, and headed out the door.

By the time I got to Landon's house, he was waiting on the sidewalk for me as I pulled up and parked.

"Hey, we gotta hurry. I saw Jeremy carrying a duffel bag to his car. I think he's about to head out."

Luckily I wore my trusty running shoes, since we had to speed-walk down the street, looking about as natural as a pair of multi-headed aliens newly arrived on Earth. Casual stroll, my arse.

Sweat trickled down my forehead and neck when we arrived at 801 Willoughby Way, and while I cursed Landon the entire trek there, the timing couldn't have been more perfect. We nearly bumped into Jeremy as he was climbing into his vehicle.

"Howdy, neighbor!" Landon called out a little too excitedly, waving his hand. "Nice morning for a walk."

When Jeremy waved back, we both approached, prompting Jeremy to step out to greet us.

"It's Jeremy, right?" Landon queried.

Jeremy's blond head bobbed an affirmative. "You're Jennifer's son, right?"

Landon stretched out his arm and the men shook hands. "Yeah. You know me?"

"I thought I recognized you. I remember when you were just a kid. You look just like your mother. Though I haven't seen you around in years."

"You've got a good memory. I tend to keep to myself. I guess I'm more of an introvert."

I noticed Jeremy's pale blue scrubs. He was obviously in the medical profession, but in what capacity, I couldn't guess. "Sorry, your name slips my mind," he said.

"I'm Landon. We were just out for a walk and I figured I'd say hi. It's a gorgeous day."

In fact, it was anything but. Gray clouds pregnant with a looming downpour darkened the sky, and a distant boom of thunder warned us to take cover if we wanted to stay dry. But Jeremy didn't seem to notice the faux pas.

"Overcoming that introvert in you, huh?" Jeremy said with a grin.

Landon nodded but said nothing.

"Hi, I'm Mia," I interceded with a stiff wave.

"It's nice to meet you. Not too many, well, friendly people on this street." Jeremy glanced at me as he said it and I forced a rigid grin.

It doesn't help that you molest children, I thought to myself angrily. I was trying my best not to punch the guy in the face.

"How's Jennifer doing?" Jeremy asked. "I've been meaning to stop by. We used to run into each other when she went for walks around the block, but it's been a while."

"She's doing pretty good. Not that it's any of your business." Landon's blunt reply felt weighted with tension. His eyes narrowed with ... was that jealousy?

Jeremy was undeterred. "Is your mom still single?" he pressed.

Interesting ... the child molester had a thing for grown women. And it just so happened that it was Landon's mother. I speculated how I could use this to my advantage—that is, if Landon would let me. I doubted it, based on his clenched jaw.

"Why do you ask?" Landon asked tersely.

"Ah, just curious, that's all. She's a beautiful woman." As Landon's fists clenched at his side, Jeremy checked his watch. "Oh boy. I'm gonna be late for work. How about I give you my number to pass along to Jennifer? I'd love to see her."

"I don't think so," Landon said, his eyes fixed on Jeremy's.

As Landon staked his territory, I noticed a name badge attached to Jeremy's front pocket. Duke Hospital—where Amy was currently recovering. I wondered how a documented child predator got a job at a hospital, unless he had already been employed with them and simply never disclosed his conviction. With no jail time—only probation—he could have easily dusted it under the rug. But that didn't matter right now. What mattered was finding out if he had any connection to the murders.

"Man, what's your problem?" Jeremy said petulantly.

"The fact that you're hitting on my mom is my problem. I thought you liked little girls, not wo—"

And that was the end of the argument and the beginning of the battle.

Jeremy didn't miss a beat before he swung, making bone-on-bone contact with Landon's cheek, snapping his head back. Landon's fingers gingerly explored the ugly gash on his cheekbone. Then he charged.

Like a bull seeing the matador's crimson *capote*, Landon bulldozed headfirst into Jeremy's gut, thrusting him against the car. The vehicle shook on impact as the two men jockeyed for position, blindly throwing blows and grunting like pigs as they grappled on the gritty sidewalk. My God, they had turned into common street thugs! My only reflex was to scream.

"Stop it! Please, stop!" I yelled, stupidly stepping into the mess of bodies to feebly try to break it up. A knuckle clipped my chin and another flailing fist knocked me backward a few steps. I was sure it'd leave a bruise.

A moment later, an alarmed Landon took notice of me nursing my jaw, shoved Jeremy aside, and sprinted to my aid. "Are you okay?" He examined me for injuries.

"Yeah, I think so," I said, tenderly rubbing my chin and working my mouth to ensure it still worked. "We need to leave … now."

"That's a good idea," Jeremy barked. "You come near me again and I'll press charges."

Ignoring his bluster, Landon circled his arm around me as we stalked down the driveway. But just as we reached the sidewalk, Landon stopped and tossed a glare over his shoulder. "You'd better stay away from my mom, you pervert, or you will regret it!"

Men.

Chapter 18

Night was my only companion when everyone else deserted me. Yet I didn't mind. I thrived in the darkness, feeling alive and whole and renewed. While victims of society snuggled beneath their security blankets of beautiful homes, endless riches, and picture-perfect lives, blissfully asleep on their 1000-thread-count Egyptian cotton sheets, outside I lurked. I watched. I waited. I plotted.

But lately my plots were unraveling, and my ego was to blame.

Amy Watson's survival was a major mistake. A mistake that could ruin everything. My weakness revealed itself, naked and vulnerable before me. I had gotten cocky, careless. I relished the release too much, too long, and my gratification could be my downfall. Now I faced losing everything, and I wasn't yet prepared. So much was left undone.

I knew there was only one way to overcome my flawed state of decadence: self-restraint. I had to reinstate my apathy for the kill. Much like a hunter's indifference as his bullet passes through the deer's skull, I must feel nothing again. Numbness was my only recourse to getting back on track.

Yet the steps that recovery would require went against everything I stood for.

Senseless murder.

I would need to kill again ... but this time one of the

sinless saints. This time I wouldn't be restoring purity to the "lost," rather I'd be snuffing out the pure from the "found." This time it would bring me no pleasure. But it would accomplish the goal and aid the mission. And I had just the person in mind.

First things first, however. The girl, Amy, had to die—and with her, her secrets. Or should I say, *my* secrets.

As far as I knew, she hadn't offered much to the police, thanks to painkillers, attorneys, and fear. A fake name and fake employer. Nothing concrete to ID me. But eventually the cops would bulldoze through Mr. and Mrs. Watson's lawyers to get more information, and Amy's memory would return, and with it her lips spilling everything, just like I wanted to spill her guts all over the cold hospital linoleum. I had to put a knot in the unraveling—and that meant one thing: Amy's time was up.

Getting past security and Amy's personal guard dogs—a revolving cast from the Durham police force—would be tricky, but not impossible. I had ways of getting things done. By casing the hospital, I had discovered she was on a morphine drip and was intermittently clearheaded, and her mother spent every evening at her bedside, with the exception of Thursdays, her ladies' poker night. The father made brief daily visits during his lunch hour, usually with an expensive gift in hand—most likely picked out by his twenty-something-year-old secretary whom he slept with on the side at the Holiday Inn down the road. Apparently his precious daughter's near-death experience didn't warrant time off from work ... or play.

Ah, life's priorities. Rarely did anyone get them right, yet we all had our mental to-do checklists nagging us during our daily routines. It was a wonder to me how our ingrained system of checks and balances could become so discombobulated that a father couldn't find the self-control to pick his daughter over his mistress. It was a shame he'd never get the opportunity to apologize to Amy once I completed my task.

Morning and afternoon visits were harder to predict, for the girl had apparently been quite popular among her peers and seemed to have an extensive family. Truant classmates stopped by regularly each morning, bringing coffee, magazines, and makeup. Yet despite the parental concerns over Amy's safety, the visitors never ceased, which was where my planning needed to be pristine in order to avoid being detected.

General precautions seemed minimal. Every entrant required permission from the guard on duty, which seemed a farce to me, since anyone and everyone was apparently granted entrance. But my patience paid off when I witnessed the guard's shift change, noting minutes-long gaps as each new shift started. Mere minutes were all I needed to complete my task.

My intel was more than enough to get me started on finishing the job. Yet recently a roadblock had popped up that made my work increasingly difficult.

Mia Germaine.

A pretty woman with an intelligent mind. More of a threat than I had anticipated when I found her lurking about, clearly investigating me. It wasn't apparent at first as she smiled sweetly and played the part of an ally, but then I smelled curiosity—the whiff of dogged snooping. That's when I decided she was my enemy.

I couldn't reveal myself to her just yet, though. The moment I popped my head up, it was over. And I wasn't up for a game of Whack-a-Mole with Mia. For while Mia imagined she was holding the bat, it would be her head on the platter in the end. And I didn't want that ... yet.

For now I would simply continue my work. Blissfully clueless, Mia would continue prying each coffin of information open—and each time she'd only find velvety emptiness within. My trail was well covered, and Mia didn't have the investigative chops to find what she was looking for. Lucky for her.

After our introduction, I had no desire to kill her, for she epitomized what I had spent decades trying to achieve with my message: Women renouncing materialism and adulterated sexuality, and instead pursuing wholesomeness and modesty.

Yet to her detriment, Mia's gifts of purity were being tainted, and her curiosity jeopardizing my mission. Left with no other option, I would send her a warning, and perhaps she would grant herself a respite from her newfound interest in my work. But I knew her type. Relentless. Determined. And thus destined to die. Yet everyone deserved at least one chance, I figured.

Sitting outside her apartment complex window in my car, humming along to Roy Orbison's "In Dreams," my eyes held fast to the white-gray flicker of her television screen two stories up, followed by the occasional appearance of her silhouette as she paced to the kitchen or bathroom or whatnot. I imagined her curled up on the sofa, her feet tucked under her plump rear, while her baggy sweatpants and oversized T-shirt shrouded her toned, slender figure.

Closing my eyes for a brief moment, I pictured her, fresh-faced and vibrant as her hair hung in a messy ponytail, the naturally curly wisps framing her face and accentuating her hazel eyes. Yes, it would be a shame to lose such a natural beauty, but it was a necessary evil if she didn't comply.

An idea occurred to me. Making a simple point could end the whole charade of girl-turned-detective. And I knew just the message for her.

My Nikon D7100 camera was always at hand, so I felt

for it along the floorboard of my backseat and grabbed the carrying case strap. After removing the camera and adjusting the focus, I took several well-timed pictures of her passing by the window, adjusting the zoom to capture a decent image of her face. It might be grainy or pixilated, but clear enough for her to recognize her own silhouette beyond the window blinds. Once I had a sufficient number of images, I slipped on my gloves and pulled out of my duffel bag an envelope with one word on the front: *Truce*.

I carefully removed the memory stick from the camera, then dropped it into the envelope along with my letter explaining the situation. It read, in a fastidious handwriting I'd perfected that was not my own:

Dearest Mia:

I write this as a treaty between two individuals with a common goal—restoring the lost among us.

Your investigation into my activities has recently come to my attention. While I appreciate your endeavors to serve what you call "justice," perhaps your vision is blurred by a false reality that you've come to accept as truth. There is no justice, my dear, for the dead leave justice at the grave. And you, too, must leave it there.

One of irony's greatest accomplishments is that you cannot punish the wrongdoing of another without committing a wrongdoing yourself. Your wrongdoing, Mia, is interrupting the purification of a vanity-polluted society. Take this as a first and final warning. I will be watching. Continued prying into my activities will result in another loss of life: your own.

Succinct and tactful, yet firm. Content with the wording, I tore off the adhesive strip and sealed the envelope shut. Overall, I felt my approach was both diplomatic and judicious. Certainly a woman of her caliber would appreciate that and abide by my wishes. And if not, well, she sealed her own fate.

After checking and re-checking to ensure no one was watching, I slipped out of the driver's seat, leaving my door cracked open, and jogged into the glass atrium containing rows of mailboxes. Finding Mia's number amid the masses, I slipped the envelope inside and trotted back to my car to resume my watch.

A few minutes passed, and I decided it was time to retreat for the evening. I had been running on fumes lately, suffering from an exhaustion I didn't recognize. Usually the thrill of the chase invigorated me, but with Amy still alive, worry consumed me.

Tonight I would finalize plans for her impending death—again—and ensure nothing got in the way this time.

Chapter 19

I admit I am a lot of things. Argumentative. Adventurous. Yet emotionally guarded. But fearful was not on the list today.

If anything, the letter I held in my hand made me more angry than afraid. I had spent the past few weeks wary of every little thing. Checking my rearview mirror for someone following me wherever I drove, sprinting to my car at night, regularly scanning the grounds outside my apartment windows, and searching the shadows ... but not anymore.

The threat I received only fueled my intensity to find the killer. Before today, it was merely a guessing game if I was on the Triangle Terror's radar or not. The idea of the unknown scared me more than the known. Now that I knew he was watching me, I knew to look for him. He was there—always there—and thus I knew where to find him.

Perhaps I was the bait needed to catch this guy.

And with my current mindset, I was willing to take that risk.

Of course, the risk could cost me my life. While I understood that, the enormity of the threat didn't penetrate me like it probably should have. Lately, all I had to live for was avenging Alexis. Brad and I hadn't spoken for God knows how long, my job was unsatisfying, and I had lost any interest in bettering myself.

I used to hike, meet up with Jackie for lunch to catch up on the latest gossip, enjoy happy hour after work, lose myself in a good book. The details that previously constituted my full life were whittled away, one by one, as I immersed myself more and more in finding this killer. I was barely eating and fitfully sleeping in my loveless, empty, pathetic life. But I couldn't return to my old life until I caught him. It was no longer a choice for me. It was a compulsion.

Come and get me, Triangle Terror. I have nothing to lose but my mind … and it's already halfway gone.

My hand quivered as I clutched the piece of paper, wrinkling it as my fist tightened. I stood in the breezy entrance where rows of metal mailboxes lined one wall and a stairwell consumed another, wondering if he was watching right now through the glass door as residents ambled in and out. I checked the parking lot, but the coward was probably hiding in his car, too afraid to face me. That's when I decided to call his bluff … and haughtily piss him off.

With resolute steps, I walked out of the mailroom and down the sidewalk, toward the parking lot. When I found a place that seemed fairly out in the open, I held up the letter above my head and tore it in half. But once was not enough. I slid the halves on top of each other and ripped it again, and again, and again, until it was nothing but a pile of tiny scraps in my palm. Then I let go.

As the shreds fluttered to the concrete curb, I regretted not saving the intact document for the police to check for fingerprints. Although, I doubted the killer was careless enough to leave any, so it probably wouldn't have mattered anyway. At least I made my point if he was watching.

I wasn't scared.

I pocketed the memory stick for now. I'd look through it later. I had somewhere to be that I hoped ended this charade once and for all.

❧❦

With help from the front desk, I discovered that Amy Watson was out of ICU and moved into room 301, but it took some coercing, and name-dropping, to convince the officer on duty to let me into her hospital room. While allowed visitors, all had to be ID'd beforehand. I hoped my little white lie—that my "good friend" Detective Evan Williams had requested that I come down and interview the girl since she wasn't talking to the cops—didn't catch up with me before I was able to extract some details from her. If Amy gave me any worthwhile information, Evan could thank me later.

When I passed through the heavy door, the first thing I noticed was all of the flowers and gifts. Either this girl was beloved, or her family was overcompensating. More than twenty colorful floral arrangements filled the room, overflowing from the mint-colored corner table onto the floor. Stuffed animals and baskets brimming with goodies took up the rolling table positioned at the foot of her bed. It was enough to become a hazard as I stepped over a basket left at her bedside while tripping on another, nearly face-planting into the electric bed from which Amy watched me with some wariness.

"You're popular, huh?" I teased with a laugh as I managed to wind past the obstacle course and approach her.

"I guess," Amy replied with a shrug as she touched a button on the side rail and raised herself to an upright position. "The nurses told me they're going to have to throw most of this away if I don't do something with it. But I'm not really hungry."

Other than the tubes connected to her arm, she looked amazingly well for a person who had nearly been killed.

Despite the harsh white overhead lighting, makeup brightened her eyes, lips, and cheeks, and a cute ponytail lolled against her starch white pillow. Save for the pale blue hospital gown, she looked ready for a night on the town.

"Hi, Amy. My name's Mia. I'm a friend of one of the cops investigating your attack. He told me what you'd been through. How're you feeling?" I probed, sitting on the corner of the bed at arm's length from her.

"I'm fine." Then she stopped. "I'm sorry, but what are you here for?" She eyed me skeptically. "The guard only told me that you were sent to talk to me. But I'm not allowed to talk to strangers, and I don't know you."

I had figured she'd be reluctant. The last time she trusted a stranger she was stabbed. I had to be tactical in my approach.

"I'm not here to ask questions, Amy. Just here to help. I knew a victim who was killed by the man who attacked you. Her name was Alexis. She is—*was*—a good friend of mine. I never got to say good-bye to her. I just wanted to let you know that I'm here for you if you need to talk to someone. Totally confidentially. That's all." I rose as if to leave, but Amy's hand on my forearm stopped me.

She pursed her lips and examined me. "I heard there was another girl—but she didn't survive."

"Unfortunately, that's right. But there was more than just one. Several. And one was my friend."

"I'm sorry." She paused a contemplative moment, then spoke again. "I'm afraid if I tell what I know that he'll come back for me."

"Is that why you haven't given the police a description of what he looks like?"

"Sorta. That, and I can't remember a lot of it. I'm scared to remember, if that makes any sense."

"Of course that makes sense, honey. But we can't

catch him if you don't try to remember what he looks like."

"Do you think he'll come after me if I tell?"

"I won't let him."

"Promise?"

I crossed my heart with my fingertip. "Cross my heart. Just between us girls."

"So your friend, Alexis, was she my age?"

I nodded. "Yes, she was twelve too. Loved *90210* and Funyuns. And had a great sense of fashion."

"Ew, Funyuns? They are so gross, and smelly. Cheetos are better."

"I agree with you. Never been a fan of onions. But I could go for some Cheetos, now that you mention it. Do you want me to run down to the vending machine and get us some?"

"No need," Amy said, reaching down with a weak grunt into one of the baskets on the floor. She pulled up a bag of Cheetos, already open and half empty. Her free hand tenderly touched her stomach as she winced.

"You okay?" I asked.

She lifted her gown to reveal a large bandage on her abdomen. "Still hurts a lot," she explained, tucking the gown back under the covers. "I'm not really supposed to eat this stuff, but snacks help when I can stomach them," she said cheerily. "The doctor said it's better than nothing. C'mon." She waved the bag at me.

"Aw, thanks for sharing. I'll bring you another bag later to restock your supply," I offered with a smile.

"That's okay. I have plenty of food that I'm not allowed to eat." I laughed at her joke as she gestured to the cream-colored tray next to her IV where a stockpile of chips and cookies peeked from a grocery bag. "I'm hoping I leave here before I get a chance to finish eating it all."

"I'm sure you'll be out in no time, Amy. You know, you remind me of Alexis. She was really pretty and super sweet."

Though the rouge hid it, I could tell she was blushing at the compliment. But it was true. I imagined that Alexis was just like this girl—full of life and beauty. My heart broke for Alexis all over again, and for this girl who would probably never fully emotionally recover from what he did to her.

"Thanks. I'm sorry you lost your friend," Amy said with sincerity, adding conversationally, "So, uh, do you have a lot of friends who are kids, Miss Mia?"

I chuckled. "Not really. No, Alexis was a childhood friend. She died about twenty years ago."

"Are you saying this guy has been killing kids for twenty years?" Her eyes widened, and for the first time I noticed how green and vibrant they were.

"Yeah, Alexis was his first victim. But I'm sure you don't want to hear about that. Do you want to talk about something else?"

"I guess. But I just don't understand. How did they not catch him yet? Do you think he'll come after me again? My mom and the cops say he won't, but I don't believe them."

It was the third time she touched on this fear, but I couldn't lie to her. "Do you want the truth?"

She nodded warily.

"To be honest, Amy, I don't know. But if we don't find him, yes, he could come back for you. That's why any information you can provide will help us find him and put him behind bars so he can't hurt you again ... or anyone else. I'm not asking you to tell me anything right now, but just think about it, okay? I know you're afraid, but you're the only person who can help us catch him."

Amy sat in pensive silence, her mind churning through scenarios, weighing her options, until she spoke again. "I want to help. I just don't know how."

"Do you remember what he looked like?" I verbally

nudged, hoping a little guidance would jog her memory.

"Just a normal guy. White. Not tall, but not short either. Like my dad's height."

Not tall but not short—which meant what exactly? I hadn't realized just how simplistic life was from a teen's perspective.

"What about his hair, or eyes?"

"I'm pretty sure he had short hair, but he was wearing a hat both times I met him, so I don't know what color. I don't remember his eyes. Said he was a talent scout. Friendly guy. And he didn't look old enough to have been killing people for twenty years."

"How old did he look?" I asked.

"I dunno. Not that old. Younger than my mom and dad, I think."

A child's perspective on age was certainly subjective and didn't give me much to go on. Especially since men aged differently than women. Men grew more "distinguished" while we women simply grew old and wrinkly.

"Maybe around your age?" she suggested.

I wondered how old Amy thought I looked. Probably ancient. Especially with the dark circles under my eyes that I woke up to every morning for the past month. I decided to leave that question unexplored.

"Okay, that helps. Um, did he have any defining or unique characteristics? Like a crooked nose, a mustache, or a scar or anything?"

"I'm not sure ... I don't think so." Amy closed her eyes as if concentrating, then suddenly started shaking her head as tears swelled beneath her eyelids. "I can't—" A tear trickled down her cheek. "I can't do this."

"Hey, it's okay." I reached over and hugged her, rubbing her back and smoothing her hair. I tipped her chin up to meet her gaze, then wiped a stray tear away.

"Sweetie, it's okay. Just relax and let's talk about something else, okay?"

She gave me a weak "okay" and rested her head against my shoulder.

It was clear that the trip down memory lane had become a bit much. I could relate. I knew the panic she felt. Alexis made sure of that. The emotional turmoil, the physical anguish, the hopelessness as death encroached. It was a terrifying experience, even in a dream. I couldn't imagine how much worse it was firsthand.

Amy needed time, and I'd give it to her. I just hoped she'd eventually grant me entrance into her inventory of memories. I needed to unlock that vault of information.

We sat, her head resting on me and my arms encasing her. Then she looked up at me.

"Do you think I'll be scarred for life?" She touched her stomach where she had been stabbed.

Probably, sweetie, but not that kind of scar, I wanted to say, but didn't.

I tugged the neckline of my shirt down, revealing a stark white line starting just above my heart that my tattoo failed to cover. "This is a scar I got from a heart transplant when I was about your age. This injury was way worse than yours, and it's faded a bunch over time. And I don't think it looks that bad, do you?"

"No, not really. I can see it, but mine's smaller."

"See? You probably won't have a scar at all."

"Cool ink, too. It's pretty." She pointed to the rose blossoming along my chest.

"Thanks." I touched the ruby-inked petals and felt a memory burden me, then flit away.

Amy must have felt the sincerity of our connection and smiled trustingly, and as I appreciated the beauty of that moment with this young, courageous girl, I wondered if the killer was watching us. If he was, he knew Amy would talk sooner or later, and he couldn't let that happen. I yearned to protect this girl, but I didn't know how. I prayed that the cops were smarter than he was.

Emotions overwhelmed me, so I hugged her, drawing her into the safety of my chest. If only I could keep her there until the threat passed. Amy must have sensed my concern, for she squeezed me tightly and didn't release.

"I'm scared," she suddenly said, her voice muffled in my shirt.

I leaned back to look at her. "Hey, do you want me to stay and we can watch a movie together? I brought a couple of DVDs with me."

"Yeah, I'd really like that. I don't want to be alone right now."

"I know, sweetie. I know..."

And I wouldn't leave her alone. For something within me—perhaps Alexis—warned me that the moment Amy was alone would be her last.

Silence swept over us like lapping waves. Then Amy's small voice splashed through it.

"You know what the worst thing about it was?"

"What's that?" I wondered aloud.

"He seemed like a nice, normal man—someone I could trust, you know? How could I be so wrong?"

I often asked myself the same thing.

PAMELA CRANE

Chapter 20

Four hours and two *Harry Potters* later, Amy's mom showed up with Ben and Jerry's ice cream and a scowl on her face. Despite Amy's protests that I was a friend, Mrs. Watson ushered me out the door and instructed me to stay away from Amy ... or else. I figured the "or else" involved lawyers or cops, neither of which I wanted to make enemies of.

On my way out I promised Amy I'd stop by again—"if your mom is okay with it," I added pointedly—and handed her mother a piece of paper with my name and phone number written on it, which she promptly threw in the garbage can beside the door. As I followed a trail of black scuffmarks down the hallway to the elevators, I visually memorized every face I passed, hoping that one would trigger a reaction. Yet nothing happened.

Alexis had no message for me—at least not one I sensed.

It wasn't until three floors down, as I exited the elevator on my way to the front lobby, when I ran into him. Jeremy Mason. He was pushing a cart of janitorial supplies and nearly brushed against me as we passed.

"Hey—Jeremy, right?" I said, stopping his hasty route around me.

"Are you really going to play dumb with me—Mia, is it?"

"Good memory."

"Hard to forget, especially when your boyfriend tried to

kill me."

"Anger management issues," I said with a shrug.

"Yeah, well, I have lawsuit issues, so tell him to watch it. He comes near me again, he'll be doing jail time."

Cowed by the threat, I held my tongue in check. "About that, we didn't mean to stir up trouble."

"Say what you want. But if I find you skulking around my house again, I promise a broken jaw will be the least of his worries. Got it?"

"No need to get pissy with me. I got it."

"Good." Now that he had the last word, he rolled past me into the elevator, embarking on a friendly chat with a nurse.

Two steps later, I felt his glower on my back and I turned around, meeting his stare as the elevator doors closed in front of him. A chill ran down my spine and I wondered if I should follow him. I watched the numbers climb as his elevator rose—1 ... 2 ... 3—and there it stopped at Amy's floor.

My pulse quickened. If I followed, Amy's mother would throw me out again and probably put me on some visitor blacklist. If I left, would I ever see Amy alive again?

I ran to the front desk and asked if I could place a call to Amy's room. The receptionist handed me the phone and recited the number for me to dial. It rang twice before it connected.

"Hello?" It was Amy.

I didn't want to scare her any more than she already was, so I chose my words carefully. "Hi, Amy. It's me, Mia. I just wanted to know if your mom planned to spend the night with you tonight."

"Yeah, I think so. Why?"

"I'm just worried about you, that's all. I really think it'd be best for you if your mom stays with you the next few nights. I don't want you to be alone right now."

"Is something wrong?" she asked. At that, I heard her mother ask who it was and what they wanted. Amy's hand muffled the receiver as she answered, "Just a friend, Mom. Chill." Then her voice came through clearly again. "Sorry, just my mom talking to me."

"Nothing's wrong, sweetie. I just feel it'd be a good idea to have someone with you at all times ... just to be safe, you know?"

"Sure," she said. "But I have the guard too, you know."

"I know, Amy. I just like to be extra cautious. Can you mention it to your mom that you'd like her to stay with you? Please?"

"I will. And Mia ...?"

"Yes?"

"Thanks for everything. I feel a lot safer with you looking out for me."

If only I really could keep her safe.

After wishing her a good night and repeating my request that her mom sleep in her room, I hung up.

There was nothing else I could do. Even if I forced my way through the cops, lawyers, and parents to stay at her bedside, I couldn't monitor her twenty-four hours a day, seven days a week. I had to trust that the police, and her mother, knew how to protect her inside the hospital. In the meantime, I'd work on protecting her from the outside.

PAMELA CRANE

Chapter 21

Genius is eternal patience," Michelangelo once said. Smart fellow; he might as well have been referring specifically to me. One doesn't achieve true success without the essential ingredient of patience. One doesn't attain his goals or complete his mission without it. Few possess it, and those who do can accomplish anything.

Luckily I was blessed with more than my fair share of it—that, and a hefty dose of fortitude.

Blending in with the nursing staff, I had arrived at Duke Hospital ... only to find myself nipping at the heels of Mia Germaine. In spite of my irritation at her blatant rebellion, I couldn't help but find it attractive. Few women these days embraced a life of sacrifice, instead choosing selfish gain that reduced families to empty shells, while homes became tombs of possessions. Mia risked her life for that of a child she barely knew, while Amy's own mother resumed her fruitless endeavors—hitting shoe sales and making lunch dates with girlfriends.

Oh, Mia—a rare gem. It was a shame I'd have to kill her after all. She knew the penalty of her actions and accepted it. It appeared we were both up for a challenge.

Five hours of wandering the hospital halls later while simulating purposeful activity—a blood pressure check here, assisting a patient there—I passed by Amy's room: 301, my lucky number. Amy's mother had finally withdrawn for the night, and it was time I made my move. The scrubs allowed me to effortlessly blend in with the staff as I paced the hallways. Within two days I had memorized the shift change times and protocol throughout the day and was almost able to predict which cop would be on duty at any given time. As they say, the devil is in the details, and I was a fast learner.

Enough time had passed since Amy's attack that the cops were letting their guard down, rarely checking staff IDs as they came and went. Getting into her room wouldn't be the problem. Staying under the radar was my concern. The moment I executed my plan, alarms would beckon doctors and nurses to her room to attempt to resuscitate her dead body, and I absolutely could not be there when it happened or else I'd be leaving in handcuffs. Timing was everything.

My plan appeared flawless. The shift change would occur in ten minutes, leaving me approximately five minutes to get in, complete the task, then get out, where I would seamlessly flow into the stream of night staff, drifting far enough away to stay unnoticed when Amy was pronounced dead.

I bustled past Amy's door at approximately 10:21 p.m. as the cop checked the time. He had nine minutes until his shift ended, but apparently he had somewhere better to be. I had anticipated the early leave and smiled. With the nine extra minutes he gave me, plus the five minutes I had until the next guard arrived at 10:35, this gave me more than enough time to execute my plan and escape.

I watched him peek his head inside Amy's door and wish her goodnight.

"I'm going to head out," he said. "I'll see you tomorrow."

Amy's reply was blocked by the man's thick frame in the doorway. Too many doughnuts rounded out his belly, mushrooming his waist above his belt buckle. After he shut her door and disappeared inside the elevator, I headed toward Amy's room.

Before slipping inside, I pulled on a surgical face mask and latex gloves, then carefully closed the door behind me. The room was dark, illuminated by the white light of the television hanging on the wall. Immediately I noticed that her heart monitor was gone, and I smiled. This meant no alarm. Could my job be any easier?

I pulled a stethoscope from out of my pocket and approached her.

"Hi, Amy. I'm going to take a quick look at your vitals, okay?"

"Sure." Without taking her eyes off her moronic TV program, she turned toward me, ready for the usual. She knew the routine … and so did I.

With a brief glance she examined me. "What's with the mask?"

"I have a cold, so I'm supposed to wear this. Can't risk infecting any of the patients."

"Mmkay."

I checked her heart rate and her blood pressure, circled the stethoscope around my neck, then pretended to write the numbers down on her chart that hung on the lip of her bed.

"How's your pain?" I asked. "On a scale from one to ten."

"Maybe a two?" she responded absently, still fixed on the television. It appeared to be a repellent reality show based in New Jersey, peopled by subhuman hedonists, and already the accents were crawling under my skin. I gave the show about two seconds of my attention before deciding that indeed I'd made the right decision to purify poor little Amy's adulterated heart before it was too late for her.

I shuffled around the IV drip, randomly checking things until I was certain Amy's undivided attention was focused on the Jersey cretins. With the wall clock ever in my sightline, I grew anxious with each ticking second. It was 10:29 and counting. I had less than six minutes before the other guard showed up, assuming he wasn't early.

Discreetly pulling a needle from my pocket, I inserted the tip into the plastic bag of morphine, which took a little more maneuvering than I expected, and filled the syringe with 60 cc of morphine—more than enough to kill a grown man. When the syringe was full, I turned back to Amy.

"Honey, I need to give you a potassium shot. It looks like your levels are low. Can you bear with me while I do this?"

"I hate needles," she whined. "Can't you stick it in the IV thingy with the other medicine?"

10:32.

I had no time to negotiate.

"Sorry, Amy, no can do. I promise it will be quick, okay? You won't feel a thing." I handed her a stuffed chipmunk from her gift hoard and told her to close her eyes and squeeze the toy, then count to five. "Before you reach five it will be over."

She reluctantly extended her arm, then did as instructed and started counting.

"One ... two ... three ..."

And in the needle went. At the feel of the prick, her hand clutched the stuffed animal and she exhaled loudly. I released the syringe into her bloodstream, relishing the grand finale of my conquest. Yet without a fight, the experience paled in comparison to our last time together.

Her reaction to the shot was almost immediate as I

watched her sway, then fall against the pillows as her eyelids dropped. Her breathing grew ragged as her fingers twitched. The chipmunk fell to the floor with a light thud. I hurriedly pulled the needle out, pocketed it, and left the room just as the next guard on duty rounded the corner on his way to stand sentry at her door. As I passed him in the hallway, I gave a slight nod, smirking beneath my mask at how close I had come.

Adrenaline pulsed through me as I made my way down the stairs to the lobby, and out the door to the parking lot. With every step I soared, freely gliding to my parked car. With my mission complete, I could now shift focus to other matters: Mia.

Killing her wouldn't be quite so easy, but the challenge excited me. I had carefully plotted through it, deciding to build her fear slow and steady until the crescendo reached its peak ... and that's when I would take her life without her even realizing it was happening.

PAMELA CRANE

Chapter 22

The blood of her death saturated my hands, and I couldn't wipe it away.

I hadn't seen the newspaper headline that morning. And because I had been running late, I didn't check the online version of *THE NEWS & OBSERVER* or bother to turn on the television before stuffing a piece of buttered toast in my mouth on the way out the door. I rarely listened to the local radio in my car. So it came as a shock when I arrived at the hospital to find Amy Watson dead. The news nearly shattered me.

Holding two stainless steel travel mugs of green tea—one for me, one for Amy—I had naively walked into room 301 where I found Amy's mother weeping inconsolably as she clutched a stuffed chipmunk. Her tears belied yesterday's formidable personality. Amy's bed lay empty, with the exception of a pile of rumpled sheets.

The scene unfolded too slowly for my brain to comprehend what had happened.

"Um, is Amy here?" I asked softly, unsure what to ask or how to ask it.

As Mrs. Watson looked up, her battered expression suddenly filled with rage—toward me.

"What are you doing here? And who are you, anyway?" She rose from the chair she had been sitting in and stormed toward me, her finger nearly poking my eyeball as she yelled, "Do you know anything about this?"

Spittle sprayed across my face, but I didn't dare wipe

at it.

"Know about what? What happened?" I asked, my voice cracking. I somehow knew the answer, but I couldn't accept it. "Please tell me Amy is okay." It was a plea for a miracle.

"No, she's *dead*! Dead! My baby girl is gone ..." Her words broke away as the weeping resumed at a feverish pitch. "That monster got to her ... because of *you*! Amy was safe until you showed up yesterday."

"That's not ... no ..." I stuttered. "I was watching out for her! I warned her not to be alone last night!"

But my defense crumbled before reaching her.

This time her finger pushed my shoulder and its impact stung.

"How did you even know she was in danger last night, huh?" she screamed. "Her death is on *you!*"

Mere hours earlier I had held that sweet girl in my arms, assuring her I'd protect her. Now she was dead?

"No ... no ... I promise you, I had nothing to do with this," I pleaded. "I'm just a friend ..." But my assurances rang hollow amid the sobs of a grieving mother. No pledge I offered could comfort this frail woman as she crumpled to the floor and covered her face with her palms.

I tentatively rested my hand on her shoulder, afraid she might swat at me. But she didn't. I wondered how she could be alone at a moment like this. Where was her husband? Where was her support? Last night I had been so frustrated with her, but at this moment I pitied her.

I dropped down beside her and tried to utter some heartening words, but they came from an empty hole in my chest. How could I offer reassurance when I felt so helpless myself?

As the chill from the cold tile floor seeped through my pants into my rear end, I shifted. That's when Mrs. Watson suddenly became aware of my presence. Her

A SECONDHAND LIFE

furious glare warned me that I wasn't welcome there.

"You never answered my question. Who are you and what did you want with my little girl? Do you have something to do with this?"

I didn't know how to answer without incriminating myself. If I told her I knew about the Triangle Terror, she'd think I somehow was connected to him, that I'd brought this on her.

Did I?

The question struck with a force that knocked me back against the wall.

Was I actually to blame for her death? Did my actions prompt him to come back for Amy? The pictures from the memory card the killer had sent me came to mind. As I had skimmed through them the previous night, I realized he was watching me. Was it my visit that prompted him to kill her?

No, it can't be because of me. Please, God, tell me I'm not responsible for this.

I struggled to my feet. I needed to get out of there. I needed air. Fresh air.

"I know your name, *Mia Germaine*, and I *will* have the cops investigate you!" she spat. "Be prepared to get a lawyer," she threatened as I backed my way to the door.

"I'm sorry for your loss. I truly am ..." I muttered, then I bolted out the door, down the stairs, not stopping to catch any strained breath I could muster until I slammed my car door behind me. My lungs weren't working; each breath felt shorter than the last, and my panting became frantic beneath the chokehold of asphyxiation.

I was drowning in my own tears.

I needed to fix this, but I couldn't. Just like everything I touched in my life, my weakness brought ruination to it all. My scar was more than a physical blemish. It typified who I was beneath the brave face I tried to show the

177

world—fragile, pathetic, ugly. I thought I had overcome my self-image issues, but the reality was written in the fine print. I was too cowardly to tumble into love with Brad, too helpless to avenge Alexis, and too afraid to stop this killer.

A flash of Jeremy Mason face to face with me.

His threat a boyish plea.

This was no beast at all, but a mere mortal.

I would take him on.

Then I let all my fears and hurt trickle onto my steering wheel for the next hour until my grief turned into fury.

Chapter 23

I tossed Tuesday's newspaper on Detective Evan Williams' desk, revolted at the idiocy of the media.

"Tragic hospital error? A broken IV regulator? Is that really what they think happened?" I seethed. I pitched a defeated look at Landon, who sat next to me shaking his head.

I had whittled the morning away by driving around aimlessly for several hours, working through my shock at the authorities' analysis of the events. According to the papers, the cops had credited Amy's overdose to faulty equipment, completely overlooking any possibility that it was the Triangle Terror coming back to finish the job. It made no sense, which made me wonder if in fact someone on the police force was behind the scenes covering up the truth. That was the only logical explanation.

After detouring past Brad's apartment three times, I eventually found myself on Landon's street, where I resigned to pull into his driveway.

When he had signaled me inside, I told him what happened, beginning with Saturday's visit and ending with seeing Jeremy there that evening, which only strengthened Landon's resolve to beat hell out of the guy. When I shot that idea down because it would only invite a lawsuit, he dragged me to the police station to recount the details to Evan, just in case I was missing something. While we waited for Evan, I vented.

"The only way it's a hospital error is if Jeremy was

behind it and somehow broke the IV drip, because it was working fine when I was there. Heck, Amy wasn't really even using it anymore. She told me her pain was minimal."

"I don't know what to say, Mia. I guess the hospital doesn't want to believe that the Triangle Terror was able to sneak in and kill a girl while under their care—and also with police protection. Look at it from their angle: What's worse—a serial killer on the loose in a hospital, or faulty equipment? I'm sure the media wants to avoid more fear running rampant."

I didn't bother to answer his rhetorical question.

"Either way," Landon went on, "the hospital bears the most scrutiny, so it's far better to blame a piece of equipment than poor security."

I disagreed. "An innocent nurse could lose her job over this, though. By saying it's hospital error that the regulator overdosed Amy's morphine, they're letting the murderer off the hook and throwing their staff under the bus. Where is the justice in that?"

Our argument came to a halt when Evan joined us at his desk carrying a cup of coffee and a handful of folders. He offered us a cup of the brew, but it looked more like sludge I'd find in the grooves of my shoes than a drinkable beverage.

He dropped the folders on top of a pile of papers that spilled out from underneath. The clutter seemed to have taken over the entire desk's surface, leaving no space for his mug. So he set it on top of more papers, leaving a coffee ring when he picked it back up to take a sip.

"Sorry for the wait. I had some pressing matters to take care of." He reached over and shook Landon's hand, then mine.

As our hands met, his blue eyes penetrated mine, and my temple seared in pain. I felt myself slipping into a memory, but I willed it to stop, forcing my eyes to remain open. Nausea slithered through my intestines, until I doubled over as a wave of sickness cascaded over me. My stomach roiled and my heart pounded so loud I was sure Landon and Evan could hear it too.

My surroundings whipped into a whirling vortex around me, intensifying my urge to vomit. I pressed my palm to my forehead and closed my eyes to stop the spinning, and that's when it came unheeded, uninvited. Another vision. A flashback. A blue-eyed guy, hardly a man—a younger Evan Williams. Standing in Alexis's old living room. He was telling her something, but his voice was muted.

"Are you okay?" I heard a voice ask. But the sounds didn't match the movement of younger Evan's lips.

"Hey," the voice said again. It was Landon, and his soothing tone was bringing me back into the present. I inhaled and exhaled, focusing on each breath, trying to regain consciousness. Eventually the blackness faded and my world of ringing phones, fluorescent lighting, and bustling police officers returned to focus.

The moment passed, and the queasiness stopped. But a thought lingered. Evan had been at Alexis's house. When? And was it connected to the night of the murder?

For a moment I wondered if Alexis was leading me on a wild goose chase, throwing red herring after red herring in front of me. But they weren't a tease; they were memories—random images tossed together. It was up to me to piece them together correctly, but this puzzle was no child's play. I felt like I was in one of those enclosed wind machines at some cheesy trade show, wildly grabbing at dollar bills as they flew around me, and coming out with nothing.

"I'm okay. Must have been something I ate."

"What brings you back here so soon?" Evan asked.

"The news, I presume." He gestured toward the newspaper's front page plastered with the headline: HOSPITAL ERROR OR TRIANGLE TERROR? The play on words sounded like a quip from a *Batman* movie.

"Good guess," I said. "Are you guys investigating her death, I hope?"

Evan took another gulp of sludge and set the mug back down heavily, oblivious to the nasty spill it made. I wondered how anything got accomplished with such flagrant sloppiness. It was no wonder they hadn't caught the killer yet.

"Before you ask, we are aware of all of the details behind the alleged hospital morphine OD issue. I can't comment about the specifics, but I assure you that we're looking into it."

"Let's cut to the chase," said Landon. "The reason we wanted to see you is because Mia was there last night."

"You were?" Evan echoed. "I thought Amy was under protective watch?"

"She was," I verified. "The cop let me in."

Evan grunted his disapproval. "I thought she wasn't allowed visitors, other than immediate family. Did the guards just let anyone and everyone in? It defeats the purpose of having one."

"Regardless, I told him I was a friend and he let me in to see her. We ended up talking."

"Oh really?" Evan leaned forward with interest. Apparently I had finally said something he found worth his time. "Were you able to get a description of her attacker? Anything that can help us?"

"Not much. Were you able to pull anything from the security cameras?" I probed.

"We tried. The mall security cameras couldn't get a clear shot of his face—only a grainy image of a white male with a hat. And the hospital footage was worthless, since the only footage we have outside of her room at her time of death caught a doctor wearing a mask. Clearly he knows how to stay hidden. Tell me you got something more from Amy."

"Well, she said that he wasn't old ... possibly my age. White male. He wore a hat, so she couldn't see the hair color, but it was short. Maybe five foot ten, five-eleven. And he seemed normal to her. So, I'm thinking he was clean-cut and maybe even good-looking. Other than that, she couldn't give any unique traits or anything. Just a normal-looking guy with an urge to kill. That narrows it down, right?"

"Yeah, to about 20 percent of Durham County residents—so roughly 60,000 suspects."

We all knew it wasn't much to go on, but something was more than nothing.

"Were you the last person to see her alive?" Evan asked.

"No, her mom came in after me. I had told Amy to make sure her mom spent the night because I had a bad feeling."

"A bad feeling, huh?" Evan probed.

I wondered if I should tell him about my run-in with Jeremy Mason at the hospital. Was Jeremy worthy of inclusion on their suspect list? I thought so, but I didn't have much to support it, other than he lived on the street of the first victim and worked at the hospital where Amy died ... and even had a shift at the time of her death. Plus, he sure looked the part—fit Amy's description perfectly. His record as a child predator could be the nail in the coffin. I figured it couldn't hurt to mention him.

"I had a hunch ..." I glanced over at Landon, who nodded his approval to continue. "You see, there's this child predator who lives on your street—Alexis's street, Willoughby Way."

183

"It's the house next to Norma's, Evan," Landon cut in.

"Jeremy's house?" Evan clarified.

"Wait, you know Jeremy Mason?" I asked.

"Yeah, remember I told you we grew up together?" Landon explained.

"Jeremy's lived there for as long as I remember, but he's never been in any kind of trouble, as far as I know. I don't normally do background checks on my neighbors—though maybe I should start. I didn't know he was a child predator. So he's got a record, huh?" Evan said, jotting notes down.

"Yeah, I found it online," I explained. "Jeremy fits the profile of a younger white male, decent-looking, and he also was at the hospital last night. And he has a record for child molestation. We just figured you might want to look into him as a suspect."

Evan's pen stopped mid-stroke and he looked at me.

"Wait—you saw Jeremy Mason at the hospital last night?"

"Yes, he works at Duke Hospital, though I'm not sure what his job is. A janitor, I think. But he'd probably have easy access to Amy's room. Anyway, we exchanged words, and he gave me this nasty look when I left. It was very strange."

"So you spoke with him? How does he know you?"

Oh boy. I hadn't intended to open this can of worms.

I sighed. This conversation wasn't going exactly as I had planned.

"Landon and I confronted him not too long ago, and Landon kind of got into a little ... well, tiff, with the guy."

"Tiff, meaning you cracked his skull?" Evan huffed. "I'm sure that could account for the nasty look," he muttered, though not enough under his breath. "Why are you starting issues with the neighbors? What even makes you think this is the guy?"

"For starters," I replied heatedly, feeling like a redundant parrot, "he has a criminal record involving children, he's been local since Alexis's murder, and he was at the scene of the crime last night. What more do you need?"

"It's not enough to convict, Mia. I need something more substantial. Something concrete. Put the murder weapon in his hands and you've struck gold."

"How do I do that?" I whined.

"I'll certainly put the guy on the suspect list and bring him in for questioning, but I'll need a lot more than this to put him at the other crime scenes. Like, say, fingerprints." Evan pushed up from his desk and stood. His body language implied our time was up, but I stayed firmly planted. "And without a murder weapon, we're kind of at a loss here."

"Can't you get a search warrant for his house?" I pushed.

"Not without probable cause." Evan heaved a sigh, rolled his eyes, and grumbled, "Is there anything else?"

There was, but I hesitated to bring it up with Landon there. I knew he'd be angry at the mere mention of it, but I didn't have a choice, did I? In light of Amy's death, I couldn't harbor information. I'd apologize later and hope he'd understand. So I blurted out, "Yes, I have another suspect I'd like to mention."

"You do?" Landon asked with surprise.

"Yes, your Uncle Derek."

"Seriously? You're still hung up on that? I thought we were past that," Landon replied irritably.

"Well, look, I can only go on what my gut tells me, and I've had a really bad reaction to him. I'm not saying he's the killer, but he should at least get checked out."

"You're basing this on a *reaction*?" Evan mocked. "Take an antibiotic, for crying out loud. I'm not pounding on

185

doors because you had a reaction—whatever that means."

"My uncle didn't kill anyone," Landon cut in.

"Can you please just hear me out? Alexis—his niece—was the first victim, and she likely knew the killer. When I spoke with him he claimed to have no recollection of the events that happened that day, so it's possible he's just lying."

Just as Landon opened his mouth to object, I rambled on. "Also, he has a pretty extensive criminal record and was—still is, apparently—into drugs and alcohol … clearly some emotional problems there. And get this—he works for a delivery company, so he has a job that gives him easy access into these houses, since none of them show a break-in. It's not that far-fetched."

"It seems to me like you're just pulling names out of a hat, Mia." Sensing I wasn't letting the conversation go, Evan returned to his seat with a groan. "I can check his alibi for the dates of both Gina and Amy's murders, but the other murders were too long ago to be able to establish a convincing timeline."

"What do you have to lose?" I proposed.

"My reputation, that's what! It may not be important to you how others view you—apparently it's not—but I have dignity I'd like to hold on to. If I go running after every name you toss at me, I'll end up questioning the entire Triangle. I'm not going door-to-door with this, Mia."

"I'm just asking for you to pay one little visit, ask a couple questions, that's all. Isn't that what cops do?"

Evan sat quietly for a moment, contemplating. He shifted in his seat, shuffled a few papers aside, then propped his chin on his hands.

"I'll tell you what. If I promise to look into these two guys—Jeremy and Derek—can you assure me you'll back off from the investigation?"

Absolutely not. I couldn't give up now. I'd already lost

Amy; there was no way I was letting the killer win this late in the game.

"Can I think about it?"

"You better think quickly. This is a limited time offer, or I may have to start questioning you. Hear what I'm saying?"

There he went with the threats again. It reminded me of a pouty little brat kicking and screaming when he didn't get his way.

"Loud and clear, detective."

As Landon stood to leave, I remembered something from my conversation with Derek.

"Can you look something up for me real quick?" I asked Evan.

"Make it snappy," he said. "I have real work to do other than helping you play Nancy Drew."

"Can you see if Derek was incarcerated on April fourth?"

Evan scratched his chin, eyeing the ceiling. "Wait, that date sounds familiar. Was that a Friday night?"

"Yeah."

"The night Gina Martinez was killed."

He turned to his computer and typed a few keystrokes.

"Derek couldn't have killed Gina then. He spent the night in the drunk tank that Friday."

"Are you sure?"

"Positive." He swiveled his screen for me to see his records. Sure enough, Derek Worthington was deposited into a cell at 11:16 that night and picked up the next day. Landon Worthington had signed him out at 4:35 Saturday afternoon.

"I picked him up Friday night. I found him facedown outside of a bar and he spent the night behind bars. I remember calling Landon to come get him, but long-suffering nephew here didn't want to post bail. Can't say I blame him."

"I gotta teach him a lesson one of these days," Landon chimed in.

"I couldn't count on all my fingers and toes the number of times I've had to call Landon to pick Derek up. It's a shame. But the good news is there's no way he could have killed Gina. It's highly unlikely the perp would commit murder and hit the bar afterward, then get intoxicated enough to get arrested. Our killer isn't that irresponsible; he's a detail-oriented stickler for order. No, Derek's not our man."

I rolled my eyes, recalling how Derek had assured me he was getting sober. So much for him being a "work in progress."

"That settles that, then," Landon said matter-of-factly. "Uncle Derek is not our killer."

But I wasn't so sure. What if he killed Gina before getting picked up? It was possible that her murder was earlier in the day, leaving him plenty of time to get smashed and arrested for public drunkenness. Furthermore, he could have purposefully gotten drunk enough to get caught simply to build himself an alibi. It was the perfect plan—if he was cunning enough to carry it out.

It still wasn't cut and dried enough for me to write him off just yet, because my gut—my heart—told me not to. So why did it seem like everywhere I turned I found one dead end after another?

Detective work was harder than I had anticipated. But I couldn't give up. Alexis, Gina, Amy—they all needed me to persist. Not to mention any future victims.

Evan and Landon must have noticed my disappointment that Derek Worthington was no longer a person of interest.

"Look," Evan said reassuringly, "I appreciate your

concern, but let the police do the police work. You go back to painting your nails or eating bonbons or whatever it is that you do."

Landon touched my arm before I had a chance to lunge forward and take a swing at the stupid ape. "You know," I said through gritted teeth, "with your condescending attitude toward others who are trying to help, it's no wonder you haven't solved this case yet. Two decades and a pile of dead girls isn't enough for you?"

With that, I grabbed my purse from off the floor and hefted it on my shoulder. "When I find this monster—and I will—you can apologize to me then."

A storm of emotions followed me to my car, threatening to spill on anyone I encountered. Too bad Landon didn't know me well enough to stay away.

PAMELA CRANE

Chapter 24

I can't believe you!" Landon wheezed after chasing me through the parking lot. "What was that all about?"

"What did I do?" I asked, daring him to start a losing fight.

Landon took a moment to catch his breath before resuming the argument. "First of all, you go accusing my uncle of being a serial killer, then you nearly attack a police officer for telling you to back off. I don't get it. What's going on with you?"

Oh, so Landon wanted to rumble? It was on.

"What's going on, Landon, is that another sweet, innocent girl was murdered and no one is lifting a finger to find the guy who did it. You're all too busy playing politics and worrying about what people will think if you were to—God forbid—ask questions. Screw that! I care about saving lives, and your buddy in there should be thinking the same way, or else maybe he shouldn't be claiming to *protect and serve.*"

Landon made a gesture to speak, but I wasn't done yet.

"And you think your uncle's so innocent? Would an innocent man be in and out of jail every other month? Would an innocent man hang the phone up on his sister-in-law when she calls to tell him his niece was killed? The man has no heart. Plus he's doped up all the time and clearly has no respect for the law."

Landon's piercing green eyes narrowed on me. He

191

stepped between me and my car, placing his palm on my door, blocking me from any chance of escaping our confrontation. "You know I didn't appreciate you going behind my back to talk to my uncle in the first place. But since clearly you think my family is a bunch of killers, are you gonna interrogate my mother too? And how about me?"

"What?" I asked, a little befuddled. "No, I don't think that ..." I stammered, unsure how to defend myself. I had no defense. True, I had gone behind his back and looked up his uncle and questioned him. But I thought it was water under the bridge that Landon wanted to burn.

"I can't play favorites. Yes, he's your family, but that doesn't give him a free pass to murder people. If he didn't do it, then his innocence will prove itself. All I'm asking is that you keep an open mind."

"What about the presumption of innocence? Have you forgotten basic American human rights in your quest to find the killer? Does it boil down to 'at all costs' with you?"

At all costs? Landon didn't know the first thing about what this was costing me. He became a hot mess at the mention of his uncle being questioned, but that was nothing compared to what I was willing to sacrifice. If not me, then who? Any decent human being should be willing to take a bullet to save a child's life. Or had decency gone out the window along with chivalry?

"What's that supposed to mean?"

"It means that you're going to end up losing everything to solve this case. Your boyfriend wants nothing to do with you, you're going to end up getting fired from your job if you don't get back on track at work, you're losing your mind, and you're going to lose me too—a friend who genuinely cares about you. When will you wake up to reality, Mia? This case is bigger than you. You can't win. It only took me two decades to figure that out."

A horn honking at the nearest stoplight drew my attention. Life went on for everyone but me. Bustling cars full of passengers heading to Arby's for a roast beef sandwich, or Food Lion for groceries, or the Goodwill for a bargain buy. Everyone going somewhere, and here I was stuck in the same place I'd been for twenty years.

I pushed past him toward my car, then shoved him aside as I opened the door and got inside.

"You know what? I *am* fully awake. I know what I'm willing to give up to help these girls. Apparently you don't want to even get a little uncomfortable. But that's fine. Just stay out of my way, okay?"

I never heard his retort over the din of traffic noise as I slammed the door and peeled out of the parking lot, leaving Landon to choke on the smoke of laid rubber.

Chapter 25

Cold. Ice cold.

A chill clung to me like a wet sweater. My teeth chattered as a result, but I couldn't make them stop. I wondered why I was shuddering so hard, why I felt so frigid.

I glanced down at my trembling hands, covered in a sticky goo that I couldn't identify. When I attempted to wipe my fingers clean, they left a crimson streak on a borrowed pair of Guess jeans, pegged at the ankles. That's when I realized it was my blood. I was going to bleed to death.

With feeble pressure I pressed my hands against the gaping hole in my abdomen, which by now had grown numb to the indescribable agony. My eyelids felt too heavy to keep open, but I needed to stay awake. I feared that if I gave into the serenity of sleep, I'd never wake up again. Remaining conscious was my only hope for survival.

Everything around me was a crooked blur. As I hung my head over the cushioned arm of the chair, my world rested wearily on its side. The television was knocked over. Beer bottles were scattered along the floor. A puddle of blood pooled below me.

All was eerily silent, like the eye of a storm. Then I heard banging behind me, followed by a garbled tenor belonging to a man, but my head was too fuzzy to make sense of the sounds.

A moment later a hazy silhouette circled around the sofa to examine me, then he knelt down at my side and touched his fingers to my throat. As he dropped down, his features came into crisp view. He examined me with intense blue eyes that scared me, for I knew he recognized death when he saw me.

He said something to me, but I couldn't read his lips from my tilted angle, and my hearing was impaired by a debilitating case of tinnitus.

With tender fingers he cupped my chin, righted it so I could see him, and spoke. This time I understood what he was saying.

"I'm so sorry, Alexis."

With that my faculties abandoned me. His farewell sent me off into another land, a land of darkness and peace and slumber. I granted my eyelids what they had yearned for and closed my eyes at last, hoping that his face wasn't the last thing I would ever see.

More than ever before, I just wanted my mom and dad.

Evan Williams. It was him. He was there.

I woke up from the dream with a twenty-year-old version of Evan on the edge of my mind—the last person Alexis saw while alive. Not to mention that it was the only face that had come into view in any of my dreams. I remember him saying that he was the first responder to the call, but he was supposed to be supervised. According to the dream, it didn't seem like anyone else was there. And how did he get there so quickly—even before the paramedics?

It felt monumental—case closed.

I had recognized him immediately in my dream. Those blue eyes, that blond cropped hair, that chiseled jaw. He had definitely been there the night of her murder, but in what capacity? As friend or foe?

I needed a better angle, more details. Was he wearing the jeans that the killer had been wearing in my previous dreams? Or was he in a police uniform? At what point during the evening of her attack did this moment take place? The full story was somewhere in the backdrop, but I couldn't fit the puzzle pieces together. The timeline was a mess; there were too many gaps in the overall picture for me to get a sense of what had happened.

Closing my eyes, I attempted to conjure up the dream again, but to no avail. I couldn't figure out how to control when my dreams came and what details they conveyed. It seemed that Alexis held the reins on that.

Then a thought occurred to me.

Dr. Weaver. She had mastered the art of dreams and possessed extensive knowledge of the dream state. I wondered if she could help me. After all, I did owe her a follow-up visit.

Picking up my cell phone, I looked for Dr. Weaver's number in my contact list and clicked the call button.

"Dr. Avella Weaver's office. How can I help you?"

"Hi, Dr. Weaver. This is Mia Germaine, the patient with the, um, organ memory."

Apparently I was unforgettable. "Ah, Mia! How are you, darling?"

"Well, that's what I wanted to see you about. I'm doing … not so good. I was wondering if I could come in this week if you have a free spot in your schedule."

"Anything you need, you can come to me. What's it regarding?"

"I'm trying to conjure up certain memories, or dreams or whatever, but I can't seem to control them. Is this something you can help me with?"

"I think so, darling. It's not always formulaic, but we can try. So there is a specific memory you want access to?"

"Yeah. I just had this dream, but I need to see it more clearly. I can't focus on the details. Is it even possible to force myself to focus while dreaming?"

"Oh, yes. I do that a lot—help clients communicate with their subconscious in order to find dream objects or clarify hazy images. Come on in and we can work through this. I have an opening in my schedule at four o'clock this afternoon. Can you make that time?"

I checked the clock. That gave me time to log in some work hours before I ended up fired. I'm sure I was already sitting in the hot seat at work for not showing up, so what was one more day? But as long as I met my deadlines I hoped Jackie would be merciful.

"Yep, I can make it. I'll see you then."

Four o'clock couldn't come fast enough. For five hours I slogged through my editing projects, snacked on Cheetos in memory of Amy, and cleaned out my e-mail inbox. For a dose of good nutrition I ate an apple—smothered in caramel, of course. Oh, how I missed fine dining at Brad's! Without him to cook for me, I relied on grilled cheese, bagged salad, and take-out, particularly over-salted chicken lo mein.

After emptying my bag of Cheetos and feeling sorry for myself, I decided to call Brad. I missed him. And with Landon not speaking to me either, I truly had no one. My only real friend at work, Jackie, had probably given up on me ever showing up back at the office. I avoided talking to my mom, for fear of the dreaded "How's Brad?" conversation and subsequent interrogation. Besides, she was happily busy with her knitting circle, her book club, and her latest passion: yoga. She didn't need dragged into my misery. Meanwhile, my social life was nil. All that I had were just me and my thoughts—and Alexis, if you wanted to count a dead girl's borrowed organ as a friend.

Yep, I was officially pathetic.

I dialed Brad's number, wondering if he had already deleted my name from his contacts. My prayer that he'd pick up was answered three rings later.

"Hey, Mia. It's been a while."

"Hey, Brad. Yeah, it has been, hasn't it? I guess I haven't been exiled from your caller ID?"

"Nah, not yet, at least," he said with a nervous chuckle.

An awkward silence drifted between us, two once-upon-a-time lovers now emotionally wedged apart. Would he ever hold me again? Would our lips ever passionately meet? Oh, how I missed his kisses!

"So what are you calling me for?" he said, his tone chilly.

And that's when I knew the hard reality. He was falling out of love with me. It was inevitable—I was losing him. My obsession with this case was costing me every ounce of happiness I had ever known.

"I just miss you. I was hoping maybe we could get a cup of coffee or something."

"I don't know, Mia ..." He sounded uncertain, which meant that I still had a chance.

"Please just consider it. I still love you."

"Do you? Or do you love yourself more?"

"Well, that's a stupid question. Everyone loves himself more than others. But that's beside the point. I'm not doing this for me. I'm doing it for the victims. Did you see the news? Another girl is dead. How can you not respect me for trying to help stop the killer?"

His heavy sigh on the other end cut my tirade short.

"Honey"—I relished his word choice, by the way—"I do respect you. And yes, maybe I'm being selfish too, by not wanting you to be in harm's way. But I haven't changed my position on this whole thing. You know how I feel, and it still stands. Maybe once all of this is over we can grab that cup of coffee, okay?" He paused, and I didn't know what to say. "Look, I better get going. I wish you the best, Mia."

It sounded like another good-bye to me—for real this time—and I wanted to plead with him, beg him not to leave me, but I still had an ounce of pride left. So I let him go.

"Alright, if that's what you want," I said. "Have a good life then."

I hung up, embarrassed that I had ended the conversation with a pathetically dramatic cliché.

When I arrived at Dr. Weaver's office at a quarter till four, she ushered me through the rain forest that she called a lobby and into the same room where we had met before. Upon entering, I noticed half a dozen candles lit around the room and soft nature sounds coming from a CD player on a corner shelf. The lights were off, and the strong scent of incense made me cough.

"What's all this for, Dr. Weaver?" I asked.

"Avella, please," she corrected while pulling me into a hug. "These stimuli are necessary to put you in the right frame of mind. We're going to practice what's called wake induced lucid dreaming. It's going to feel like a dream, but you'll be awake and can control it. I'm going to try to help you nudge the dream state along by probing your organ memories. I can't guarantee that this will work on our first try, but since you already seem to have an aptitude for connecting with your dream state, I'm hoping we'll have some luck."

I thanked her as she glided toward the sofa and waved me to follow. On the table sat an antique Wedgwood tea set. Avella poured two cups of a flowery herbal brew from the cheery teapot into two cups. The heady aroma was almost overpowering.

"Sugar and cream?" she offered.

"Yes, please."

She plopped a spoonful of sugar into the liquid, then poured a stream of milk in, stirred it, and handed the steaming beverage to me. I sipped it and grimaced. The flowery taste was a bit strong.

"I know it's a bit tart, but this will help relax you before we begin."

In one big gulp I downed the drink, wanting to get it over with as quick as possible. I set the teacup down and relaxed.

"Well, don't enjoy it too much," Avella chided with a

smile. "Now, I need you to lie down and close your eyes."

She patted a velvety green pillow at one end of the sofa and I took the cue to rest my head on it. I wiggled off my shoes and let them fall to the floor with a thump.

"Get comfortable and just breathe. In ... and out. In ... and out."

As she spoke, I heard her move to her own chair and sit down. The mechanical rhythmic sounds of pattering rain and chirping birds soothed my nerves.

Her comforting voice continued. "Think about how you fall asleep at night. I'm going to help you replicate that process, but as your body falls asleep, your mind will stay awake."

She talked me through releasing my body and embracing my subconscious awareness. "As you inhale and exhale, you'll begin to feel your limbs grow heavy and your mind chatter will fade. Allow the sound of my voice to transport you into a state of tranquility."

As I began to feel swept into a deeper state of mental and physical relaxation, I noticed a subtle hovering sensation. My body began drifting along freely, as if timeless and unguarded.

"I want you to empty your mind and gaze into the blackness. If a thought comes into your mind, don't focus on it. Allow it to pass. You may start to feel like your body is softening, or floating. As you soar, think of the dreamscape you want to envision. Detach yourself from the real world and visualize yourself stepping into your dream state—your past."

The darkness enveloped me, its weight almost suffocating, until colors started filling in the blackness. The swirling patterns began to hypnotize me, drawing my awareness away from Avella, from her office, from my worries and my crumbling life.

"Imagine below you the room where the murder took

place. You're looking down on it, hovering above the day that caused you grief. Now stop and descend into the room. What happened that caused you pain?"

With each passing moment my physical body sank further into the sofa, growing numb, as my mental state let go. Soon my internal dream world evolved into what felt like a tangible place.

I heard Avella's voice resume, distant now, remote. "The scenery ... explore it. What do the walls look like? Imagine the room. What is under your feet? Can you feel the flooring? Where are you? Sitting, or standing? What do you smell?"

The more I let go of my current reality, the more I submerged into the alternate one, instead of viewing it from above. Once I dropped out of my lucid state, I felt a vibration, like electricity pulsing through me, clouding out Avella's words with the noise. Then I found myself there, in Alexis's home. Only I'd left myself behind and had taken over Alexis's body.

The walls came alive with their old-fashioned floral paintings. The cold of stained hardwood floors seeped into my feet. I felt the scratchy wool of the armchair beneath me. And the smell ... the smell of blood, almost metallic—rusty, like iron.

"What do you feel?" Avella's soft voice broke through, conjuring more scenery to life.

A stabbing sensation in my abdomen suddenly pierced me, and my hand reacted, grabbing where it cramped.

"Are you hurt? Are you bleeding?" she prompted.

"Yes, I've been stabbed," I mumbled, unaware that I was speaking. "Pain. Blood. Afraid." As I spoke, I didn't recognize the voice. While the words were coming from my lips, they sounded like they belonged to a young girl.

"Look around you. Is anyone there? Do you hear someone coming?"

PAMELA CRANE

A loud thud. The rattle of a doorknob. Booted footsteps approaching. Then the man approached me and cupped my chin. Evan.

I looked harder at him, but the seconds were passing too quickly.

"Stop," I ordered myself.

In one tidy instant my dreamscape halted, like an unblemished scene from a movie on pause. Upon suspending the events in my mind, I was able to examine Evan further as he stood before me. As if frozen in time, the setting and its players stood motionless, like mannequins in a storefront window display. Finally I found what I'd been searching for.

Evan's clothes—he was wearing jeans and a long-sleeved shirt, not a uniform after all. I couldn't have forgotten it if I tried. It was the same attire that the murderer had been wearing.

Detective Evan Williams was the killer.

Chapter 26

The revelation jarred me from my semi-conscious state. An officer called to serve and protect the innocent was in fact the villain killing them. As my dream world collapsed around me, an overwhelming nausea hit me.

"I'm going to be sick!" I yelled, bolting upright and heaving just as Avella thrust a garbage can under my mouth. When the Cheetos and apple I had eaten earlier emptied from my stomach, I apologized profusely. I was mortified.

"I don't know what's wrong with me." I stifled a sob while wiping orange-ish chunks of *yuck* from the corners of my mouth.

"You must have experienced something pretty traumatic to provoke such a violent reaction. Do you care to share with me what you saw?" Avella offered gently.

Was it even safe to tell her? I wasn't sure. The last thing I wanted to do was put another person's life in jeopardy.

"I don't know if I should. It has to do with the man who killed the girl whose heart I have ... and he's responsible for several deaths since. I mean, what if he goes after you?"

Avella brushed away the worry with her hand. "Comes after me? Honey, I'm not concerned about that, and neither should you be. I can handle myself. Now, as your therapist I can assure you that anything you tell me will be held confidential. Okay?"

I gave a barely perceptible nod of agreement.

"The murderer ... I saw him. I know who it is. But I can't tell anyone, because he's a cop."

"Oh, my. That does complicate things."

"What am I supposed to do now? No one will believe me if I told them how I found out who the killer is. I mean, 'it came to me in a dream' doesn't exactly sound credible, does it?"

"You just need to think things through, Mia. If this police officer did indeed do it, and most likely plans to kill again, eventually he'll slip up. You know what—and who—to look for now. But before you go barking up the wrong tree, are you absolutely sure it was him? Is it possible that you might have mixed up the details within your dream state? Perhaps you stopped at a different point in time, not necessarily during the murder?"

"What do you mean?"

"Sometimes your mind can create things when in a lucid dream state. If you want to see something, you see it. If you want to do something, you do it. I just want you to be sure about what you saw and its accuracy before you pursue this angle. Accusing a cop of murder is a pretty serious accusation, so you must be sure. Does that make sense?"

"Yeah, I guess. So it's possible that because I'd already seen what the killer was wearing in a previous dream, maybe I projected that on Evan this time?"

"Precisely."

I didn't know what to do with that. I felt like I was back at square one. Although, hadn't I always been at square one? Nothing I knew was based on evidence, only on conjecture and a bunch of subjective dreams. But there was more than just my dream to back up Evan's inclusion on the suspect list—namely, my dramatic flashback in his office.

So for now I'd have to widen my list of persons of interest to include Jeremy Mason, the creepy child molester; Derek Worthington, the incorrigible drunk and dopehead; and now Evan Williams, an upright officer of the law. It didn't make any sense for Evan to have done it, but who was I to question the mind of a serial killer?

For the remainder of the session I shared with Avella my grief over Amy's death, heaping the responsibility on my own shoulders. If only I would have stayed ... If only I would have confronted Jeremy ... If only, if only, if only.

Although the kindly doctor assured me it wasn't my fault, that I was only doing everything in my power to help girls like Amy, her consolation felt empty. We moved on to discuss Brad, but the conversation only intensified the aching longing I felt. I loved him. I missed him. And yet I gave him up on my own accord to pursue ... what, exactly? Misery?

Again Avella listened with undivided attention, but her advice only reinforced what I already knew. I was playing with fire, and I ultimately held the power to change my fate. I could easily quit searching for the killer and resume my happy-go-lucky life again if Brad was still available—or even interested in me—by then. She obviously didn't understand. I wasn't in the driver's seat anymore. Alexis was. My screwed-up life was merely collateral damage.

At the end of hour two, I insisted on paying Avella, despite her initial refusal to take my money, and left the session feeling more confused than ever. If I could control the dreams, then how could I trust anything I witnessed in them?

My fragile, fragmented state of mind was slowly deteriorating beyond recognition. Who was I? I didn't know anymore. Just a shattered mess of unrecognizable shards.

❧❧

In the twilight I couldn't get a good look at the make and model of the car three vehicles behind me, but I knew it was following me. Ever since I pulled out of the Mexican restaurant adjacent to Dr. Weaver's office complex, the car persisted to tail me, always leaving a short row of vehicles between us to block my view.

My eyes continuously checked my rearview for a peek at his face, but a ball cap and sunglasses masked his identity. But even with the disguise, he was growing sloppy. Tailing me in public seemed highly risky for a suspected killer. It was enough to at least discredit the man if I could identify his car and report it.

He must be getting desperate.

I slowed down to let him catch up to me, but he would equally slow and hold back. Then I punched the gas through a yellow-almost-red light to lose him, but sure enough, he sped through the red light and kept close behind, always within sight.

Anxiety rose with each turn I made as I frantically tried to lose him, and yet there he was, every time.

About thirty minutes into the chase, I realized he wasn't giving up. And the more he persisted, the more my fear transformed into rage.

I had had just about enough of him—of his games, of his threats, of the power he held over life and death. It was time to lose this jerk and strip him of that power.

For some reason, imagining that it was Jeremy or Derek or Evan gave me the fearlessness I needed to be strong. They were mere men. No longer obscure shadows in the night or whispers in the dark, but people ... with faces. Faces that I would claw off if any of them got too close to me.

I had a plan to trap and confront him, or else lose him.

When the car continued its pursuit after four more turns and through two yellow lights, I steered into a busy shopping plaza, cruising past an Italian restaurant, then an Ollie's Bargain Outlet, and at last pulling into a parking space in front of a martial arts studio. I waited for him to drive past, but he never did. Instead he turned onto the main road and blended in with traffic as he fled.

Coward.

I cursed at him through my windshield, and laughed to myself that I had won.

Sitting for a few minutes, I waited to make sure my stalker was gone. Shoppers came and went in a faceless crowd, until one particular face coming out of a dollar store caught my attention. I rolled my window down and squinted to get a better look.

"Landon!" I yelled out the window.

But he didn't seem to hear me. Or else he did hear me and was ignoring me after our little spat the other day.

"Landon!" I called again when he got a little closer.

Nothing.

He was either really pissed at me or going deaf.

He walked with a shambling gait, body bent, shoulders slumped. He didn't look well at all; dark circles ringed his dull green eyes, only accentuating his pale skin. His hair looked unkempt, sticking out in all directions as if he hadn't showered or bothered to brush it in days. I wondered if he was okay, but when I opened the door to walk after him, he glanced past me, then jogged the rest of the way to his car and zoomed out of the parking lot before I had a chance to see where he went.

Upon getting back into my car, I reached for my purse to call Landon, but after rustling through all the junk I carried around with me, I realized I had apparently forgotten my cell phone at home. Had I known I didn't have my cell, I might not have acted so brazenly with the killer. Thank God for false bravado. I felt a belated pang of fear and shook it off.

I considered driving to Landon's house but thought better of it. Obviously he didn't want to talk to me. Maybe he needed to sleep on it ... because from the looks of him, it appeared he hadn't slept in days.

I hoped I hadn't burned the last bridge of friendship remaining in my life.

Chapter 27

I'm not a cat person. But of all the species in the animal kingdom, they are among the few that I respect. While often misunderstood, a cat's greatest traits are its sense of self-preservation and observation. Carefully plotting its course of action, a cat practices the genius of eternal patience before it pounces on its victim. Undetected, it watches the prey's movements, waits until the perfect moment, then strikes. Rarely does it miss its mark.

Once it captures the animal, the cat has enough sense to wear it out in order to avoid sustaining injuries. Methodical, deliberate, and vigilant, the cat is a respectable animal with impressive instincts. It's these attributes of the cat that inspire me.

The curvature of the wall hid me from outside observers as I swiftly pushed an old credit card up along the bronze strike plate to unlock Mia's front door before slipping inside. Cheap apartment complexes, this being one of them, were notorious for poor security.

I was careful not to turn on any lights, in case someone noticed my hooded figure through the window.

I expected Mia home at any moment, so I hurried to the bedroom. Her bed was a rumpled mess of pillows, sheets, and comforter, which would make it all the more difficult for her to notice my message. It would only take a minute to make the bed, and I quivered with excitement at the thought of her realizing someone had been here ... in her room ... touching her things.

Once her bed was made and the pillows fluffed, I placed the letter on the soft bedding, smoothing it with my gloved fingertips. I checked the time.

8:43.

I had less than a minute before she arrived, and I would be waiting, watching, and, much like the cat who takes pleasure in his taunting, I'd be enjoying every minute of it.

It was 8:45 when I carried my purse and Styrofoam to-go box of enchilada leftovers into my apartment and set them on the dining room table. An ideal evening was all planned out—chocolate chip cookies and a romantic comedy in my Netflix queue.

Without turning on the lights, I navigated through the dim living room into my bedroom, where I flipped on the light switch. Stepping out of my clothes, I tracked them along the pale blue carpet, dropping various articles as I went until I was naked. As I stood at my dresser, rummaging through my lounging clothes for a T-shirt and sweatpants, I noticed my bed.

The covers were neatly made.

And I knew for a fact that I had been too flustered that morning to make my bed.

My heart thudded harder, and suddenly I felt vulnerable. I hurriedly threw on my clothes and warily approached the bed. In the middle of the bedspread was a handwritten note. It looked much like the one I had torn to shreds on the sidewalk.

I picked it up and read the overly neat, almost prissy script:

My dear, obtuse Mia:

I warned you, and yet you neglected to obey me. I gave you three strikes, and still you insisted on continuing your forbidden extracurricular activities. So it comes to this.

Your life is no longer my concern. While killing you would stop your pursuit, I would take little pleasure in it. It would only serve to end your antics, but perhaps there is another way.

I've decided to take the life of someone you love.

Brad Thomas.

You, my dear, are an open book. It isn't difficult to track your affections. You really ought to be more careful where you leave your cell phone. If someone were to get a hold of your contact list, they might know how to contact your friends, your mother ... or your lost lover.

This is no longer a threat, Mia. This is a promise. Brad is next. So I urge you to bid him a proper good-bye before it's too late ... unless too late has already arrived.

PAMELA CRANE

Chapter 28

I'd placed a dozen or so frantic calls to Brad's cell phone, showed up at his apartment to find no one home and the lights off, and his car was nowhere to be found. I checked the restaurant, but he had called off work. Was Brad okay?

Short of breaking his door down or reporting a missing person, I didn't know what to do. Contact the police department—which perhaps had the killer working for them—about the letter? Call my mom? I had no one to turn to, and I was petrified of making the wrong move, which clearly I had already done.

Brad was right. I had bitten off more than I could chew, and yet he would be the one to pay the price. The irony was bitter.

After losing track of time searching for Brad everywhere I could possibly think of, I eventually made my way home well after midnight. I was exhausted—mentally, physically, emotionally. Helplessly frustrated, I attempted to distract myself from my anxiety with a movie, but I couldn't pay attention. Anxiety over Brad's safety consumed me.

It was after four in the morning when I finally dozed off, warding off nightmares of Brad's murder from corrupting my sleep ...

Today's newspaper sat on the coffee table, and I wondered how we could afford the daily News & Observer but not cereal for breakfast. Heading to the kitchen, I found a stale piece of bread and slid it into the toaster while I rummaged among plastic containers of crusty leftovers in the fridge looking for butter or jelly.

As the toast popped up, I checked the time. I was already late for school, since I had spent the better part of the morning trying to wake Mom up from her alcohol-induced stupor. Most kids probably would have called the paramedics, but I had learned over time that it was a waste of effort.

I smothered the remaining tablespoon of butter on my toast and sat at the table, nibbling bland bites with nothing to wash it down. Upstairs I heard Mom retching in the toilet, then five minutes later her bedroom door closed. I knew I was on my own getting to school today, so I grabbed the phone and dialed.

"Uncle Derek?" I asked when he answered.

"Yeah, kid, what's up?" he slurred.

"Can you take me to school today? Mom's out of it." While the sight of him creeped me out, and being in close proximity to him within a moving vehicle made me nervous, I had gotten used to his ways over time. I couldn't change my life, couldn't get away, so I might as well face it. At least that's what my dad always said about having a tough life. Though I never told Dad or Mom about Uncle Derek's secret, I figured the logic

applied to that too.

Forty-five minutes later Uncle Derek honked outside, and I ran up to his Ford Escort. A burly man with a long, grizzled white beard already occupied the front seat, so I climbed in the back. The passenger almost reminded me of villainous version of Santa Claus.

They were in the middle of a conversation, so I didn't bother to say hi as I slid across the plastic bench seat.

"Derek, I just think you're pickin' the wrong place. I'm pretty sure the owner's got guns there. It's a death sentence," Seedy Santa whined. "Are you sure this is the place Dan told you about?"

"Hey, dude, shut your pie hole," Uncle Derek said, nodding over his shoulder at me. "My niece be in the car. We don't talk business with her eavesdroppin', got it?"

"She's just a kid. She don't know nothin'."

"Yeah, well, we don't need her spoutin' on about it, y'know? Besides, I already got everything figured out, and Dan's already got all the details planned."

The two men fell silent, and I wondered what they had been talking about as the car bumped along the concrete. Knowing Uncle Derek, it wasn't good, and I worried how my dad was mixed up in it … especially with guns involved.

Uncle Derek was cooking up something, and it tasted sour.

❧❧

I came to from the hazy dream and my first thought was of Landon. While it was barely five o'clock in the morning, I had a hunch that he would be awake. After being snubbed by him at the shopping center, I sensed it was time to talk things out—now, regardless of the hour.

I texted him a brief good morning and waited for a reply.

The beep came back less than a minute later.

Hey.

Can you talk?

The next sound I heard was my phone ringing. I picked up on the first ring. "Sorry if I woke you," I said meekly.

"Nah, I was awake already. Not sleeping much."

"I saw you at the Willowdaile Shopping Center and you looked kinda tired. Are you okay?"

"What? You saw me? When was this?"

"Just yesterday. I tried to get your attention but you ignored me. Are you angry with me? I feel horrible about the way I left things at the police station."

"Please, don't worry about it. And I'm sorry I didn't see you at the shopping center. I must not have heard you. But I'm not mad. Things feel a little … I dunno, tense between us, though. But I'm over it."

"I'm glad," I said with a sigh of relief.

"So, what are you texting me at"—he paused, then resumed—"5:13 in the morning about?"

The idea of confessing the dream involving his Uncle Derek oscillated in my mind. But if I even mentioned the words "Uncle" and "Derek" in the same sentence, it could be disastrous to our friendship. On the other hand, somehow I felt like it was important. It involved his dad, after all … and perhaps it had something to do with his father's incarceration. It was a wild guess, but it seemed to fit together.

I decided I'd let Landon decide if he wanted to know.

"If I had a dream that involved your Uncle Derek and your dad, and possibly what put him in jail, would you want to know?"

"What are you getting at, Mia? Stop being so cryptic and just spill it." His attitude immediately put me on the defensive.

"I don't want to cause a fight, okay? I'm asking because I'm already on thin ice with you and I don't want to fall through." I heard my voice growing shrill, so I pulled back and added calmly, "Do you want me to tell you what I dreamt?"

I heard an exasperated groan, then a grudging "yes, please tell me."

"Now it may be nothing, but here goes," I began. "It was before Alexis's death, obviously, and your Uncle Derek picked her up for school with some big guy with a long, nasty white beard—like a redneck Kris Kringle. Sound familiar?"

"Nope, but go on."

"They were in the car talking about casing a place, I think, and I guess the owner had guns. He mentioned your dad being in on it, but I thought you may want to ask your dad about it. Maybe he knows Redneck Santa, since he was clearly part of it. But anyway, I think it had to do with the robbery your dad was charged with."

"You think Uncle Derek was involved?"

"If the dream was about the same robbery, then yeah. I don't have proof or anything, but I'm not so sure your dad's the only one who should be behind bars."

Landon didn't respond for a long minute or two, and when he did, it wasn't what I had expected.

"Are you making this up because you *want* my uncle to go to jail? Because it sure sounds like you're grasping at straws here."

"What?" I screeched. "You really think I'd make it up?"

"Maybe unintentionally, yeah. Maybe you're so focused on blaming Derek that your subconscious is making things up."

"Look, it's not like I can prove anything. I just wanted to tell you that your dad might not be entirely to blame."

"Why can't you stay out of my family business? Sometimes it feels like you're trying to save us, but we don't need saving. We just need to be left the hell alone, okay?"

"You know what, he's your dad, not mine, so it's your problem if you don't want to look into it. I gotta go."

I hung up before giving Landon a chance to toss another biting retort back at me. I was tired of being persecuted for being honest. Tired of being threatened by a killer. Tired of chasing down ghosts. Just tired.

I wanted out. Out of it all—Alexis's monologues, Landon's life, even my own life.

As far as I was concerned, I didn't care if I ever woke up from the nightmare that had become my existence.

Chapter 29

The pounding on my front door rudely awakened me from my light slumber on the sofa. After hanging up with Landon, I had put on another mind-numbing movie I'd afterwards regret, *The Human Centipede,* which had ended hours ago, but the TV screen had steadfastly captured a screenshot of a distorted figure plastered against the movie's cover.

I clicked off the television and listened. Had I actually heard someone knocking, or was my imagination in overdrive again?

Last night was a blur of panic.

I remembered receiving the letter last night, but after that my brain had become a befuddled mess. My only recollection was the killer's threat. Jolting upright, I forced myself awake, conjuring up a distant recall of events.

Yes, the haze was clearing. I had tried calling Brad to warn him, but his phone was turned off. Seven urgent voicemail messages later, I recalled heading to his apartment, but his car wasn't in the lot and no one was home. I figured he was at work, so I detoured to Bella's Cuisine next. When I had arrived and asked to speak to "Brad the chef," a cute and perky hostess working her first day—she was a bit of a talker—told me he wasn't on the schedule. Eventually I went home and feebly tried to shut my brain down for the night, since there was nothing else I could do at that late hour.

Brad is safe, Brad is safe, I had repeated to myself like

a desperate mantra.

I ultimately suffered through two forgettable movies before finally closing my eyes sometime around four in the morning. And then my fight with Landon.

What a night.

It was now—I checked my cell phone for the time—a little after nine.

The rumble of my stomach reminded me that I hadn't eaten much for dinner. I glanced behind me at the dining room table. Sure enough, the unopened box of Mexican leftovers still sat there. I wondered if they were still any good.

Bang bang. I jumped at the intruding sound. This time I had no doubt that my brain hadn't made it up.

With hesitant steps I tiptoed to the entryway, wondering if the killer was on the other side of the door. To be prepared, I grabbed a knife from the kitchen counter on my way to the peephole.

"Mia!" a familiar voice called from the other side. "It's me, Brad. Can we please talk?"

"Oh, thank God!" I said as I broke down into grateful sobs. I hastily unlocked the deadbolt and doorknob locks, my fingers fumbling with the mechanisms, and I hopped into his arms, wrapping my legs around him. "You're okay!" I cried into his shoulder as I wiped a stream of snot on his shirtsleeve. "I was so worried. Where were you last night?"

"I, uh, was out with some friends. A little drinking therapy, y'know? Hit a bar in Raleigh and crashed at my friend's house for the night. It was a rough day."

"Okay..." I said suspiciously. It wasn't like Brad to drink his sorrows away. The cryptic nature of his explanation waved my internal red flag. "Well, I'm just glad you're safe." I squeezed him even harder and planted a dozen soggy kisses on his cheek.

Brad kicked the door closed behind him and carried me into the living room, then plopped me down onto the sofa.

"Mia, what's going on? I got half a dozen messages from you last night, but you were freaking out so bad that I couldn't really understand what you were saying. Is someone after me?"

"The killer, Brad. He knows I'm tracking him and left me this." Picking the note up from the coffee table, I showed it to Brad. He reached to grab it, but I moved it aside and out of his reach. "Be careful not to touch it. I want to see if there're any prints. Hold it like this." I held it out to him by one corner edge, and Brad took the other.

His eyes scanned the document, then he looked at me.

"This explains why I got this." He shifted over and pulled a folded piece of paper from his back pocket. "I had hoped it was a twisted joke or something. But apparently not."

He handed me the paper, which I unfolded, dreading what I was about to read. My stomach churned and I felt myself growing faint. In the same meticulous script as my two notes, I read the following:

Brad:

Your girlfriend Mia doesn't know how to follow orders, so now I place the burden on you to teach her this valuable exercise. I will be looking for an opportunity to meet with you, so be prepared.

See you soon.

"Where did you find this?" I whispered.

"It was on my bed. I didn't know if someone you know left it or what. To be honest, I didn't know what to think."

"So he broke into your house too? That's where I found

mine."

"Does this mean what I think it means—he's actually coming after me? What should I do? Should I go to the police?"

"I don't know if it's safe to do that. I think one of the cops may be the killer. If that's the case, God only knows who's covering for him over there. Why else would this be a cold case if the cops were actually investigating it? And why haven't they called in the FBI to help?"

"Mia! Stop and listen to yourself!" Brad exclaimed, cutting me short. "We need to get out of here ... *now*. This is getting way too dangerous, and now you've put me—and possibly my family and friends—on this guy's radar. I know you don't care about getting yourself killed, but don't you care what happens to us?"

"Of course I care. Why else do you think I'm risking life and limb to catch this serial killer?"

"Because you want the dreams to stop!" His voice rose, causing a cup of water on the coffee table to shudder. "That's really what this is about, isn't it? You want to solve this so that you can feel peace with yourself. You've made this about Alexis resting in peace, but it's really about you."

"What? That's ludicrous."

"Alexis is dead. She has no care in the world anymore. But you—you're the most intricately, beautifully damaged person I know. You tattooed over your scar to hide what you think is ugly, but all along it's what makes you beautiful. Mia, you are amazing. You don't need to prove it to anyone but yourself."

"Are you trying to psychoanalyze me? Look, I'll admit I'm a mess, but only because I'm losing sleep over this. Once he's caught, I'll be better. I'll be me again."

"That's no reassurance, Mia. I know you. You're afraid of love because you think you're not worth it. But you are—to me. I love everything about you, but I can't lose you to this … devil. The demon you face isn't the killer, honey. It's you."

I didn't know what to say to that. What was my defense? I had none. He was right. I had been a wreck long before my dreams. I was insecure, dejected … and by no one's hand but my own. I hid behind my scars, feeling hideous, so I kept love at arm's length. And it wasn't just because of my scar, but because some days I felt like an unwanted orphan. Had I really become the villain in my own horror story?

"Mia," Brad said, much more serenely this time, "I have a confession to make."

The words lulled me from my self-realization as I met Brad's distressed brown eyes. What could he possibly have to admit? He was perfect. Unflawed. Mr. Knight-In-Shining-Armor.

"Go ahead," I encouraged him.

"I know you've been seeing a dream specialist. Dr. Avella Weaver."

"Wha—?"

It didn't make sense. I never told him about her. How could he have possibly found out … unless …

Oh. My. God.

In that heartbreaking moment my trust shattered into a pile of unrecognizable pieces. I felt so betrayed, so deceived. More than anything else I had experienced—watching my father die, undergoing a heart transplant, experiencing Alexis's murder, losing Amy, facing a killer—this marred me the worst.

A mental image flashed into my head. The ball cap—with the Durham Bulls logo. My stalker had been wearing it, trying to hide from me.

I gasped. "How could you …?"

It wasn't the killer who had been following me all this time.

It had been Brad all along.

Chapter 30

She wasn't as vain as the others, Lilly Sanderson, but she was the easiest target by far. With her homely appearance, mousy brown hair, and dull blue eyes, she had never struck me as corrupted ... at first. Until I saw her kissing a boy on her front porch outside of her house.

It had never been my intention to pick Lilly. First of all, I didn't even know she lived three streets over from mine until I recognized her, once her face wasn't plastered up against that boy's. Plus, I knew Melody Sanderson, Lilly's mother. She was a single mom, divorcee, who worked at the Sun Trust bank in the Kroger plaza. I often exchanged greetings with Melody when cashing my paychecks before I switched to direct deposit. She seemed nice enough, and her modest clothes and professionalism toward me demonstrated that she took her responsibility as a role model for Lilly seriously.

Lilly, her daughter, sold me Girl Scout Cookies—the Somoas being my favorite—every year until this year. The year Lilly apparently tossed her childhood innocence aside and took a detour down the primrose path.

It pained me to consider taking the only thing left in Melody's life—her only child. For all intents and purposes, I was taking a break from my calling. Things had been strained since Amy, and I needed some time to regroup. But that kiss—it was an adult kiss, not the kiss of a thirteen-year-old girl. Tongues. Passion. Fingers clamoring for more. Just seeing their lips touch made me spew right there behind the wheel as I drove past.

At that moment Lilly added herself to my list. Poor, simpleminded Lilly.

I didn't have the patience today to develop some elaborate ploy or to plot out my attack. I intended to deal with Lilly right now. When life throws you curveballs, you must hit a home run.

Killing Lilly would be my home run. My saving grace.

The first thing I noticed when I pulled over along the sidewalk across from her house to clean the vomity spittle from my lap was that Lilly hid a key under her doormat. How predictable. I parked and watched. In plain view of the entire neighborhood she pulled it out.

Upon retrieving the key, Lilly opened the door, invited the boy inside, and returned the key to its hiding place before she and her beau resumed their forbidden acts within.

I checked the time—10:08. Melody's work followed banker's hours, so she would likely be at the bank right now. Plus the door had been locked, so presumably no one was home. I'd tread carefully just in case.

I wondered where Lilly had been that she was returning home when she should be in school. The question didn't go far without an answer. She had probably faked going to school, then went home with the boy to do who knows what. I shuddered with repulsion. God only knew what she had planned for the rest of her day playing hooky.

Luckily I carried my "toolbox" with me in the car—just the essentials hidden in a duffel bag. My knife, latex gloves, and a few other odds and ends if I needed them.

Today I would do the bare minimum—in, out, and onward. I didn't have the energy to devote much more than that after a sleepless night. But I'd have to wait until the boy left to make my move.

It was a predictably short wait—he was a teenage boy, after all, not known for their endurance.

The hour was closing in on eleven o'clock when the boyfriend left, trotting merrily down the sidewalk, no doubt with dreams of defiling her again. Of course he was happy. He had plucked the purity from a witless child and had the gall to leave so quickly after.

Clearly he was no gentleman.

I tucked my knife into my pocket and marched up the sidewalk, admiring the variety of flowers lining the concrete—begonias of every color, a sprinkling of Asiatic lilies, complemented by a row of purple irises. Melody had quite the green thumb and took pride in her yard, which was hard for a single mother to find time to do. I almost felt sorry for stealing her last remaining joy ... but the bigger reward would come when her daughter was free from her filth.

When I reached the door, I checked the handle.

Unlocked.

I snuck in and let the door linger open as I peered around the entryway. In the living room at the back of the house I heard a television conversation. It sounded like young girls talking in adolescent gibberish ... and something about Hannah Montana.

Yes, the decision was made.

Lilly deserved to die.

PAMELA CRANE

Chapter 31

I cannot even look at you right now!" I screamed at Brad, pounding my fists against his chest. "You were *stalking* me, and it never occurred to you how terrifying that was for me?"

Brad took each punch in stride, not bothering to hold me down or stop me or protect himself from my pummeling. This was so like him not to fight back. It was one of the traits I loved most about him—his conciliatory nature. He was an excellent punching bag and I hit him with everything my fists and motor mouth had to give.

Several intense moments later, I felt the energy drain from me. As my arms went limp and my throat dry, I looked up at him.

"Can you please just answer one question?" I asked weakly.

"Anything," he replied.

"Why did you follow me? Why didn't you just ask me where I was going? *Why?*"

He nibbled on his lower lip, glanced upward, and sighed.

"Because I didn't trust you to be honest with me."

"What? Why not? I've been nothing if not honest, Brad. I even let you break up with me to preserve my honesty. If I wanted to be dishonest, I would have lied and told you I'd stop tracking this murderer in order to keep you. But instead I told you the truth—that I couldn't give up—and as a result I lost you."

He held up his hand. "First of all, you didn't lose me. I've always been waiting for you to come back ... no matter how long it took. And secondly, you weren't totally honest with me about everything."

"Name one thing," I snapped.

"Landon Worthington."

Landon? What did he have to do with anything? It took a moment for my memory to catch up to the conversation. But when it did, everything became clear.

Brad's run-in with Landon and me at the coffee shop— clearly he thought I had been cheating on him. If Brad had been the one following me the night I went to Landon's, I probably sealed my own coffin in Brad's eyes and buried any uncertainty with it.

"So you thought I was hooking up with Landon, Alexis's brother?"

"Sure, why not? He's good-looking, supportive of this whole investigation you're doing, and obviously has a lot of free time to be meeting up with you at ungodly hours. What more could you want in a man?"

And there it was—the jealousy that makes a grown man act like an idiot. I exhaled a heavy breath.

"Brad, I only wanted you. I've always just wanted you. Landon and I were never a thing." I paused, unsure how to continue. My feelings had changed since this discovery.

"Wanted—as in past tense?"

"Right now I feel ... torn. I love you, but you betrayed me. I need some time to think things over. Not because I want to be with Landon, but because I'm not sure I can be with someone who trusts me so little. And by the way, there are better ways to get information than stalking a girl when a murderer is on the loose."

"I'm realizing that now," Brad grumbled as he rose from the sofa to leave.

I walked him to the door, and when he turned to say

good-bye, I kissed him on the cheek. "I do still love you, Brad. But I don't trust you. I'm not sure if our future can survive if neither of us trusts one another."

In the recesses of my soul I knew it would take a miracle to rebuild what we had together broken.

"Daddy, please help me."

My father's headstone jutted up from a bed of freshly cut grass, a striking contrast between the green of life and the gray of death. The cemetery's vast emerald lawn was dotted with marble slabs as far as the eye could see. Packed dirt paths meandered throughout the grounds, lazily winding their way back to the entrance. Despite the morbidity associated with it, the cemetery felt serene. A calm rest area before venturing off to heaven.

Even though death surrounded me, I never felt afraid when visiting. After all, my father was here to protect me.

It had been months since I last stopped by, but my mother never missed a week. Freshly cut lilac adorned his marker—my mother's favorite flower, which I adopted as well, and one that my father had planted every variety of at my childhood home. My father was the kind of man who did anything for the woman he loved. Why couldn't Brad?

If he truly loved me, he wouldn't have followed me. If he truly loved me, he would have stuck by me during my compulsion to help Alexis—no matter how unfounded my reasons were.

I wiped remnants of the mower's spray off the face of the stone, revealing the shiny surface dedicated to my dad:

Eric Germaine
July 10, 1951–April 11, 1992
Beloved husband and father,
until we meet again in heaven

Sadly, these words were all that remained of his life, along with distant memories of his laughter and charm. I remembered as a kid being able to turn to him for advice on anything and everything; he always had an answer to every problem. Not always did I take his advice or like his answers, but he respected me enough—even as a child—to let me decide for myself.

Today I needed his wisdom.

Not just about Brad, but about everything. About my job. About my relationships. About the risks I was taking pursuing this investigation. About the dreams and Alexis. Was I messing everything up? All along I thought I had been given a gift—my heart, and Alexis's memories—to use to save lives. Now this gift was becoming a curse, costing me everything I loved. It was breaking up relationships and tearing people apart, making villains out of the innocent.

No longer could I look at a man and see him as a human being. They were monsters, all of them potential suspects. Since when had my view of humanity become so gloomy?

"Oh, Daddy, I've made such a mess of my life. I don't know where to turn or who to have faith in anymore. I need your advice on what to do about Brad. I love him, but I don't know if I can forgive him. And this whole issue with bringing Alexis's killer to justice—it's taking everything out of me."

I dropped to my knees as I poured out my soul to the only one who made me feel safe.

"How am I supposed to help her when I think

everyone's the killer? I don't trust Evan because he rubs me the wrong way. I'm suspicious of Jeremy because he has a sordid past. And I'm ready to convict Derek because he's an addict. I'm so confused that I can't see the reality around me. What has happened to me? Who am I? I don't recognize myself anymore. I mean, where is my grace and understanding? I'm not much better than those men, am I?"

The confession felt freeing, exonerating me from a burden I had carried far too long. Somewhere along the way I had lost faith in humanity. Every time I added a new suspect, regardless of missing facts or lacking evidence, I villainized them all, with prejudice. It was time to restore my hope, my love, and my convictions.

It was time to forgive Brad.

Time to embrace love.

Time to embrace myself for who I was, scars and all.

But first I needed to put Alexis's retribution against her killer to rest.

"I thought I could figure out the killer, but I'm finding out he's 'a riddle, wrapped in a mystery, inside an enigma.'" I smiled as I said it. My father often quoted Winston Churchill.

Then the rest of the quote formulated in my head as I said it aloud: "'But perhaps there is a key.'"

Was this my father's message to me all those years ago? There was a key to solving every problem, even this one, but I needed to figure it out. If there was one thing my dad had taught me, it was that there's an answer for everything, a detour around every roadblock. The resolution may not always be black and white, but it was there, somewhere in the gray.

I possessed something that no one else alive had—a firsthand glimpse of the murderer and a heart that was guiding me. If I took a moment to stop running and instead start observing, I'd find him and I'd bring him down. The answer loomed right in front of my face. I simply needed to listen to my heart and stop directing it. My heart was the "key" to solving the problem.

My heart had a lot to say, after all.

It was still in love with Brad Thomas, and it always would be.

Chapter 32

After leaving the cemetery, I arrived home to an unmarked police car parked outside my apartment building.

My nerves sparked as I pulled into a spot and headed to my entrance. Once inside, I could overhear a man's voice echoing down the hall into the lobby. He sounded awfully close to my apartment ...

As I headed up the flight of stairs and rounded the corner to my front door, sure enough, Detective Evan Williams stood there, in a cheap grey suit, holding a manila envelope and talking into his cell phone.

"Hey, I'll call you back," he said, abruptly ending the conversation.

"Can I help you?" I asked, bewildered at what could possibly bring him to my doorstep.

"I come bearing bad news," he replied obscurely. "May I come in for a second?"

Bad news?

My first thought was if Brad was okay. My second thought was that the killer had taken another female victim. My third thought was that this was a setup to get me alone so Evan could kill me.

The third thought stuck.

The last thing I wanted was this man in my home, but if some greater force was controlling these events to help me catch the killer—*Dad, is this you helping me?* I wondered to myself—I needed to go along with it.

"Um, okay. Come on in."

I unlocked the door and held it open for Evan to lead the way to the living room, then left the door open a crack behind me. No way was I closing myself in, in case I ran into trouble and needed a hasty escape.

As I followed Evan into the belly of the apartment, I eyed my computer—which I'd left open out of long habit—on the dining room table and an idea struck me. My webcam. I had often used it to video chat with Brad as we talked ourselves to sleep at night. If only I could discreetly turn it to face the living room and send a live video feed to Brad so he could witness anything that happened.

"Can I get you something to drink?" I offered, forcing myself to be as hospitably charming as possible.

"No thanks."

"Well, then excuse me while I grab a water."

On my way to the kitchen I "bumped" the computer, spinning it around to face us. "Oops, clumsy me," I muttered to myself while I swiped a key to turn on the camera. With a quick stroke I dimmed the screen so that Evan would be none the wiser. When it was set up, I trotted to the kitchen and returned with my bottled water.

"So, what's this all about?"

"Perhaps you should sit," he suggested.

"No, I'd rather stand," I insisted.

"Your choice." Evan handed me the envelope he was carrying. "I wanted to give you a heads-up before the sheriff's deputy shows up. I got wind that you're being sued, Mia."

I pushed the envelope back at him.

"What?"

"Amy Watson's parents are suing you for emotional damages because of your visit with Amy the night of her death. They feel you're responsible for her death in some way, mainly because of the timing. They're in the process of pressing charges as well."

I wasn't sure if I should believe him or not, but the sympathy etched in his frown lines told me all I needed to know. This was no act. He was for real.

"Are you kidding me? I was trying to help Amy and protect her! That's all I've been trying to do. How can they accuse me of hurting her? I didn't do anything wrong."

"I know, Mia. Unfortunately, we live in a world of frivolous lawsuits. When I saw this complaint come in, I wanted to warn you about the charges and help you, if I can. I don't think they have much of a case, but it's being presented to the prosecutor's office to see if it'll stick. I'm guessing not. They have no evidence. But as for the lawsuit details, here they are. The deputy's on his way to officially serve you."

This time I regretfully accepted the document.

"I'm so sorry," Evan added.

Could things get any worse? I doubted it.

Evan rose to leave, but as I walked him to the door, I knew this would probably be my only chance to ask the question that had burned in my mind since my vision.

"Evan, can I ask you something?"

"Maybe," he said, turning to face me.

It took a deep breath to muster the courage to voice the words that resonated in my mind. Evan's shifting toward the door spurred me to speak. "The night of Alexis's death, you were the first one on the scene, even before the EMTs, right?"

"Yeeesss," he answered cautiously.

"You were just an officer back then, right?"

His eyes narrowed. "Yeah. Why do you ask?"

"Why weren't you wearing a uniform when you showed up at the crime scene?"

Cocking his head and eyeing me warily, Evan's mouth dropped open. Deafening silence reigned for a long moment, then, "How did you know that?"

I wanted to backpedal, to take it back, in case I just pushed him too far. But then again, lives were at stake. Shoving him over the edge was a risk I had to take. "I just do. Please answer the question." I hoped the webcam was picking up the audio on this, since it was missing his body language.

"I don't owe you an explanation, and I thought I warned you to stay out of that case!" he bellowed. "Isn't this lawsuit enough to prove you don't belong in this investigation? Stay out of it, or you'll be dealing with more than a lawsuit."

The door slammed shut behind him before I got a chance to wipe his spittle off my cheek.

Murderer or not, whatever Evan was hiding was crucial to solving the case. From day one with me, he'd been elusive about the details of that night, but I was determined to uncover his secrets. Evan was my key to everything. I just needed to find the right door to unlock.

Chapter 33

My eyes panned up from my mind-dulling computer screen to the panorama of lush foliage beyond the windowpane. Squirrels scampered one story below me, frolicking in a mating dance that involved bouncing from tree to tree. My office window revealed the perfect spring day outside, yet a darkness loomed over me that I couldn't break free from.

Another victim—Lilly Sanderson. Thirteen-year-old daughter of Melody Sanderson. Attacked but barely made it through, currently in critical condition and recovering in an undisclosed hospital.

The numbers of victims were climbing, and no one was stopping it. It seemed like the more involved I got, the more lives he took.

Should I give up? Should I press on? There was no correct answer, and I was losing everything to the pursuit. And yet, for some reason I was okay with that because I didn't deserve what I wanted anyway.

All day I was stuck at my desk playing catch-up. It had been days since I last stepped foot inside my office, and at least a cameo appearance was long overdue. I was lucky to still have a job. But today I couldn't pull my brain out of the rut it'd been trapped in all morning—how to get information out of Detective Williams and Derek Worthington.

To me, which one was the killer was a toss-up. Detective Williams came across as elusive and threatening, while Derek was a womanizing derelict—both reasonable choices. I even wondered if they were in on it together. It wasn't out of the realm of possibility since Evan was pulling strings to keep Derek out of trouble at every turn. Landon's sights, however, were still set on Jeremy Mason, and since our run-in at the hospital, I couldn't deny his logic.

During an apologetic phone call to Landon the previous night, where I told him about the charges being pressed against me, he felt sorry enough for me to agree to a make-up dinner at Meelo's, an authentic Italian and Greek joint that served the best gyros this side of town. We instantly reconciled, and I promised not to bring Derek's name up again—though not before securing Landon's word that he'd talk to his father about the day of the robbery and take one quick look into it.

Landon spent the rest of the dinner conversation arguing his case that Jeremy Mason was our guy, while my gut told me otherwise. I knew Landon just wanted someone to blame, but my heart felt he was wrong. Something didn't strike me as "murderous" about Jeremy. Vile, yes. And on paper he fit the profile, but I had no reaction to him. Alexis was leading this parade, so certainly I should have felt a reaction—sort of like I did upon meeting Derek. With Derek I felt disgust and fear; Jeremy, nothing. Plus, I couldn't get my mind off Derek.

Despite Landon's protests, and Evan's proof that Derek was incarcerated the night of Gina's murder, Uncle Derek remained at the top of my suspect list. The timeline was too loose to certify that Derek hadn't first committed the crime before getting picked up—by Evan, of all cops. Coincidence? I thought not. Why was he—a detective— bringing in a drunkard? A diabolical serial killer could have plotted it to happen that way to create the perfect alibi. It was ingenious for avoiding detection.

Reaction or not, I kept Jeremy on the list anyway, since someone capable of inappropriately touching a child is certainly capable of God knows what else ... including murder. Plus, he worked at the hospital where Amy was killed. So I promised Landon I'd look into it. I figured I could ask around the hospital to see what people knew about Jeremy.

My eyelids drooped heavily as I returned my focus to my work computer. A beige ceramic clock in the shape of a horse—horses being a childhood passion of mine— promised I only had another hour until quitting time, so I decided to waste the rest of the workday browsing online. Jackie never acted like a stickler about how we spent our time, as long as the work got done. Gotta love her.

I searched for popular, credible background check services and found one that was relatively cheap. After entering my credit card information, I provided the information I knew, which wasn't much:

Derek Worthington
Durham, North Carolina

It was barely a start, but it was enough to pull the right guy up from a virtual lineup. A page-long catalog of debts and criminal activities popped up under his name, mostly just petty theft, public drunkenness, and DUIs. Nothing involving assault or a sexual offense.

As my eyes filtered down the list, beneath his name was a list of possible relations. No surprise, there I found "Dan Worthington," along with a hefty dose of unpaid parking tickets, a heap of delinquent debt, and a handful of petty crimes. His latest convictions of burglary, theft, and attempted manslaughter, along with the subsequent sentencing, stood out in a bold font.

As I continued scrolling down, another name caught

my attention. Bewildered by this unwelcome surprise, I clicked on it and held my breath as another webpage popped up. First the name, date of birth, and address—all basic facts. But then, a little further down, I saw something I hadn't expected, something that collided into me, physically rocking me back into my chair:

Landon Worthington
Crime Details: Arrested for misdemeanor death by vehicle
Disposition Date: 04/28/1992
Disposition: Charges dropped

The same year my father was killed ... and the charges were dropped only two weeks afterward. Was it possible that it was the same accident? I couldn't stomach the thought. The coincidence struck me like a blow to my head.

No, this was no happenstance. It couldn't be.

Another guy I trusted turned out to be a liar, betraying my confidence. How could he have not mentioned this to me? I was fuming, and he had some explaining to do.

I stormed up the walkway to his front door, banging relentlessly while screaming his name. My anger burned so hot that I barely registered a familiar vehicle parked in front of the house when I peeled into the driveway. Too angry to give it another thought, I continued hammering.

"Landon! I need to speak with you right now!"

My heart pounded in my ears as the door trembled beneath each blow. Several thuds later, Jennifer calmly cracked the door open just enough for me to push past her into the living room.

"Where's Landon? It's urgent I talk to him."

"He's in the basement, honey. Are you okay? You seem really worked up." She wrapped her manicured fingers around my forearm, halting my fervent stride. But I was too frenzied to explain.

"I just need to speak with Landon," I insisted curtly.

Releasing me with a gentle pat on my shoulder, Jennifer walked me through the living room, past a man sitting on the sofa sipping from a mug. I did a double-take—Jeremy Mason. I suddenly remembered—the car outside belonged to him. For a brief moment I wondered what he was doing here ... until I remembered what I had come for.

My brain was too befuddled, careening in too many directions, to deal with his presence.

With timid steps Jennifer led me to the basement door and swung it open.

"Landon, Mia is here," she called down to him. "I'm sending her down." She turned back to me and asked, "Please tell me, Mia, is everything alright?"

"No, it's definitely not alright."

I slipped past Jennifer, through the open door, and bounded down the bare wooden steps painted a dull grey. A rough-hewn railing guided me to the bottom, where a shaft of light feebly illuminated the unfinished open space. The mildewy scent of damp cement wafted over me. I heard the door click shut, casting me in semi-darkness. I followed the trail of light and found Landon seated on a worn, outdated, green plaid sofa, eyes fixed on a small television with a Wii remote controller in hand darting back and forth as his avatar navigated the on-screen terrain.

A large oak entertainment center housed the television, along with an array of knickknacks. An eerie dead-eyed ceramic doll. A headless Barbie. Several framed pictures—mostly of Alexis and a younger Landon. Childhood memorabilia. Macaroni artwork—presumably Alexis's creations. It almost resembled a shrine to the girl.

Without a glance in my direction, he greeted me. "Hey, Mia. What's up?"

I stalked over to him and planted myself in front of the television. He leaned to the right to look past my body. Dark circles rimmed his bloodshot eyes, as if he'd been playing for days. His food-encrusted gym shorts and pit-stained T-shirt suggested he hadn't changed clothes, either.

"Hey! What's the deal? You're in the way," he whined.

Turning behind me, I found the power button and pressed it. The television screen went black.

"Well, I'm guessing this is important," he said with an eye roll. Tossing the remote on the cushion beside him, he sank further back into the sofa and crossed his arms defiantly.

"Yeah, you can say that. I was doing some research online, Landon, and I found something ... interesting." I paused, unsure how to continue. Tears pooled, ready to pour. I wanted the truth, but then again, I didn't.

"Okay, tell me what you found about Derek this time," he prompted after a moment of overwrought silence.

"Oh, it's not about Derek. It's about you."

"What?" he said, his voice high-pitched, girlish.

"Why do you have a record for vehicular manslaughter?" My scathing tone defined just how serious this was.

I watched him turn from smug and calm to panicked and shocked. Landon's eyes widened like a rabbit's in a trap, and he shrunk back into the safety of the sofa cushions.

"Wha—what are you talking about?" he replied with an uneasy chuckle.

"You have a record. April of '92. What happened?" I demanded.

"Okay, okay. Can you please sit down? You're making me nervous."

"I don't want to sit. I want to hear the truth ... from your lips ... right now."

"Fine. Now, please understand," he began, "that I didn't intend to keep this from you. I just didn't know—"

"Spit it out, Landon," I interrupted with a shout. My patience was trickling away like a leaky faucet.

"Geez," he huffed. "So, judging by your anger toward me, I'm guessing you already figured out that my car accident was the same one you were in."

"You tell me."

"Yes, but there's more to the story," he said simply. "A lot more. But before I explain, I need you to promise me something."

"What?" I said sharply.

"You can't tell anyone. And I mean anyone. This must never come out. Can you promise that?"

I thought about his request. Whatever it was, it had happened years ago. Water under the bridge and all that, right? Though it didn't feel that way. I had trusted him, and he was about to tell me he was responsible for my father's death.

The ache over the loss, even so many years ago, surged anew with a force that left me breathless. Time that I thought had healed ticked down to nothing. Years of missing my father cascaded over me, bringing the pain of loss back in all its ferocity.

A salty tear surfaced, edging past my eyelashes. I didn't bother to hide it as it slid down my cheek and dangled from my chin. Another followed, and another, until I stopped them with the palm of my hand pressed roughly against my eyes.

I couldn't show my weakness ... not now, anyways. I was too angry to cry.

"Please promise me, Mia," Landon urged.

"Fine, I promise," I said, choking on the words. I needed to hear the truth, so I'd give him my word to guarantee secrecy, but that didn't mean I would forgive him ... again. Long ago, when he was merely a nameless boy who lost control of his car, I had forgiven him. But now—now he was my *friend*. And a liar. Our relationship, friendship—whatever it was—would never be the same after this. He had known all this time and never said a thing—the sin of omission had the potential to be the deadliest of sins among friends.

Although I couldn't imagine what extra details loomed in the depths of his memory, I figured I already knew what he was going to tell me.

Boy, was I wrong. If I thought my mind had been blown an hour ago, my brain was about to experience Hiroshima.

Chapter 34

Please just tell me already," I ordered when Landon hadn't spoken a full minute later. My feet had remained planted in front of the television this whole time, until Landon patted the cushion next to him.

"I insist that you sit. I can't do this with you standing there like that."

With numb movements I guided myself beside him and descended stiffly into the seat. Half a butt cheek rested on the edge of the cushion. Every muscle in my body tensed as I waited ... and waited ... succumbing to a sensation of dread.

"Okay, I guess I'll start with earlier that night," Landon began tentatively. "It was the worst night of my life ..."

He sighed heavily, then continued. "After a rough day, I had been walking along the street to clear my head when it happened—the accident, Mia. I heard the collision, the crushing metal, screeching tires. I saw your car coming around the bend, and then Evan—"

"Wait," I stopped him with a raised hand as I shook my head. The facts were still pouring in, but nothing was making sense. The puzzle pieces weren't fitting together. "What does Evan have to do with that night?"

My eyes bore into his, watching the vibrant green being swallowed by a darker shade of olive. They pierced me with their pain as a transformation unfolded within him.

"Mia, Evan was the driver."

"What? How is that—possible?" I stuttered.

"He had been drinking at the bar when he was supposed to be on duty. Apparently he was trashed when he hit you guys. I just happened to be there, so I ran up to help ... that's when I saw the driver's face as he stumbled out of the car and I realized it was Evan. I knew as soon as I saw him staggering that it wasn't from an injury—he walked away without a scratch. He was drunk. So, I offered to take the blame for him."

I shook my head. "No, that can't be right. The kid who hit us wasn't driving a police cruiser. He was driving a regular car."

"Like I said, he was *supposed* to be on duty but wasn't. He had gone home, changed into plainclothes, and switched cars so he could go drinking. When the cops showed up to take my statement, I told them Evan had let me borrow his car to meet up with some friends. They didn't question it, since they knew we were friends."

The hazy fog began to lift, but there was one thing I couldn't understand. "Why would you do that?" I whispered hoarsely.

Landon looked ashamedly down at his lap, tracing a jagged white scar that ran up his kneecap. When he noticed me watching him, his nervous fingers began picking at a tear in the sofa's abrasive wool fabric. He ran his hand over his face and I noticed exhaustion lines etched into his pallid skin. He looked downright ragged, but that wasn't my concern anymore. Today I only cared about answers—the truth.

"You don't understand," he pleaded. "When everyone else rejected me growing up, Evan stood up for me. He had always been a true friend, even though we were years apart. If he were to have gotten caught driving drunk—and killing someone on top of that—he would have lost his job and done jail time. It would have ruined his family and marriage, which were already on thin ice. It was the least I could do for him after everything he'd done for me when we were kids. I knew that if I took the blame I'd get a slap on the wrist at worst. An innocent, responsible teen loses control going around the bend—just a tragic accident. I had no other choice, Mia. Besides, Evan's repayment over the years was more than I could have ever asked for in return."

The realization washed over me in a heavy wave, crushing me beneath its weight. Landon covered for my father's killer. My life could have been fuller, happier, whole, if not for Evan. We would have gotten to my gymnastics practice in one piece, while Dad cheered me on from the bleachers. After an evening of uneven bars and floor routines, we would have stopped for ice cream and lived happily ever after. I would have had a whole childhood and adolescence of beautiful family memories instead of spending two decades recovering from the broken shards of my life that remained after his death.

It was too much to handle, especially right now. First Brad breaking my heart, now Landon deceiving me. Any ounce of faith I once had in mankind diminished into nothing. People were liars and thieves—stealing our trust and destroying it with their carelessness. I was right to have guarded myself.

A heaviness settled on my heart, steeling it from Landon's excuses. No longer would I be that naïve girl. I would be just as heartless as the rest of the world.

"You lied to me. I trusted you." I rose to my feet, but Landon jumped up beside me, grabbing my arm to pivot me toward him. I shouldered him away, refusing to face my betrayer.

"Please! You *can* trust me. I didn't tell you at first because I wasn't sure it was the same accident, and when I did finally realize that it probably was the one your father died in, I didn't know how to bring it up. It wasn't an intentional secret—you have to believe me! I never meant to hurt you. I ... I love you ... like a sister. You're the sister I lost, Mia. Please don't abandon me after all of this."

I stared at the wall in front me, then glided to the entertainment center, my eyes blankly skimming the pictures of once upon a time ... a time when Landon was innocent, just a kid. Before the accident, before Alexis died ... though for him life had always left him callous.

The pictures didn't reveal a happy child, rather a somber blond-haired boy reflecting on the sorrows of his life. In those green, tortured eyes, all I saw was an ache. Perhaps we weren't so different after all.

Except for one thing: I never covered for another person's murder.

"It doesn't matter what you say anymore. Don't you get it? You let the man who killed my father get away with it! Evan was drunk, a murderer, and you hid that from me, from the world. You say you love me? Prove it! Evan should have paid for what he did—by suffering the consequences. But you freed him from that obligation when you had no right to do that."

"You don't understand, Mia. He did pay—in his own way. You don't understand the guilt he carried ... and still does. Plus, he's better now. He changed because of that accident. He's a dedicated father, selfless husband, been sober ever since ... Doesn't that count for anything?"

"At the expense of my father's life? No, it doesn't count. And no, justice was never served. I'm done with you, I'm done with Alexis, I'm done with everything. I hope you sleep well at night knowing you're responsible for a lifetime of suffering and lies, Landon."

Furious, I stormed toward the stairs, fleeing for my sanity, for freedom from the hell that had become my life. I needed to leave all of this behind, but it continued to pursue me. How could I ever break free from the past? Everything felt so futile.

Chapter 35

I don't sleep, Mia."

Landon's dejected voice echoed against the hush that engulfed us. His words bridged the widening gap between us, causing me to pause in my retreat.

"Why's that?" I asked flatly.

"Because I'm sick."

"Humph. They make over-the-counter meds for that, you know."

"Not that kind of sick. Besides, meds don't work for me. It's not that simple. I've been sick a long time."

I turned around, wondering where he was going with this. No matter how far I wanted to run, my heart would never let me stray.

Something within me splintered in that accident twenty-two years ago. The shell that took over my body refused to let anything in. No love. No security. No passion. I spent my lifetime resenting and hiding my scarred existence. But I wasn't the only disfigured one.

Here, before me, was a man deeply wounded like me, only his scrapes lurked beneath the skin. He was damaged goods, and I could relate. Suddenly I felt sorry for him and sorry for hating him.

"Why are you telling me this?" I asked softly.

"Because you want the truth, you want justice, and because I love you."

Yet I wasn't so sure I wanted honesty anymore. All it did was torment me. But I had no choice. It was my nature to want resolution. I had been fighting for it with Alexis, a dead girl, all this time, to the point of risking my life for it. What was one more dirty secret laundered and air-dried for all to gawk at?

I walked toward him and sat, and he knelt down before me, his haunted eyes searching for help.

"What are you doing?" I wondered aloud.

"I am begging for your forgiveness for not telling you about Evan. But my past is, well, complicated. I have a mental illness, Mia. It's why I can't sleep. It's why I was out walking around that night. It's why I took the blame for Evan. I'm sorry. I was so ashamed of you finding out about my mental problems, which is why I didn't want to bring it up. Nothing in my life makes sense without that context. But no one knows other than Evan—not even my mother. And I'd like to keep it that way."

I exhaled the breath I had unknowingly been holding during his confession—although what exactly he was confessing wasn't registering.

"What kind of mental illness?"

"I don't know. I've looked it up, and the only thing that seems to fit is dissociative identity disorder."

"I've heard of it—like multiple personality disorder, right?"

He nodded. "Though, I've never been formally diagnosed. I can't bear to know if it's true. But the insomnia, losing track of time, extreme mood swings, amnesia ... that's the only thing that makes sense."

"You need to get help, Landon. I know someone who can help you—a psychologist I've been talking to."

"Don't you dare!" he shouted, jamming his finger into my shoulder with a quick jab. As quickly as his temper flared, it abated. "I'm sorry. I just don't want anyone to know."

"It's not your fault you're sick, Landon."

"I suppose, but what I do when I'm not me is my responsibility. I mean, I don't really know what I do, since it's all hazy and I black out a lot, but I should have gotten treatment and I didn't."

Placing a reassuring hand on his arm, I attempted to comfort him. "It's not too late to get treatment now, Landon."

"Maybe ... but maybe nothing can help me," he whispered.

On some level I knew what he was dealing with. My compulsion to help Alexis overwhelmed any sound judgment. But something about Landon's admission still plucked at me. A detail was missing ... a very significant detail.

"You said that Evan 'repaid' you—what did you mean by that?"

Landon rose to his feet and wandered around the room, pacing nervously. "Let's just say he took care of me when I wasn't feeling ... myself. Still does."

But that wasn't all. I just *knew* it. In my heart of hearts—or perhaps Alexis's heart—I discerned the truth behind Landon's black veil of secrets.

Closing my eyes, I let my brain and heart connect. A flood of emotions pulsed through me, resulting in a kaleidoscope of images. The blond boy in the photographs. The scar on his knee. A mentally ill teen wandering the dark, lonely streets. Each thought spurred on another, until a complete picture formed within my mind's eye.

A horrifying picture.

Landon had killed his own sister.

My heartbeat quickened to the point that I was certain it would burst under the pressure, and at that moment I knew I was correct. Which meant one thing: He could easily kill me too.

Yet oddly, I wasn't afraid to face this demon. In fact, I

urged him on. I knew the man beneath the killer, and I loved him too much to cower. He couldn't hurt me because I knew he wouldn't let himself.

Plus, I was ready for this to end … even if it ended badly.

I was tired of the taunting, the fear, the threats. I knew Landon, and this wasn't like him. It was some darker evil beneath the soul that lashed out. And I planned to bring it out and annihilate it. But I had to be strategic.

"There was a reason why Evan showed up at Alexis's murder scene first, wasn't there? You're not telling me everything there is to tell, are you, Landon?"

Landon's pacing stopped, and he stumbled, then dropped in a heap to the floor. With a crushing grip he clutched his head, violently shaking it back and forth like a scene from an exorcism. The thrashing scared me, and everything went still—an eerie calm that terrified me even more.

He rose slowly, then turned to glare at me with shark-like eyes—all pupil, cold, cruel. His appearance was no longer his own, but I refused to let on that it frightened me.

"Landon?" I whispered, unsure if he still existed beneath this monster's façade.

"Do *not* call me Landon. I am not Landon!" he screamed.

"I'm sorry," I stuttered. "What should I call you?"

"It doesn't matter what my name is. What matters is what you mean by your question—are you implying that I have a dark secret tucked away in my pocket?" he seethed.

Clearly rage had subsumed any vestige of humanity.

Was it safe to answer? Was it safe not to? I had come too far to strike out this late in the game. I had to know for sure. "Let me guess what happened. When Evan saw you show up at the car accident, you were covered in blood, weren't you?"

Not-Landon gave a mock laugh. "Why would I be covered in blood?"

"Did you make a deal with him that if he cleaned up your mess, you'd clean up his?"

The question must have pushed him too far, for at that moment he lunged at me, cornering me on the couch between his muscular arms.

"I know what you're insinuating. How dare you accuse me of killing Landon's sister! I loved Alexis, but she was losing her innocence. Much like you've lost yours. She was no longer a sister. And likewise, you are no longer a friend. Your words, not mine."

I never saw it coming—the knife sitting on the end table, his swift movement, the blade now pressed firmly against my throat. All of my time searching for Alexis's murderer would be in vain if I died. I was supposed to give Alexis peace, set the memories of all the victims free, give closure to the families and myself. I felt overwhelmed with regret for not fixing things with Brad, for not being a better daughter, for being ashamed of my past. Thirty-four years I had to grow and learn and live, and I squandered them with regret.

This moment was my biggest failure yet. I had finally realized my purpose for living—to actually live! And here I was, dying just when I'd discovered this. It felt Shakespeareanly tragic.

"You may feel that way," I said, gulping, "but no matter what I said, I still care about you. I have Alexis's heart, and I feel all the things she felt for you when she was alive. Admiration. Respect. Sisterly love. Dependence. You can't erase the past by using the present, but you can face it, Landon."

"Maybe I can't delete it, but I can keep it hidden. And

as I said, don't call me by that name. I don't know *Landon* anymore. He's not here." He tapped his forehead with a wicked sneer.

A moment later, I felt a pinch as the knife's steel edge sliced across the flesh of my neck. It stung, but it wasn't deep enough to bleed me dry. An icy chill slithered down my neck. He was going to torture me first.

I debated trying to reason with him, but it would have been futile. He wasn't in his right mind. Logic and crazy go together about as well as pickles and ice cream. There was nothing I could say to reach the void where his brain once was.

"Can you just answer one question before you kill me? A final request, please?" I begged, hoping to buy more time—enough time for maybe Jennifer to waltz down the stairs carrying a plate of cookies and thus come to my rescue, or for Landon to return to his body.

"Sounds reasonable," he answered calmly.

"Why? Why Alexis? You say she was losing her innocence, but how?"

At least I could die finally knowing what made him tick.

"Isn't it obvious? Look around you, Mia. Look at the clothes these young girls wear. Look at the pressures they face to grow up too fast. Look at the television shows that turn virgins into whores. They become victims of their own fleshly desires, leaving their purity behind. It's a shame, Mia. A damn shame. All I want is to protect them from themselves and from the society that corrupts them. Make them wholesome again—unpolluted. Don't you think that's a worthy cause?"

He scraped the blade against my cheek as he spoke using another man's gritty voice.

I contemplated his explanation for a moment. In his dementia he had become a self-styled crusading avenger obsessed with righting a societal ill—albeit in a most deadly and unorthodox fashion. Every killing had purpose, each one perfecting his craft and achieving his goal of "making them wholesome." Each murder was well planned and precise in preserving the child's innocence. It's why he stabbed them in the abdomen instead of randomly killing them in a myriad of ways. A gunshot to the head would demonstrate violence and mutilate them, but Landon's alter ego wanted order and perfection.

And that's when it hit me. I knew he couldn't kill me— not like this. Not by marring me. He was methodical. I just needed to wait for the right moment, and I'd know it when I saw it.

"I think it's noble what you're trying to do, but killing doesn't seem like the way to fix things. Isn't showing them another way toward purity a better solution?" I was grasping at straws here, and I hoped he didn't ask me to elaborate, because I hadn't prepared that far ahead for a discussion of morality versus social norms.

He became pensive for a moment, then shook his head.

"There is no other way. They're too tainted to come back. But you, you could have changed the world. And now I have to kill you."

With a tsk-ing sound he swiftly raised his arm up to strike me in the stomach, but my reflexes had been waiting for this moment. A sliver of space opened up between his chest and mine, just enough for me to kick him hard enough to propel him backward into the entertainment system, sending framed photos crashing. As he slumped on the floor in a heap, shaking off bits of glass, I jumped up and ran like hell for the stairs.

A hand coiled around my ankle. I fell with a fleshy thud onto the unforgiving concrete with Not-Landon's full weight on top of me. Kicking and gouging, I squirmed out from beneath him and crawled to the stairs. When I glanced back, I saw droplets of blood trailing me and I grew woozy.

With another tackle he pinned me face-first to the floor, and I felt a rib or two break under the impact.

"Bad move, *sis*," he hissed in my ear.

All I could hear was his heavy breathing against my neck and my grunting as I fruitlessly attempted to kick him off of me.

"Now you'll finally get to meet Alexis face to face."

A dull thump battered the back of my head with such force that I nearly bit into the concrete under my jaw. Then everything faded into black oblivion.

Chapter 36

I double-checked my outfit in my full-length bedroom mirror, hoping that the ensemble would meet Luke Perry's approval. In two-dimensional form, he watched me with those dreamy eyes from beside my bed, next to my door, and above my dresser. Landon argued that no twelve-year-old should have posters of boys, but rather horses, but give me Luke Perry on horseback and I'd settle for that.

Landon didn't find that funny.

My best friend Sammie had loaned me the super-short acid-washed skorts and tie-dyed midriff top, and I added my own suspenders just like Jennie Garth's outfit in last week's episode of 90210. I even curled my hair using my mom's curling iron, which I could never let her find out about. She'd kill me if she saw me with it, I'm sure. Not that she ever noticed where I was or what I was up to.

A knock at my door startled me. "Come in," I said.

It was Uncle Derek, which didn't surprise me, since he had a knack for showing up when he needed money, which was all the time.

"Wow, don't you look all grown up," he said in a crude

tone I'd become all too familiar with. Uncle Derek often said sleazy things to Mom, and sometimes said things to me that made Dad threaten to kill him. Plus he dated girls way younger than him, but the comment still made me feel uncomfortable.

"Um, thanks," I said. I didn't really know what else to say to him, so I said nothing.

"So, uh, your mom around?" he asked, each word smearing the next. "I, uh, need to talk, um, to … uh, to her."

"She's at work. Should be home soon, though."

He nodded slowly, taking another shaky step forward, and I suddenly felt really creeped out. I moved away from the mirror and started toward my dresser to widen the space between us. The alcohol on his breath and the slurred speech scared me.

One more step forward, and he closed the bedroom door. Another step toward me, then a stagger, then another step. He was less than a foot away from me, and his breath reeked of pot and beer.

My eyes started to tear up, and panic seized me. I attempted to walk around him, but a vice grip that belied his drunken state stopped me in my tracks.

"Um, I gotta go," I pleaded.

"You're not going nowhere, pretty girl. I mean, woman."

He grabbed me near my collarbone and leaned forward, lips puckered. I shook my head and faltered backward, until

264

the wall blocked me.

"Please, Uncle Derek, don't!" I shrieked.

"You know you want it," he insisted, fumbling with the straps of my suspenders.

I shoved his hands away, but that only egged him on as he ripped one strap undone, then the other, with a brutality I was no match for. A moment later his lips smashed up against mine, silencing my cries for help. When the waistband of my shorts and weekly "Tuesday" underwear began to slip downward, I threw my knee up against him, hitting the meat of his thigh.

Bad move.

Instead of releasing me, he only pressed and pulled harder, squeezing my arms with such vengeance that I was sure they'd break.

I felt Uncle Derek's disgusting tongue in my mouth, tasted the rotgut whiskey. My body shook with silent sobs. I prayed that God would just let me die before "it" happened … before he took me and left me a cracked shell time could never mend.

God must have heard my prayer.

The sound of a creaking door jarred us both, and when it swung open to reveal Landon, I seized the chance to break free, darting into the hall where I could hide behind his lanky frame.

"What the hell is going on in here?" my brother, my

savior, bellowed. He quickly sized up the situation, noting my suspenders dangling to the floor and my shorts near my knees.

"Your sister's what's goin' on," Uncle Derek retorted. "She made a pass at me. You got yourself a little whore for a sister, all's I'm sayin'."

"What? Alexis, what's happening to you?"

I couldn't believe Landon was taking Uncle Derek's side and protested, "I swear, Landon, I didn't do anything!"

"Dressed like that, I don't believe you, you little slut! He's our uncle, for God's sake. Who else have you been screwin'?"

"No one, I promise." With tears streaming down my hot cheeks, I begged for him to listen.

"You look and act like a tramp. I don't know you anymore," he said, looking away from me with disgust.

"You gotta get your sister in check," Uncle Derek warned as he barged past me and Landon. On the way to the stairs, he glared at me, then pressed his finger to his lips, the universal sign for me to keep quiet. He ran his thumb across his neck and I knew exactly what that meant too.

I vowed to myself never to speak of it to anyone.

As Uncle Derek descended the stairwell with heavy footsteps, Landon pushed me hard against the wall, his eyes penetrating me.

"I don't know what really happened in there, and I don't want any details."

"You have to know it wasn't me, Lan—"

"I know you didn't do anything wrong—in this instance. But something's gotta be done about the way you handle yourself. Look at your clothes! And the garbage you watch. You lost your purity, Lex. I'm your big brother, supposed to take care of you, but I have no idea how to do that anymore. You act like a woman, but you're only a kid."

"I'm not a kid, Landon. I can take care of myself." I burst past him, heading toward my room.

"You think you're grown up, do you? Then why did you need me to save you from Uncle Derek? If you're not going to protect yourself, then I'll have to do it for you, since I'm your brother and I love you. Unless you want to end up like Mom— a whore."

A lump throbbed in my throat—not from sadness but from anger. *"I'm nothing like Mom!"* I insisted. *"I just wish you'd stop treating me like you own me, cuz you don't."*

"If you're not going to save yourself, I guess I'm going to have to do it for you, Alexis."

Alexis—he used my full name, which meant he was acting parental and serious. Instead of arguing in circles with him, I slipped into my bedroom, wondering what he meant.

I couldn't pin down what changed in him that day, but it was there, underneath the mask. A darkness brooded as black as his eyes when he walked in on me and Uncle Derek. I sensed the vigilante within him growing, evolving, but the justice he served was no justice at all.

It was murder.

⛬

The dreamy fog drifted over me, then slowly dissipated, leaving me helpless in my current reality. Facts bumped together in my mind in a frantic rush, like bumper cars at a carnival. It all added up to one thing: I was about to be killed.

Pinned to the floor on my stomach with Landon's bony knees in my back, I waited for the final stab to my abdomen, just like I'd witnessed too many times in my dreams. Then I waited a second longer. Why was he hesitating? A moment later I discovered why.

Both hands were holding me down.

Only one thing could explain why there was no blade tip piercing my side. He must have dropped his knife during his fall and hadn't realized it yet.

"Any last words?" he offered with mock courtesy.

Nothing witty came to mind. I was too focused on finding a way to get to the knife or call for help, but my mouth was planted against the concrete, muffling any sound I could make. Besides, my chest was so constricted beneath his bulk that I doubted I'd have enough air to bellow loud enough for his mom to hear me upstairs. I couldn't believe she hadn't heard the commotion and come to investigate, but I guess she was preoccupied with entertaining the friendly neighborhood child molester.

I was pinned and definitely outmatched.

My only chance was to dig up any ounce of brotherly compassion left in the corpse that once was Landon.

"Alexis forgives you, you know," I squeaked softly.

I sensed him budge, giving me a little more space to breathe.

"I don't care. Why are you telling me that?"

"Because she still loves you. She misses you. And she knows why you took her life."

Not-Landon cackled. "Oh, really. And why's that?"

"Because of Uncle Derek. You saw what he did to her that day in her room, and you didn't want her to live with the burden of that memory. And ever since that day you've tried to protect other girls from becoming sex objects."

The grip on my neck softened, and I hoped I was reaching the heart buried somewhere within.

"Yes, you understand then? I'm protecting them from people like Jeremy and Derek—men who will use them and throw them aside. I'm saving them. You understand … you understand."

"I do. You did save Alexis, in a sense, from her own downfall. Only you could see the signs, and you acted on it. You've accomplished your goal. But please don't kill her again, because then everything would be in vain."

A stillness enveloped us. A long moment passed. All was calm. Then something wet tickled the hairs on my neck. Landon was somewhere in there, and he was crying.

I strained to turn my neck around to see him, and his hold released when his hands covered his face as he wept bitterly.

"Hey there," I soothed. I scooted upright and hugged him, my eyes searching behind him for the knife. There, under a fractured picture frame. The blade reflected hope back at me. And Alexis's smiling face beneath the spider web of shattered glass gave me strength.

"I didn't know how else to help her," Landon sobbed. "But the other me, the me I can't control, it knew. So I let it take over sometimes. For years I kept the bad me hidden inside, but I can't stop him anymore. It's overcoming me. I just … black out. Then wake up with vague recollections of events, but it's not me. I promise it's not me. Please help me stop him, Mia."

"Don't worry," I said, calculating how I could retrieve the knife without him suspecting anything. "We'll figure this out together."

"I just don't think so. I'm not fixable, am I? I'm a killer … " As the words slipped out, Not-Landon did the same—slithering out of my grasp and toward where the knife remained hidden.

"The knife," he muttered. "Where's the goddamn knife?"

I had caught a break—he hadn't spied the knife yet. I could beat him to the stairs this time, but I knew better than to turn my back on him. I'd seen too many horror movies watching the naïve female attempt to flee, and the moment she looks away from her captor—dead.

As Landon kicked and pawed, searching for the knife, I glided my feet slowly backward, feeling for any obstacles that might impede me. I needed to get Jennifer's attention.

Oh crap, he had found the knife. He looked at it oddly, as if he had forgotten its purpose.

"Landon," I spoke loud and clear, "please put down the knife! You don't want to do this!"

I hoped the volume didn't give my scheme away, but Landon seemed too overcome with guilt or self-doubt at the moment to register what I was doing.

A couple of steps later I bumped into the bottom stair and sprinted up the staircase, tripping and fumbling my way to the top.

At the landing I threw open the door, screaming for Jennifer.

"Call the cops, Jennifer! Now! It's Landon!"

Jennifer, trailed by Jeremy Mason, rounded the corner of the kitchen where a phone hung on the floral-wallpapered wall.

"What's going on?" Jennifer demanded with a

sternness I'd never expected from such a sweet old lady.

"He's got a knife, and Landon, he's not himself—" I tried to explain, but the words came out in a jumble.

"You're bleeding!" she said with shock as she grabbed a cream-colored dishtowel with pansy trim from the counter. I held it to my neck, watching with a kind of fascinated terror as the fabric grew red with my blood.

While I was distracted by the red easing its way through the fibers, Jennifer snatched the receiver from the wall and dialed 9-1-1. "Please send an officer and an ambulance to 721 Willoughby Way. My son stabbed someone. Please get here soon."

A couple of questions and answers were exchanged, but I was starting to feel too dizzy to catch what was going on. Dark circles began rimming the edges of my vision, so I slumped down against the partition separating the stove from the dinette, fixing my gaze on the pastel paper flowers dancing along the wall.

Jennifer hung up, then her shadow crossed over me as she stooped to help me up. Once on my feet, she sat me in a chair.

"Sit, honey. I'm going to check on Landon."

Immediately I perked up. "No! He's dangerous right now. Let the cops handle it. Just keep him away from us."

My warning came a moment too late. Landon appeared through the doorway, bloodied knife in hand.

In sacrificial boldness, Jeremy rushed him and grabbed both his arms. *Thwack*! A lightning-fast head butt sent Landon to the floor. Jeremy leapt on top of him, throwing punches. They scuffled, while Jennifer screamed for them to stop. The next thing I saw was Jeremy pinned in a vice grip under Landon's arm and the knife was pressed against his throat.

"Please, Landon, don't hurt him! Talk to me, Landon. I know you're in there, sweetie," Jennifer implored.

The vacancy in Landon's eyes told otherwise. No one was home. No one with a heart, that is.

"Landon's dead, Jennifer." His voice was jagged and heartless. "I'm not the son you thought I was. I failed."

"No, honey, you didn't fail. You'll never fail me. You're more precious than you'll ever know."

Clearly Jennifer's words offered no comfort to this tortured man.

Outside, the peal of sirens grew closer with each passing moment, hollering their call as an announcement to the rubbernecking neighborhood that drama was happening at number 721.

Hurry. Hurry, I prayed silently.

"Don't come any closer," Landon threatened. "This ends now."

I knew exactly what that meant, and it wasn't good.

He was about to kill again.

Chapter 37

D on't hurt Jeremy, please, Landon," Jennifer begged. "I know what you think of him, but you're wrong. He's a good guy, I swear. We're friends, honey, and have been for a while."

"He's no good for you, Mom. He's done horrible things … to children, when my mission has always been to protect them."

Jennifer wiped a tear away, leaving a wet trail along her cheek. "Oh, honey, that's not true. I know what really happened—Jeremy was the victim, sweetie. Please don't punish him more than he's already endured."

"I don't want to hurt anybody, but sometimes it must be done. Sometimes it's the only way to free someone from their pain."

Landon looked directly at me as he said it. *Free from pain …* the words echoed. And then I became conscious of where he was heading with this as I read his mind.

Help me, Mia, his eyes beseeched. *You know what I have to do. It's the only answer. The only way to right my wrongs.* Or was it Alexis speaking to me?

Either way, I couldn't let him do it. No matter what he had done, he couldn't take this route. It was selfish. An easy way out.

"An eye for eye. Or in my case, a life for a life. Right, Mom? Isn't that what the Bible teaches?" Landon crowed. The blade indented Jeremy's skin as he tensed for the final cut.

"Don't you think enough life has been lost?" I pleaded. "Enough blood shed? This won't put things right. It's a weak reaction because you're too tired to think straight. Let's talk about this."

"I'm done talking. And I am weak, don't you understand?" he screamed. "But I'm not like you, Mia. I can't fix what I see in the mirror like you can... like you *should*."

His words were terse and urgent. His gaze was fixed on me.

"Look, the cops will be here any minute, and I'm guessing Evan's with them. I don't want him to see me like this. I didn't want any of you to witness this. I know too much that I can't hide anymore. The voices are too loud. I'm scared I'll never be good. I just want to be good, to be enough. This is the only way. Mia, you understand, don't you?"

And in that awful, sick, life-changing moment, I understood. I knew. I felt it all. This was me I was looking at—the insecure and fearful child in the mirror. Landon was a timid boy beneath the blood covering his hands. But there was just too much blood. Maybe he was right. Maybe it was time to kill the demon, to let go, to be free. With it, all of Landon's secrets—about the victims, about Evan, about Alexis, about his past—would die too.

I wouldn't tell. I promised him that with a nod. This was his final confession of all the sins he had covered up, and I was willing to be his priest today.

"Yes, Landon, I understand. Go be with your sister. Alexis is waiting for you."

With my blessing, Landon pushed Jeremy forward on his knees and drew the blade across his own neck, a symbol that only I could comprehend. He wasn't worthy of dying the same way he'd killed the innocents—a stab in the side. No, he was vanquishing the evil within in this way, a fitting end.

Jeremy backed away from the spreading puddle of gore and, striking the wall, slowly raised himself against it to his feet. He inched over to Jennifer, her mouth frozen open in a grotesque silent scream, and drew her close, averting her view.

For a moment I felt time cease, then I ran to Landon and clung to his frail form, watching the life waver in his eyes, feeling his ragged breaths as I firmly pressed the towel to his neck.

"Don't be afraid, Landon. You're going to be all better now."

He smiled. "I know. You are too," he said gutturally, his voice wispy and frail.

I grinned down at him knowingly. "Yes, because of you."

By now the sirens wailed outside the house. Jennifer scurried to the front door at the sound of footsteps stampeding up the front porch.

"It's Landon," I heard her say. "He ... he's in the kitchen. Badly hurt."

"The paramedics are on their way." Evan's voice. He had come, just as Landon had foretold.

Evan and another officer entered the kitchen, their guns drawn. Landon's eyes met Evan's in a frank, unspoken exchange, a naked, vulnerable little boy looking to a big brother for understanding. Evan holstered his gun and took a hesitant step forward, then knelt down beside us.

"Hey, buddy. What'd you do to yourself?"

Landon coughed a barely audible chuckle. "Don't worry, man. Brothers forever, right? And brothers never tell. I'll see you on the flip side."

Evan nodded weakly and gripped Landon's hand in a man-shake. "I love you, man."

The sentiment of the moment wasn't lost on me. Landon was closing the chapter that had probably held Evan captive to his Good Samaritan for years. I didn't know the details—if Landon had been blackmailing Evan all along, or how deep Evan's involvement went. Right now I didn't care. Alexis's murderer had forfeited his own life, and my father wasn't coming back, and that was enough for me.

Evan's eyes met mine for an infinitesimal second, long enough for me to read the guilt and embarrassment and regret in them. He gave Landon's hand a final squeeze before he rose.

It was all I could do to look at the obscene gash in Landon's throat and to listen to the gurgle of words coming so painfully from his blood-filled mouth. "You're a strong woman, Mia," he said, "but no matter what façade you put on, I know the real you. Don't hide that scar anymore. Be proud of it, okay? For Alexis."

"Okay, I will. For you both."

"Thank you, sis," he said with his final breath.

His eyes drooped lazily closed, and I imagined him peacefully sleeping—at last the restful, deep sleep that he had been longing for. As his limp hand fell to the cool linoleum floor, I couldn't help but be proud of him. Maybe in another context his choice would have been selfish, but today it wasn't. Today he chose to bury the past with him, a past full of painful memories and waking nightmares. The Triangle Terror hadn't been a terror after all, but a victim to his own mental illness.

At least he got the final say.

Chapter 38

After Landon's suicide, Evan suggested everyone head down to the station for questioning. A police cruiser and ambulance were parked in front of 721 Willoughby Way as I strode out the front door with Evan leading the way. Blue and red lights strobed hypnotically against the windowpanes. As I headed to my car, Evan waved for me to follow him.

"How about you ride with me?" he suggested with a firmness that gave me no alternative.

His offer made me uneasy.

"Alone?" I asked.

"Don't worry. I don't bite."

He opened the rear door of a black Chevy Impala for me to enter and stepped aside waiting. Likely he wanted to know exactly what I knew, and what I planned to do about it.

"I would prefer to drive myself," I asserted.

"This isn't a choice, Mia. Get in. Now. Don't make a scene."

With nerves sparking, I obediently slipped into the backseat, separated from the front by a security screen, prepared for the worst. I'd need to assure him that other than a last-minute confession that he was the Triangle Terror, Landon had taken his confidences to his grave.

I just hoped I was convincing.

The last thing I wanted was Evan taking matters into his own hands to guarantee that I never told about what actually happened during the accident that killed my father. Ignorance was my best plea, and I'd have to play it well. Besides, I didn't want more trouble. Twenty-two years and a moment of clarity have a way of cleaning the slate.

A minute later we were silently cruising down Roxboro Road, but in the wrong direction.

"Where are you taking me? I thought we were heading to the police station," I spoke as firmly as I could feign.

Yet Evan said nothing. Just kept driving.

"Please tell me what's going on," I begged. I had survived too much to lose the game now.

With stoic resolve he ignored me, until fifteen minutes later he pulled into a vacant lot that appeared to have been a gas station of bygone days. Weeds sprouted from chunks of crumbling concrete, and the vintage pumps had no sign of modern technology. Beneath a film of dirt I could barely make out an outdated Texaco logo on a cracked globe.

Evan pulled around to the back of the building out of view of passersby. Angst crept up my spine, and my fight or flight impulse roared to life. I tugged on the door handle, but the child safety locks held the door firmly shut. I pressed the button to roll down the windows, but again—nothing.

My purse. I had it with me. And my phone. As I grabbed it, ready to dial Brad, Evan's voice stopped me.

"Mia, put the phone down. I'm not here to hurt you. Just to talk."

"About what?" I said, clutching my phone to my chest.

"Show me your phone isn't recording this, then we'll talk."

I did as instructed, then tossed it on the leather seat beside me. "Happy?"

"Not really. One of my best friends died today," he

replied coolly.

"That's not what I meant—" I fumbled for words, then gave up.

"Did Landon say anything ... about me?"

"What do you mean?" I edged around answering his question.

"Did my name come up in your conversations with him, and if so, what did he say?"

I had two choices at this juncture: Tell Evan the truth about what I knew, or lie to his face. Each choice had its own set of conflicting consequences, but which one was my safest bet?

And that's when it hit me. Screw safe. Screw running from the truth. I'd rather come clean and pay the price with my life than hide in the shadows of lies. Lies took Landon's life. If only he'd have told someone about his problems, gotten help, maybe he'd be alive today. Maybe he'd never have gotten blood on his hands.

"I know," I whispered. Then with bravado I continued, "I know what Landon did for you on the night of Alexis's murder, and I vaguely know what you've been doing for him since. I didn't ask for details, and to be honest, I don't care anymore. How you've been protecting him doesn't matter. He's gone. And I won't tell anyone, if that's what you're worried about."

A penetrating hush engulfed us. I wasn't sure what to expect—a gunshot to my head or a reconciliatory hug.

"Why should I believe you?"

"Because I just want to move on. It's over. I can't bring back the dead. And I know you were just trying to help him. Please believe me."

"Give me one reason why I shouldn't kill you—you know, get rid of all loose ends?"

What could I say? I was indeed an unpredictable loose end, as far as Evan was concerned. He was perfectly capable of covering up my murder, and what incentive did he have for letting me live?

There was one thing, though ...

"Because Landon told me you changed. You're a good guy now. And I believe that."

Neither of us spoke for several moments. Perhaps I had given him a good enough reason to let me live. I prayed that was the case, because I didn't want to go out like this.

Then Evan sighed, shattering the calm before the storm.

"I'm going to confess, Mia, to the accident. I've already decided this a long time ago but never had the balls to come clean. But if there's anything Landon taught me today, it's to do the right thing—no matter how much sacrifice it demands."

After everything that had happened, and completely unlike me, I was speechless.

"To set the record straight, I never really knew if Landon was the Triangle Terror. I had hoped and prayed not, but a hunch has haunted me since I found him covered in blood the night his sister was killed. At the time I didn't realize what I was seeing, but ever since then, details about the whole night felt ... off to me. My guilt wasn't in covering up evidence or anything, but not following up on an obvious lead that pointed to Landon. That's how I protected him all these years—never mentioning what I saw that night. He knew I protected him just like he protected me—through turning a blind eye. Mutual silence. I guess that makes us blood brothers," he said with a cynical laugh.

Evan's vow to confess shocked me, especially since I had assured my silence, but my appreciation for his integrity wasn't the feeling pulsing through me at that moment. Instead I felt sorrow, pity. While he didn't mention my father's death in his discourse, he held responsibility for it. That was his burden to bear all these years.

"I'm really sorry, you know. You were right." His voice was etched in sincere remorse.

There was only one thing I could say to offer solace.

"I forgive you for what happened to my dad."

I heard air mixed with relief exhale his lungs, and from my angled view of his face, I saw a tear slide down his cheek.

The interrogation was an exhausting ordeal, but it seemed to go well enough that the cops let me go home afterwards with no follow-up required. Mentally and emotionally I felt transformed. I had battled my own demons that day, facing down the thing that imprisoned me since the accident—a scar and the diffidence it created inside me. But it was just a physical blemish, not something that made me who I am. It took a mentally disturbed murderer who gave me a sneak peek at death to show me that. The real scars are never seen on the exterior, but on the inside.

I had plenty of those too, but nothing I couldn't overcome.

That same night Lilly Sanderson, the only surviving victim of the Triangle Terror, confirmed from Landon's picture that he was indeed the killer. She had ID'd him immediately before being rushed to a psychiatric care unit for the emotional trauma brought about by the resulting media frenzy. I made plans to visit her the next day—if I could get past the paparazzi following my every move—so that I could help her see past the murderer and into the victim that he was. I'd tell her about his personality disorder and how he was sick, never intending to hurt anyone. Maybe humanizing him would help her sleep at night. It was worth a try.

It was well after midnight when I finally got home, weaving through a slew of reporters waiting outside my apartment. My newfound celebrity status as the Triangle Terror's confidante inspired me to take an overdue vacation ... somewhere tropical and remote.

Despite how tired I was, I strode inside with confidence, not letting the shadows chase me. When I opened my front door, I almost thought I was sleepwalking. Certainly I was in a dream ... this time not one involving murder but romance.

Brad stood there holding a bouquet of lilacs, their enticing fragrance permeating the room. Candlelight flittered from various places around the room casting a warm glow, and soft background music added to the ambiance.

"What's this?" I asked with a coy grin.

"You've had a rough day, to say the least. I wanted to give you a happy ending. Does this work?"

I chewed playfully on my lower lip. "It's a start. You know, lilac is my favorite scent in all the world. How did you know?"

"Lucky guess."

"You visited my dad's gravesite, didn't you? You're a stalker, you know. That's unhealthy."

Brad laughed good-naturedly. "It's called research, not stalking. Which I'm sorry about, by the way. I didn't mean to be overprotective or harassing."

I sighed forgiveness. "Water under the dam, or over the bridge, or whatever the saying is. All's well that ends well."

"Enough with the clichés. Get over here and kiss me," he ordered as he drew me into his arms and touched his lips to mine—first gingerly, but when I didn't pull back, the sweetness turned spicy. Our tongues clashed as I nibbled his lip and he suckled mine. His lips traced down my jaw line as he guided me to the sofa and pulled me down with him onto it. I straddled his lap as his mouth covered mine, teasing me with his tongue.

As the intensity burned, I stretched out my neck, inviting his kisses to wander along my flesh. He devoured me, and I raked my fingernails down his back with fevered gratitude, urging him on with murmured groans.

My hands slid down his thick, muscular arms, savoring their power. When I reached his groin, I tenderly palmed him through his pants, then tucked my fingers under the hem of my shirt. Slowly I raised my arms and lifted the shirt up and off, to Brad's delight, then unclipped my bra. I'd never felt so bold, so liberated.

He didn't mind, to say the least.

Instead of staring at my scar, he lovingly kissed what I had formerly despised. His passion for me never wavered—if it had, I would have sent him packing. But no, he loved me, scars and all.

Tipping my chin up to hold my gaze, he examined me, penetrating me with those brown eyes that had wooed me from the moment we first met.

"Hey, you know I love you—every part of you, right?"

"I do now," I said.

"So then, I need to know something."

"Shoot."

"Well, you never told me what this rose tattoo was all about."

He pressed his lips to it, moving upward to a spot along the base of my neck where he tongued the flesh until it tickled. I squealed and squirmed away from him until I broke free.

"Fine! I'll tell you. I've never told anyone this before, though. Pinkie swear you'll keep this between us." I held out my pinkie.

Brad grumbled. "What are we—five?"

"Play nice … or I'll put the girls away."

"Fine, you win." He entwined his finger around mine.

"The secret handshake among women. This is some cloak-and-dagger stuff here. I feel privileged to be inducted into it."

"Okay," I said, resting my head against his chest. "I trust you. My grandmother's name was Rose, and I loved her dearly. She even helped raise me after my father passed. But after my grandfather died, she just became a basket case. My mom and I took care of her, which was a job. I mean, I had to change her diapers and she went to adult daycare because she couldn't be trusted home alone."

"That bad, huh?"

"Yeah. She almost burned down the house one time by leaving a rag on the gas stove while it was on. Short story long, she had dementia and eventually died from its complications. Not physically—at first. But mentally, she had no idea who I was. I never told anyone how much it broke my heart to see her like that—the woman who cared for me as a child had become one herself. I loved Grandma Rose so much, so my tattoo was kind of a tribute to our shared suffering and to her life. With Grandma Rose I could be anyone I wanted to be—a better version of myself, because Grandma Rose didn't judge me, didn't notice my flaws, you know? All she saw was a beautiful flower in me, even though the thorns were there."

I wiped away a tear that threatened to fall and swallowed the nostalgic lump in my throat.

"That's really sweet," Brad said with a light peck on my chin. Then another. And another. "You wanna know how I got my frog tattoo on my thigh?"

"Let me guess. You had one too many drinks with the

boys in college and ended up at the mercy of a tattoo artist with a cruel sense of humor?"

"Bingo!" Brad laughed. "It's almost as if you were there. Maybe I'm not the only stalker among us."

"You got me," I said with a giggle as I wrapped my arms around him and pulled him on top of me. "Now take me like you mean it, you fool," I playfully ordered.

And he obeyed ... boy, did he obey.

PAMELA CRANE

Chapter 39

THE TRIANGLE TERROR'S FINAL ACT

Durham, NC

In a stunning turn of events on Thursday, Durham native Landon Worthington professed to being the Triangle Terror moments before taking his own life.

"After receiving a 9-1-1 call from his mother, officers found a white male identified as Landon Worthington laying on the floor after stabbing himself," Detective Evan Williams stated in a press release.

Beginning with the murder of his sister, Alexis Worthington, twenty-two years ago, Worthington was responsible for the deaths of four known victims, including Violet Hansen, Gina Martinez, and Amy Watson, and possibly several others. His latest victim, Lilly Sanderson, survived but is being treated for emotional trauma at an undisclosed location.

Dr. Avella Weaver, a Hillsborough psychiatrist, sheds light on his mental condition after interviewing the last person Worthington spoke to before his premeditated suicide.

"Based on an analysis of his symptoms—blacking out, insomnia, mood swings, and auditory hallucinations—it's likely Mr. Worthington suffered from an oft disputed mental illness called dissociative identity disorder, formerly known as multiple personality disorder."

While authorities are uncertain whether the diagnosis is credible, Dr. Weaver goes on to explain that "dissociative identity disorder is a severe form of dissociation where a lack of connection occurs in a person's thoughts, feelings, or actions. Case studies reveal that it stems from trauma and can be a coping mechanism as the person dissociates himself from an experience that's too painful to assimilate with his conscious self. It's a mystifying disease, and one that is difficult to diagnose or treat."

Authorities believe the murders of five other local girls between 1993 and 2008 are also attributed to Worthington, though evidence has yet to prove his ties to the victims.

The witness, Mia Germaine, who heard Worthington's private confession, says it's likely the true scope of who he was and what he's done will never be known.

"There are secrets that my son took with him," his mother Jennifer Worthington says, "but no matter what he's done, he was my son and I love him. And he paid the price for his crimes with his life by his own choice. In the end, he did the right thing."

Epilogue

Two months later ...

Following Landon's death, I had kept in contact with Jennifer Worthington, dropping by for the occasional cup of tea to catch up and make sure she was all right. Losing both her daughter and her son to death, and her husband to jail, I couldn't imagine how she coped. But with each visit she seemed to be healing more and more, giving me reassurance that she'd survive.

And I'd be there when her days got dark. After all, we were now family.

But the day I got her frantic phone call would be a day I'd never forget.

I had been at my office when my cell phone rang, and I immediately recognized her picture when it popped up on my caller ID.

"Hey, Jennifer. What's up?"

"I have the most incredible news, Mia. Can you come over to my house after work today?"

With it being a Wednesday, I had nothing planned other than a quiet home-cooked dinner with Brad, so I promised to stop by on my way home from work.

Gratefully, the media circus was mercifully short-lived and my fifteen minutes of fame were long gone, but the unwanted reporters shoving mics in my face every time I stepped foot out my door had given me a greater appreciation for nights at home. If I had ever dreamed about being a movie star, after the past few weeks I was glad that fantasy never came true.

"Can you give me a hint of what it's about?" I probed.

"Nope," she said firmly. I imagined her graying bob swaying as she shook her head—a haircut decision she had agonized over for two weeks. When she admitted that she needed a change to get her out of her emotional rut, I suggested a fresh hairstyle could do the trick. Plus a visit with Dr. Avella Weaver. Jennifer took my advice on both counts and thanked me a million times over for recommending Avella, the heart healer.

"Just come over when you can. I'll be home all day. All I can say is this is big with a capital B."

Intrigued, I rushed through the rest of my editing projects so that I could beat the traffic. I arrived at her house a few minutes after four o'clock. I had barely made it to the door when Jennifer opened it.

"C'mon in, honey. I've been dying to tell you the news."

"Wow, this must be important," I oohed, tossing my purse on the coffee table as I sat down. She poured me a cup of chai tea—my favorite. A dollop of cream and two spoonfuls of sugar later and it was perfection.

I sipped, anxiously waiting for her to spill all.

"So? Tell me!" I scolded playfully.

"Dan is getting released from jail!" Jennifer nearly screeched.

"What? Is his time up? I thought he had a few years left—or did he make parole?"

"No, better than that. He's being exonerated."

I set down the teacup and waved my hand. "Wait—back up a bit. Exonerated? You mean he didn't do it?"

"That's right. I'm not sure who did the crime, because I only heard the basics from the district attorney, who swore me to secrecy until the hearing is over, but he told me I'll have my Danny back by the end of this month. And his record will be cleared! But you can't tell a soul—not until this is over. The DA doesn't want the media catching wind just yet, since it could screw up the investigation."

I felt my jaw drop in amazed joy. Dan, innocent after all. But the bigger question remained to be asked.

"What prompted them to open this case back up, twenty-two years after the fact?"

Jennifer beamed. "Landon. My darling Landon went to Evan with some information he found out before he died. Apparently it involved proving faulty eyewitness testimony, which was a good enough tip that Evan presented it to the district attorney before he resigned, God bless him. Evan really came through for us, considering what he's going through now."

I remembered that his vehicular manslaughter trial was coming up. I hoped he'd catch a break, considering he came clean on his own.

"So," she babbled on like a bubbling brook, "the DA agreed to look into it more. They've spent the last two months digging into its validity and found some evidence that clears Danny. How about that, my Landon, a hero after all!"

The elation I felt for Jennifer overwhelmed me. She needed this. Something good, finally, coming her way. Months ago I would have been wary about Dan's freedom, but not now.

While the prodigal Dan of the past returning home would not have been welcome news, the new Danny whom she'd been writing to and visiting in jail was a transformed man. Jennifer spoke of him in a girlishly giddy way, and she had shared with me the long love letters he'd written her, in which he'd taken responsibility for his bad life choices, which was the biggest step anyone could take on the path toward personal growth. Whoever said people don't change was full of it.

He was a slice of sunshine in her gray life. It was time she basked in the sunlight with the rest of us. This was welcome news, and I knew life was turning around for this woman who had lost everything.

I couldn't wait to hear the details.

Heck, maybe Alexis and I could be of service.

The End

Author's Note

A couple years ago I met a man who had undergone a lung transplant. After a risky, painful surgery that kept him bedridden for several weeks, doctors warned him that things would change. "Take it easy," they reminded him. No more sports with the kids. Keep stress triggers to a minimum. No air travel for the foreseeable future. Even day-to-day details would never resume to "normal" as he relied on oxygen support every few hours to sustain him.

Yet the daily life changes weren't all he endured. Never would he have guessed how one lung transplant would forever impact who he was—both inside and out.

It started with a distaste for foods he used to love. Then television preferences. Not long afterwards he had dreams—odd dreams that didn't belong to him. Upon sharing his experiences with me, it sparked my curiosity. What could possibly be causing my friend to "lose himself"? Was it possible it had something to do with the organ transplant? Because it sure seemed too coincidental.

That's when my research led me to the scientific phenomenon called "organ memory"—a theory that our organ cells retain "memory" from the original owner, which can be passed on to an organ recipient.

A Secondhand Life, inspired by my friend's personal experiences after his lung transplant, is based on this theory of organ memory—a "what-if" exploration of the aftermath when a murder victim's organs are donated to another. Some may call it science fiction or pseudoscience, but countless others who have shared similar life changes would call it reality.

I hope you enjoyed the tale and will stick around for the novella that reveals what *really* happened to put Dan behind bars.

And for those of you who want to leave a legacy after you depart this world, consider becoming an organ donor. You never know how you'll impact another person's life and live on in a powerful way ...

Discussion Questions

1. *A Secondhand Life* is loosely based on the author's friend's experience of organ memory after a lung transplant. What do you think about pseudo-science—are our bodies more complex than we realize, or are such things figments of our imaginations?

2. Did you figure out who the killer was? What gave it away for you?

3. What do you think the title *A Secondhand Life* means?

4. If you could get a second chance at life, what would you do differently? What would you do the same?

5. Mia struggles with her self-esteem due to scars that are a reminder not only of her pain, but also her flaws. Do you think we put too much stock in physical perfection? If so, how do you think we can overcome that societal pressure?

6. If you could get to know one character in the book better, who would it be and why?

7. Mia pushed Brad away when things got tough. Do you think distance can help clarify relationships, or does space push people apart?

8. If you could ask the author one question about the book, what would it be?

9. Mental illness is a major theme in the book, particularly multiple personalities. The character Landon was based on the author's family member's diagnosed dissociative identity disorder, but many argue it's not real. Do you think it really exists? What is your perception of mental illness and the mentally ill?

10. Landon took his life in the end as his own form of justice. Was this act selfish or selfless, and why do you think so?

11. Landon is a killer, but he's also a victim of mental illness. Do you see killers as humans, or monsters?

I hope you enjoyed the book as much as I enjoyed writing it. Are you part of a book club? I'm always happy to connect with reading groups—simply email me to plan the details.

Or if you'd like to connect with me to share your thoughts, I love meeting my readers. Feel free to email me anytime at pamela@pamelacrane.com. Hugs!

A Final Word...

If you enjoyed *A Secondhand Life,* browse my other titles at www.pamelacrane.com.

If you'd like to be notified of my upcoming releases or enter my giveaways, join my mailing list at www.pamelacrane.com for chances to win free prizes and pre-release offers.

PAMELA CRANE: Horse tamer. Book editor. Mom of four. Reading addict. Literary reviewer. These are just a few of the roles I play, and I relish them all. I'm a proud mama of a crazy brood that keeps me on my toes, and I can't turn away stray animals, which is how I ended up with a farm full of misfit pets. I hope they never find a cure for my reading addiction, because it's what keeps me sane. I love writing women's fiction and anything mystery or psychological thriller, because the crazier the characters, the more sane I feel!

Discover more books at
www.pamelacrane.com

Made in the USA
Middletown, DE
11 January 2025

69311788R00187